The Trilisk AI
(Book 2 of the PIT series)
by Michael McCloskey
Copyright 2012 Michael McCloskey
ISBN: 978-1478149484

Cover art by Howard Lyon

Learn more about Michael McCloskey's works at
www.squidlord.com

For my mother and father.

Thanks to Maarten Hofman, Tom O'Neill, and
Howard Lyon.

I'd also like to thank many fans who encouraged a
new indie author.

Chapter 1

"What do you need me to find?"

The man glanced around the dingy office before answering Cilreth's question. No doubt he was not impressed. Who would be? The office was small, with modest furnishings and little or no decor. Cilreth did not even like being there herself.

She knew his name was Leonard. He had alerted her to his visit, but he had been short on details. He had asked to talk in person. More and more, it seemed like the kinds of jobs Cilreth got involved in had clients who wanted to talk incarnate to avoid the government snoopers. It was the only reason Cilreth even had an office.

Admit it, old girl. You like the mysterious ones.

"I'm looking for someone. I have a lot of solid data on her, but she's since gone missing, and she wants to stay missing," he said. Leonard sat before her on a ceramic chair. He looked athletic, though a bit past his prime, with short, gray hair and brown eyes. His skin was clear and clean-shaven. His nose was slightly bent.

He looks like a hardass. Ex-military, Cilreth thought. She decided she liked him. "Runaway?"

"Yeah. A Space Force officer's brat daughter. She's been to the frontier for sure. Most likely she's still there."

"What's her overall temperament? Is she prone to violence? Involved with drugs?"

"She's intelligent and stable. Used to be, anyway," he said. "But she fell in with a mean crowd. Smugglers. The assignment I'm offering requires a lot of travel, which of course is included in the pay offer."

Cilreth nodded.

"Then what happens when we find her? Is it going to get ugly? What are we supposed to do with the guys she's shacked... the people she's working with?"

Leonard hesitated.

"Nothing personal, see? I need to understand what's expected before I sign the dotted line."

"If she's gotten in over her head, we're there to give her a quick out. If the smugglers get in the way, I'm going to put them down. I've got a man for it. It won't be just you and me."

"And if she doesn't want to come home?"

"If she's not under any kind of mind control, and wants to stay, then she stays. If she really thinks everything is great, being hunted by the Space Force and hiding out on the frontier, then we leave her alone. I'd be disappointed, but we'd be done."

Sounds like he has a personal stake in this. Maybe he's getting paid a lot more to bring her back.

"She's wanted by the Space Force? Her father must be a high-ranking officer."

"No, actually it has to do with the smugglers. They're wanted by the Space Force. If we can extricate her from that mess, too, then all the better."

Leonard opened his mouth to continue but hesitated again.

I don't like it when he does that.

"Please tell me everything," Cilreth prompted. "It's going to help me do this job, if I take it."

He nodded. "I understated it. Those smugglers are *really* wanted by the Space Force. They met with an unprecedented level of success, and they have some heavy duty alien tech in their possession."

Cilreth looked the client in the eyes. "How did you hear about me?"

"You did some work for the family of a friend of mine, Lieutenant Commander Barnes. Joseph Kane Barnes."

"Okay. Assuming you check out, I can find her for you," Cilreth said. "If you can accept I'm not signing on for kidnapping, then we're good."

Cilreth's left hand jumped a bit on the table.

"You use twitch," he noted.

"Yes. It enhances my performance. As for the downside, what do I have to look forward to? A long retirement in a tropical paradise? Let me tell you something: it's better to burn out than to fade away."

She referred to an inevitable cost of long-term twitch usage: about ten years off the human lifespan. She was forty now, and she could expect another fifty years on the twitch. Leonard appeared to accept her attitude.

"I'll send you what I've got right now. It's a lot to sift through."

"The more the better," Cilreth said, finally remembering to stand. The clients did not like it when she sat there and waited for them to leave.

Leonard walked out. His footsteps echoed down the worn hall. At the same time, Cilreth's link saw the data package he'd sent her. Cilreth prepared a mental workspace for the target: Telisa Relachik.

Something familiar about that name.

She reviewed the ID on the payment information.

"Oh," she said to herself.

Michael McCloskey

Chapter 2

Telisa lounged in a small, domed shelter on the planet Averian. Her eyes were closed, allowing her to concentrate on information retrieved from humanity's vast network. She moved thousands of Earth Standard Credits around, shuffling money into her new accounts from illicit ones through a complicated web of services offering help to individuals seeking to avoid the attention of the Core Worlds' government. She lost some of the funds in the process. That was part of the arrangement.

Telisa and Magnus, the two survivors of the last expedition of Parker Interstellar Travels, had managed to make a shady deal to use a proxy service for their net connections. The service disguised their activity by creating an aggregate of data queries from many other people like themselves, mixed in with fake queries, all wrapped up and accessed via a dummy corporation on Averian. The planet was far out on the sphere of Terran expansion, filled with frontier types who had a more practical approach to life than the typical Core World citizen who followed every rule of the government. It was simply too expensive to police everyone, everywhere, all the time, even with the help of machines.

Telisa tapped her fingers impatiently. Part of the obfuscation often introduced time delays so her actions could be mixed together with other real and fake queries, sent out as queries for larger blocks of data, or split up into smaller actions in a giant blender of electronic communications.

Making the first connections to create new accounts after the incident at the Trilisk ruins had been nerve-wracking. They tested the waters with the UNSF. If the Space Force were actively hunting for them, they would be waiting, ready to track Telisa and Magnus whenever they accessed data caches, bank accounts, or business contacts.

On the other hand, if the government had not identified them as the culprits, avoiding their old accounts could just as easily raise a red flag. If the government was looking for smugglers, and everyone from a certain travel agency suddenly dropped off the grid, it could be a sign of their involvement. Luckily, given the size of Terran-controlled space and the number of people who wanted to conceal their activities from the prying eyes of the Earth government, it would be a red flag in a sea of red flags. Telisa took on the responsibility, getting a crash course in illicit dealings.

The bottom line, Magnus had asserted, was one of priority. If the UNSF knew who they were and wanted them badly enough, then they would eventually be brought in. Otherwise, they might be able to keep a low profile and avoid some of the most basic (and cheap) methods the government might use to catch them. If they were really lucky, then the UNSF was not after them at all. Telisa thought he was probably right and tried to accept her fate. She could not live her life on the constant knife's edge of fear.

Magnus cycled through the door. He wore his favorite military skinsuit and a light helmet equipped with an air filter. He took the helmet off and put it on a small side table. The main room was about the right size for two people, with little space to spare. It struck Telisa again how they lived like poor hermits even though they commanded substantial financial resources.

"How's the *Iridar*?" Telisa asked.

"Pretty good. She's ready for action if it comes to that."

Telisa nodded. Her eyes remained closed. Magnus hesitated.

"I got death packages from Jack and Thomas," he said. "Now we have access to their accounts. Medical records. And of course, everything for Parker Interstellar Travels."

Telisa opened her eyes. "We should tell their family they're gone."

Magnus was quiet for a moment, then shook his head. "I think we can skip it. They didn't have much family. And they weren't close. After all, they were often gone from Earth for months at a time. The messages they've gotten aren't very urgent."

"Still, we should tell them. It's the right thing to do."

"If the family was close, then I'd agree. But these folks don't have close ties to either Jack or Thomas. Better to keep a low profile. If it was so important, they probably sent packages to their family, too."

"How could you dream of not telling them? It's not right."

"We aren't exactly angels ourselves. Our whole operation is unethical."

Telisa bristled. "Unethical?"

"Well, we illegally obtain artifacts and sell them on the black market. Our whole business is a secret, PIT is a front... you know all this."

"We're the ones in the right! The UN doesn't have any business keeping us from learning about alien civilizations!"

"It's against the law."

"It shouldn't be! The government is only interested in preserving their power and you know it!" Telisa's voice was rising.

Magnus replied with more fire himself. "Yeah, they do want to stay in power. Everyone with any power always wants to keep it. That's just smart. But another part of the reason they keep artifacts from people is because they can be dangerous. An alien machine can destroy a whole city. We're not completely in the right ourselves, selling dangerous artifacts."

"That's why we evaluate them in the field, and again before selling them," Telisa said.

Magnus started to answer, but stopped to take a deep breath before continuing. "Let's wait, cool down a bit, and have this conversation later. We can wait a few days, right?"

Telisa nodded. She was still angry.

"I'm going to contact Jason, the guy we have babysitting the agency while we're on expeditions," Magnus said. "There's a fair chance the UNSF will be listening in, if we were identified, but I'm going to take that risk. I won't tell Jason where we are."

"All right."

A high priority news item tripped an alert in Telisa's link. Magnus looked away and became still at the same time.

Emergency announcement going out of the office of the United Nations secretary-general in one minute.

They stood in uncomfortable silence. Though the argument had ended, Telisa stood with arms crossed, her mouth compressed and downturned. She fought inside, unable to concentrate fully on either the possible meaning of the announcement or the argument. Finally the secretary-general came on. Telisa focused on the man in her mind's eye.

The secretary-general stood straight at a podium as the archaic tradition demanded. He had graying hair above a long, narrow face, and the wan complexion and thin build of a man kept fit with toning pills rather than real exercise.

"Citizens, this evening I bear grave news for humanity. There has been an incident involving unknown, and presumed alien, forces that resulted in the deaths of men and women in our Space Force."

"Five Holy Entities," Telisa whispered. *Are they going public about the incident at the alien base?*

"The UNSF scout ship *Seeker* was investigating a possible ruin site at this location approximately 115 parsecs from Sol," said the secretary-general. He paused

8

for a three-dimensional map to appear in their links for reference.

"The *Seeker*!" Telisa said aloud.

Magnus put his hand on her shoulder. "That's not where we were."

"The ship sent us detailed scans of six constructs of unknown origin. These constructs reacted to the presence of the *Seeker* by altering course. Objects were launched from the unknown vessels. Our scout was tracking those objects and scanning the other vessels. When the objects approached dangerously close, on collision courses with no signs of slowing, the *Seeker* responded with a drone and laser countermeasure suite, destroying the incoming objects, presumed to be missiles.

"The scout ship was destroyed shortly thereafter by means unknown," the secretary-general said. "We do know it was destroyed because of other probes that survived its destruction for a matter of minutes before they, too, were destroyed. I would like to make it absolutely clear that the *Seeker* took no offensive action against the mysterious vessels."

The secretary-general paused. "As a result of this unprovoked attack, I'm declaring a state of martial law across the commonwealth. We are assembling a grand fleet to defend ourselves. I assure you that we will protect each and every settlement with our full capability. No outpost is too small to receive our full support. Whenever, wherever these unknown forces appear next, we will be ready to deliver a strong counter to their aggression."

At that point, the secretary-general started to discuss the names of new ship classes being assembled, the types of local defenses being prepared by UNSF forces across the known worlds, and the things civilians were being asked to do to help the cause. But Telisa was not ready to listen. She was trying to absorb the news about her father.

"He's dead. We'll never be reconciled," she said.

"I'm sorry."

"I'm okay. It's not like I really knew him anymore, anyway," she said. Despite her words, she felt a nebulous loss that threatened to break her surface calm.

"You know, he died doing what he wanted to do. From everything you've said, it sounds like the Space Force was his life."

"Well, this time it was his death. And it sounds like aliens did it, too."

***

A man's face appeared in Magnus's PV. The man's eyes hinted at Asian ancestry. He had short black hair, except on the crest of his head, where long hair stood straight up then turned out at ninety degrees to form a T shape. Magnus did not own a hairbender, but he was vaguely aware this was the new trend.

"Jason. Good to see you."

Jason smiled. "Magnus? I was beginning to wonder."

"How's the agency?"

"Everything's good. We've been contacted by several clients," Jason said. "I thought the news of the alien attack would make everyone scared to leave, but it only caused a shift of clients. Everyone who gets ahold of the agency now is asking to be taken out to look for the live aliens."

"What did you tell them?"

"I put them on a waiting list."

"Okay. I have good news and bad news. Good news is, you're promoted. I'm doubling your salary. We have a few tasks for you."

"That's... that's great!"

"The bad news is, we're not coming back for a while. I'm sending you some money. Get two androids. Model them after Jack and Thomas. I'll send you their bio data."

"Uh... okay."

"Here's the deal. Someone may be snooping around. We want them to see the androids and think Jack and Thomas are back, see? So don't let the androids go outside. Have them clean the agency and hang out, and leave some of the windows unpolarized. If someone's determined to spy on the agency, they'll think Jack and Thomas are back. Got it?"

"Sure thing! Could be fun," Jason said.

"Set up a bit to flip if the Space Force shows up there. It's officially the status of the second waste receptacle in Jack's office for our trash service. I'll monitor it from here so I'll know if they show up."

"The Space Force?"

"You didn't think I was doubling your salary for nothing, did you?"

Michael McCloskey

Chapter 3

Captain Relachik was not a captain anymore. He had lost his command shortly after the fiasco at the alien starbase, where he had made "incompetent" decisions that enabled the smugglers and the alien to escape. Now he was just Leonard Relachik.

Relachik had taken a calculated risk to save his daughter. He had since revisited that decision a thousand times in his mind. Sometimes he called himself an old fool. He scolded himself for ruining a lifetime of hard work. But at the core of his being, he knew he had made the only decision he could live with. He had saved his only daughter, at least for a while.

He walked through a drizzle near the spaceport on Malgur-Thame. The algae growing in the clouds gave the rain a green tint, which made him feel like he was swimming through a slime pit.

He had missed a big announcement. At the time, he had been working off his sorrows in the gym, his version of escaping reality. Now he allowed himself to return to the world. He scanned the headlines in his link's interface. A news viewpane was full of them.

Seeker Lost... Space Force Defeated... Aliens Attack!

"Five Holies," he said, stopping in his tracks. He stood and read the stories. He watched the speech of the secretary-general. Slowly the green rain leached away the residual heat of his workout, but his thoughts raced too fast to care.

His ship, destroyed. His crew, dead. And he had not been there to prevent it. The only victory in all of it was that no one even suspected he had made those decisions to save his daughter.

This was his reward.

Relachik started walking again. Now his muscles were cold. He headed back to his cheap hotel to take a shower and think over what he would do with the rest of his life. He stayed in the shower a long time, meditating on his life under a thin stream of hot water, though in this remote locale it cost him almost a standard credit to use so much water.

I have enough.

Fortunately, a Spartan life in the service had left him with a considerable amount of savings built up. That money could keep him comfortable for a long time.

Or, he could double down on finding his daughter.

Relachik did not need to think on it. He opened a new metapane in his mind's eye and started to peruse the net for private military firms.

***

Relachik walked into the moldy office building. The place was deserted. The water containment had started to fail, turning the place into one giant green stain. The only way to recover a building after this happened on Malgur-Thame was to re-establish the water barriers, block out all the visible light, then UV gun the place for days. The wall struts, at least, were inherently water impermeable, but every inch of textile in the place teemed with microorganisms.

He had an FTF with another potential hire, a man called Arlin Donovan. Of course the man offered virtual business consultations, but for what Relachik wanted... better to keep it offline. Relachik found the man in a single-room office. A real wood desk and a couple of chairs dominated the middle of the space. A dusty filing cabinet took up space in the corner.

Probably empty, Relachik thought. *Or filled with weapons.*

Arlin stood tall. He had light brown hair and blue eyes. His nose looked smashed by a few too many solid jabs from a cage fighter. The man was in shape. Relachik's first impression of Arlin was positive. This was exactly what a mercenary should look like: strong, fit, determined, and a bit roughed up around the edges.

It reinforced what he had already found on the net. Arlin had a solid military background and it all checked out.

"I'm Relachik. You look the part," Relachik verbalized his thoughts.

"Arlin Donovan. You look like a soldier yourself," Arlin observed.

"Navy man, actually," Relachik said. "But you knew that already."

Arlin nodded.

"Then you know I can afford the contract. We're going to find my daughter. She's... fallen in with the wrong crowd."

Arlin nodded again.

"I know you aren't broke, and I know you're not a screwup—which puts you two points ahead of my last employer. So I'm glad to work with you. Just one concern," he said. "With due respect to the man footing the bill: Your daughter's of age. She's old enough to choose her own course. Are you asking me to take her back against her will? That could impact the bottom line."

"We should agree on a contingency for that. If she's being abused, or if she's been brainwashed, I can imagine scenarios where I'm going to take her back against her will."

Relachik had told Cilreth that he had no intention of taking Telisa back if she did not want to go. But he had since reflected on the possibility that Telisa might have been coerced with violence, drugs, or more sophisticated behavior modification. In those cases, he had decided, he would extract her from that environment and rehabilitate her before letting her decide what to do with her life.

"I tell you, though," Relachik continued, "What I'm mostly worried about is the other smugglers. If they're bad news, it may get ugly."

Arlin nodded. "Okay, I'll touch up our agreement to include that possibility."

"Your info packet said you could cover the transportation angle," Relachik said.

"I have an arrangement for transport. I can get us wherever we need to go, on the frontier or beyond."

"Is there another man involved? I mean, will we have a pilot tagging along?"

"No. The ship's reasonably modern. I can handle her. As long as we don't run into those aliens that deep-sixed the *Seeker*."

Relachik nodded.

"Do you feel lucky or unlucky you missed it?"

"Unlucky," Relachik answered immediately.

He understands me well to ask such a question.

"But since I'm still around, I'm going to try and clean up this mess with my daughter," he continued.

"And if your daughter logs me?"

Relachik understood Arlin meant: What if Telisa logged him as the target of her weapon and prepared to open fire? Arlin could hardly be expected to hold back and allow himself to die.

"This isn't a suicide mission. I know I can't pay you enough to lay down your life. But I hope you focus on the extra 5000 ESC you get if we come back home with her still breathing."

"Then we understand each other," Arlin said. "I'll be ready to go tomorrow."

***

Relachik sat in his small room on his last night on Malgur-Thame. The woman before him looked fit enough, though he suspected it was from the pills as much as the dancing she did for her VR packages. She wore a sleek black dress that caught the eye. Her narrow face was clear and beautiful.

"You're about to get your money's worth. No doubt about that," she said, walking to the end of the small room and twirling around. "No more virtual encounters. This time, in the flesh!"

In contrast to her sensual overture, Relachik was all business.

"About that. You're making some assumptions, and I didn't bother to alter them. Sorry about that. I know you're famous, and I'm sure you get your share of people who come to Malgur-Thame to enjoy the presence of The Emerald incarnate. But I'm here about something else," he said.

Emerald's pleasant smile dropped quickly. Her body tensed.

She's probably thinking she's made a mistake, that I'm a psycho. Hurry before she sends for help.

"I need you to contact a friend of mine," Relachik said. "The fee stays the same." He spread his hands as he spoke, universal body language for 'I mean you no harm.'

Emerald's shoulders relaxed. She glided over to him.

"Okay. I can't say I'm not disappointed. You're attractive. I have a soft spot for Space Force guys, I guess. Why don't you talk to this person yourself?"

"I might be flagged for surveillance. I'm not a criminal. I'm just not Space Force anymore. I need to make sure a friend of mine in the force is on board for a plan and exchange a few secrets for further communication."

"Your link will still show up in the conversation if you join in," she said. "You have to know."

"I have a way around that. As I said, I used to be in the Space Force. I have a few tricks."

"I see. I agree, but I have conditions."

"I already paid well," Relachik said warily.

"Have you ever used one of my VR modules?"

"Can't say that I have. But I've heard they're great. My friend is a fan of yours. I'm pretty sure he'll take your call."

"If you had, you'd know one of the reasons I'm so good is that I enjoy it. I take pride in my art, so I want a chance to win you over. I'll help you, then we conclude the deal exactly as I'd assumed."

"What?" Relachik shot out forcefully. *That was a bit sharp,* he told himself. He softened his voice. "I mean, why would you want that?"

"I like you. And I know what you're missing. You don't. Trust me, you won't regret it. And you'll tell your buddies all about it."

Relachik stared for a moment. He allowed himself to look at her again in a new light. She was attractive, exotic, and apparently, ambitious.

"Okay, fine. Deal."

"Of course we have a deal. Okay, so how do I contact him?"

"Nothing special. You give me permission to link into a conversation. My software will take care of the rest."

"I have a lot of friends—"

"I know. If I hack your link, you have people who will hunt me down and do terrible things to me."

"Right."

"Okay, please contact Nick Vrolyk. Here's his ID. Mention you know he's a fan, but don't mention me except as a friend in common. Then sit tight, give us five minutes or so to talk, and we're done."

"Then we start phase two, you mean," she said smiling.

"Right."

"Oh. Is it that you want him to listen in on us? That's no problem."

"No, it's as I said. By the Five, don't let him listen in, please!"

She laughed.

Emerald tried to establish communication. They waited for the connection to be accepted or blocked by Vrolyk. A net authority would vouch for the authenticity of the caller, but there was always a chance Nick would laugh, disconnect, and put it down as a hack from a friend.

"Nothing yet," she said. "He may be asleep."

Relachik nodded. When Nick answered the query, Relachik tunneled through without letting his link ID appear on the channel.

"Sorry, Nick, it's me, Captain—Leonard—Relachik. Emerald is really here, though."

"You bastard. Called me to show off, did you? That's great, though. I thought you'd be crushed, but I see you've adapted quickly."

"I need a contact in the force. Under the table. Can I count on you?"

There was a moment's hesitation.

"You know you can," the answer came.

Relachik sent an information module he had prepared which would allow them to communicate indirectly. It contained several seemingly random message drop points and shared secrets. They would use any four of five seemingly unrelated sources of data to combine and use for exchanging messages.

"I don't need anything now. I'm still setting up," he said.

"I hope it won't be often. I'm a busy guy and I don't need to take more risks. We have to fight the goddamn aliens now, you know. Looks like my days may be numbered."

"Then this risk just got a lot smaller," Relachik said, but at the same time he felt guilty asking his friend to cooperate, especially now that the aliens were on the scene.

Nick laughed. "True enough. Watch yourself, then, *Captain.*"

"You too. Thanks."

Relachik closed his tunnel and ran his finger across his throat to tell Emerald to stop the conversation.

"Thanks for being a fan, Nick," she said, then closed the channel. "Good. I'm glad it worked out. And now..." Emerald ran her hands over her dress.

Maybe this won't be so bad after all, Relachik thought.

Chapter 4

Telisa looked at the three remaining artifacts from the Thespera expedition. That failure still grated on her. She had managed to survive the harrowing experience and escape with what she thought was a collection of Trilisk artifacts. As it turned out, none of the artifacts provided the clues she sought.

Telisa had pored over them, researching each one. She had identified two as items from known, but extinct civilizations. A Talosian water distiller and a Capacite's charge core. The distiller was suspected to be a minor pleasure rather than a critical survival device: a Talosian might have enjoyed a vial of water the way a Terran might enjoy a cigar. The charge core had probably come right out of an alien's body. It was believed to be a cybernetic enhancement to Capacites' ability to store electrical energy after which the long-gone race had been named.

In the end, she was convinced almost nothing from the collection was of direct Trilisk origin. Telisa theorized the items belonged to creatures who had inhabited the Trilisk facility at other times. Whether as prisoners, zoo exhibits, or guests, she did not know. Even if the items had been created in the complex itself as part of an environment, then carried out by someone or something, it meant beings from several different races had been there at one time or another.

I should have known immediately they weren't Trilisk. Simple examination shows they're too externally complex, too gadgety to be Trilisk. I shouldn't have taken it for granted that anything at the site would be Trilisk.

The mind-recording egg, which apparently held a Trilisk memory, could have been Trilisk. Its method of operation was a mystery. How the recording could be experienced by Terrans remained unexplained. Telisa thought of it as a recording of Trilisk events for an alien friend (or an ambassador, as she liked to imagine). Trilisk artifacts were elegant, outwardly simple things that seemed to work as if by magic—when Terrans were able to get them to work at all.

At least the finds generated a lot of money for Telisa and Magnus to live on while they avoided the UNSF and planned their next move.

Magnus had taken to studying alien gadgets as well. He had concentrated his effort on the alien walking machine Shiny had let them take from the space station. He had been pulling his hair out over it for some time.

Telisa strolled through the *Iridar* to the cargo bay where Magnus liked to work. The bay was a mess. Tools and components littered the floor. Racks on the walls held piles of parts on every shelf.

"I hope you're ready to train," Telisa called out.

"Well, I guess I should," Magnus's voice replied. It did not sound enthusiastic.

"You never pay attention to me anymore, darling," Telisa said in a singsong joke.

"Ha! You're going to like this though," Magnus said.

Telisa walked over to the robot standing in the center of the bay. It was a spider-legged machine the size of a German Shepherd.

"Nice! It's great to have a robot to use. Think of all the things he can do for us."

"It's not ready yet, but I think it could scout for us," Magnus said. "It can back us up, too. It has a stunner and a grenade launcher."

"Whoa. Really? This thing's not coming back to Earth, that's for sure. I see Shinarian walker parts in here."

"Shinarian? Ha. Yes, we'd get in quite a bit of trouble with this. But no reason to ever bring it back, if we ever do go back to Earth."

"How depressing."

"Well, we made our choices," Magnus said.

22

"Have you learned how the walker worked?"

"No. Not really."

"Too bad it didn't come with a manual."

"It probably did. For all the good it would do me, if I could even ask the walker for it."

Something asked Telisa's link for a connection. Her locator told her it was the gutted remains of the Shinarian walker. She shrugged and accepted it.

"I didn't know you had any interface with the walker working at all," she said.

"I don't," Magnus said.

"Greetings, hello, howdy," a buzzing voice announced. It was Shiny's voice.

"What the...!"

Telisa shot a look at Magnus at the same instant he looked suddenly at her. The look on his face was enough to know he was on the channel.

"Is this a recording?" Telisa asked.

"Apologies, regret. How to initiate negotiations?" It was still Shiny's voice.

"Where are you? How did you...? Interesting that you can fool our links."

"Orbiting, rotating, circling above."

"I'm surprised to hear from you," Telisa responded mentally. She traded looks with Magnus, then opened a private connection to him.

"Should I be worried it's a trick?"

"Would anyone else know exactly how he sounded? But we may as well see what he wants," Magnus responded to her privately.

She nodded. Telisa remembered she had asked Shiny to imitate his original buzzy voice, generated by rapid vibrations of his attending sphere devices.

"Why have you sought us out again?" she asked.

"Telisa. Objective: collect artifacts. Shiny. Objective: collect artifact. Suggest cooperative mode."

"I missed the funny way he talks," Telisa said.

"Did you notice he said 'artifact' singular?"

"Shiny, do you have a particular artifact in mind? Which one?"

"Industrial seed. Very valuable."

"You suggested cooperative mode," Magnus noted. "Shiny, what other modes do you have?"

"Social modes: cooperative, competitive, reproductive."

Magnus nodded. "What about some kind of independent mode? Where you just ignore the other guy."

"Ignoring peers not optimal, safe, recommended. Never ignore. If not cooperating, reproducing, default to, prefer, select competitive mode."

"If we're not with you, we're against you, huh?"

"We sure as hell aren't going to put him in reproductive mode," Telisa said to Magnus. "It could be like those VRs where the aliens lay eggs in your paralyzed body."

"Ugh."

"Yes," Shiny said.

"Would you change to competitive mode while we're out there? Are you going to kill us if you switch?" Magnus asked.

"When benefit of conflict outweighs, is greater than, is more beneficial than, Shiny switches. Could kill you. If optimum, most performant, most efficient solution to long-term goals. Estimate, guess that probability is low."

Telisa and Magnus exchanged concerned looks.

"Five Holies," Telisa sent to him privately.

"At least he's honest. Kind of," Magnus responded.

"Yeah, he's honest unless he's lying because that's optimal."

"Okay look, whenever you fully trust anyone, Terran or otherwise, you're taking a risk."

"Yeah," she conceded.

"Well that sounds less than optimal to me," Telisa said on Shiny's channel. "Why should I work with an alien who might kill me?"

"Potential benefit for Telisa," Shiny said.

"Potential of dying. How can I keep you from killing me?"

"Remain useful, desirable, beneficial. Stay alive," Shiny buzzed. The voice sounded happy.

"Unbelievable," Magnus breathed out loud.

...or alternately, become too expensive to kill.

"We'll have to take out an insurance policy. Something that can damage Shiny if we die," Telisa sent to Magnus.

"Right. Make our deaths suboptimal."

"Shiny, where do you suggest we go to get these artifacts?" she asked.

"Shiny. Homeworld. Origin."

"Five Holy Entities," Telisa said. "Your home planet! Will it be safe for us?"

"No. Danger. Peril."

"You are so failing to sell me on this," Telisa said.

"Why do you need us?" Magnus asked. "Are you an outcast like us? Hunted by your government?"

"Shiny homeworld is ruined, derelict, destroyed."

Telisa frowned.

"I'm sorry. I didn't know."

"Telisa, Magnus retrieve artifacts. Destroyers, invaders, conquerors, less likely to attack primitive species."

"How wonderful. The destroyers of your planet have occupied it?"

"War machines linger. Hunt. Eradicate."

"But they won't hunt us, right? That's why you're sending us down?"

"Likely you will survive," Shiny transmitted. "Likely success for both parties. Benefit, profit, gain to be had for all three."

"Likely we'll survive? Your salesmanship needs work."

"Shiny is not a salesman. Shiny is not a man."

"We need to talk about it privately first," Magnus said.

"The channel is secure," Shiny transmitted.

"Telisa and I need to talk for a moment, so stand by please."

"Acceptable. Telisa and Magnus negotiate terms as a sub-alliance?"

"Perhaps," Telisa said.

"Sounds dangerous," Magnus told her on a private channel.

"It is. But as he says, we have a lot to gain. And I'm tired of hiding. At least on an expedition, we'll feel like we're out of touch, not fugitives."

"I'm up for it, too. But I wonder what we can do about Shiny. I think we're playing with fire here."

"Like you said. Make ourselves dangerous to lose. We can set up an info drop to the UNSF in the event of our deaths?"

"Something like that may work. He mentioned negotiation. We should ask for more."

"Like what?"

"What do you want? His race is older than ours. Or at least more advanced. He probably has a lot to offer."

"Like information about the Trilisks," Telisa said.

"Perfect. Yes. Ask for information. I'm thinking about the robot. I could use his help. I'm sure he could give me all the pointers I need to incorporate those walker parts."

Telisa shifted her attention back to the shared channel. Magnus must have done the same. He prompted Shiny first.

"Okay then. We're in," he said.

26

"We have conditions," Telisa added.

"Shiny offers benefit. Profit. Gain."

"Yeah, I heard that part. The conditions are easy for you. Magnus has questions about your walker. The one we took from that base? You help him enough that we can incorporate parts of your walker into our new robot."

"Agreeable. Possible. Acceptable."

"And my condition is... you give me the location of every Trilisk ruin your race ever encountered."

"Agreeable. Possible. Acceptable."

"When are you thinking to leave?" Telisa asked.

"We may leave immediately."

"Are you coming down to pick us up? You'll cause a panic if anyone detects your ship here. Aliens recently attacked a Space Force ship. Wait. Was that you that destroyed the *Seeker*?"

"Rendezvous in space. I will board your *Iridar*. I have not engaged, fought, combatted any Terran ships."

"We have to take the *Iridar*?" Magnus asked. "You have an advanced Shinarian starship, wouldn't we be safer in that?"

"Negative. Unsafe, precarious, risky."

"Why is that?"

"Homeworld... unsafe. Destroyers—"

"Invaders, conquerors, right. They still have a presence in space around your planet."

"Correct, accurate, right on."

***

Jason appeared in Magnus's link pane.

"Jason. It's Magnus again."

Jason did not react.

Damn sheltered connections. I am so tired of waiting for stuff to go through the masking layer.

"Magnus, are you there? Oh. Hi."

"How's the agency?"

"Calm," Jason said. Magnus summed up Jason's demeanor. He used a program designed to detect stress. Jason's reading was fairly low.

Let's hope it really is calm.

"I'm altering our death packages significantly. They've also become much more important. Are our drop locations all still valid?"

"What the hell, Magnus? You guys really dig into the shit out there on the frontier, don't you?"

"Just a precaution. Do you have what I asked you set up?"

There was another delay. Magnus gritted his teeth and waited it out.

"Yes. Jack and Thomas are doing fine. And I'll still see anything appearing at our drop spots."

"Okay. Go ship shopping, then. Do some research. Get us a good deal. I'll send the funds. We'll put together another crew and send these people you have on the list out to find... who knows what."

"A ship? Uhm, okay."

"That's everything then."

"Hey, uh, Mag? I'm not going to have to head out to the frontier myself, am I?"

"No, I need you right there at PIT headquarters."

"Good. All right then."

Magnus smiled.

Chapter 5

Leonard Relachik gathered his few belongings and headed for the sole starport on Malgur-Thame. Most people would have taken the elevator to the top of the housing building and rented a glider to whisk through the green mist to their destination. Relachik hoofed it. Even though the ground was spongy, wet, and eternally green, he had a spaceman's appreciation for real exercise across a real distance as opposed to a VR helmet or a link program hooked up to a treadmill.

When he arrived at the spaceport, he entered the facility at an automated checkpoint and headed down to the berths below ground. Squat robots scuttled and rolled about on errands for their unseen masters. The chemical smell of whatever the locals used to kill off the tenacious green slime filled the air.

He looked up the berth number and found the name: *Violet Vandivier*. He smiled. The vogue for naming civilian vessels was an adjective and a name, supposedly necessary to sufficiently differentiate vessels for casual conversation (of course, their unique identifier was simply an obscenely long number). Relachik knew already the name would be shortened further to the *Vandivier* in shipboard conversation.

Relachik found the ship in another fifteen minutes. It was a small ship by his standards, round, and predictably violet in color. The ship rested like a flying saucer over a dish-shaped depression. He examined the depression for a few minutes until Arlin arrived. Relachik decided it was thick metal or ceramic. His link told him it was powered down, but it was capable of drawing a lot of power from the spaceport reactor.

"What's up with this berth?" Relachik asked.

"You don't know? Hmm. I guess there would be no reason for you to know if you're used to capital ships in deep space. You probably spent all your time off-planet. Anyway, a lot of the spaceports on the fringe are finally getting these spinner shields. You can run your gravity spinner up much higher here above this plate to save yourself some propellant taking off."

"Oh," Relachik said. Typically, a modern craft could only use a small fraction of its gravity spinner capability when taking off, or else people and debris would go flying for a kilometer.

Cilreth showed up on Arlin's heels. She had brought two silver luggage cases.

"What do you think of the ship?" Arlin asked her.

"How big is the data cache?" she asked.

Arlin and Relachik laughed.

"I actually don't know," Arlin said. "But I gave you both the permissions you need for all the services."

A boarding ramp descended. Cilreth marched on board with her head down. Relachik imagined her mechanically perusing its network capabilities. He connected to the ship and summed up their new home. He could not help but do it as a series of comparisons to his old ship, the *Seeker*. The ship was clean but cramped. It was so much smaller than the *Seeker*.

The *Vandivier* had two levels. The ship was designed to support up to ten people, though only six could reside inside comfortably. The gravity spinner was newer and reasonably efficient for long distance travel. Relachik could see from the interior layout service that each of them would have tiny personal quarters. A small mess area and a modest lounge dominated the center of the main level. The lower level of the vessel as it now sat held a small cargo compartment. It was not of much interest to Relachik, who had brought so little it would all fit in his cramped living space.

The ship had no bridge. There was simply no need to set aside valuable space for piloting a ship that was controlled through links. The *Seeker* had possessed a bridge—though it was merely an armored space designed to protect the officers from harm. The crews of the Space Force vessels could do their jobs from anywhere on board through their links.

Notably missing were laser turrets, a particle accelerator, and a battalion of marines.

Oh well, it's a step down. Two steps down.

In one way, the smallest ships were as amazing as ships like the *Seeker*—everything had to be cleverly designed and super-compact in order to pack everything in.

This damn thing is a tin can. Oh, well. That's what VR is for.

"We're well stocked and ready for a long trip," Arlin said.

"Looks newer than I expected," Relachik noted.

"Only three years old. The gravity spinner is a monster. Very nice ship. It's also not mine. On loan from a relative."

Relachik's eyebrow rose. "None of my business, but sounds like a good way to destroy a family."

Arlin smiled. "He's a big company man. Doesn't care about this much. Besides, it was to pay off an old family debt."

Then why isn't it really yours? Relachik shrugged. "As long as he's not going to show up in the middle of the search and demand it back."

Arlin nodded. "Won't happen."

Cilreth looked around the ship quite a bit. Relachik did not ask her about her plans to begin the search. Cilreth was not a soldier and probably would not tolerate micromanagement. She was a professional and he knew she would dive in as soon as they were underway. Cilreth continued to the second level.

Relachik stayed in the cargo area as the ramp retracted. He looked around at the many cargo containers. His link allowed him to rummage through the container inventories, but he asked about them anyway just to get to know Arlin better. "You said we have enough for a long trip. These are food supplies? Weapons?"

"The cargo hold has everything we could possibly need. Everything on board has multiple functions, like a collection of a thousand Swiss Army knives. We have plenty of decent food. As for weapons..."

"Yes?"

"Come with me."

Arlin walked to the end of a tiny walkway on the second level. The mess was directly behind them, and a reactor room was to Relachik's left. His link told him Arlin was headed to the armory. Once again, Relachik could have inquired electronically, but it would be more polite—and more interesting—to let Arlin show him the contents FTF.

Arlin opened a sliding metal door, revealing the small room. An array of weaponry lay upon lit racks. "This section is all the usual. Stunners, a laser, smart glue bombs, and projectile launchers."

"Impressive," Relachik said robotically, though he was actually underwhelmed. He had seen much better on the *Seeker*.

You're in a different world now, he told himself. *This is a good arsenal for a small independent vessel.*

His eye caught a glint of metal on his right. Several swords were secured there.

Well, that's something different.

Relachik took one by the handle. It was held in place by a clamp.

"Careful, please," Arlin said. Relachik smiled. "Those are sharper than you might believe. That thing could cut through a landing strut in one swing. If you drop it to the floor, I'm going to have to replace a deck plate."

"They're dangerous even to have on board," Relachik said, withdrawing his hand. He examined the clever mounting mechanism on the wall. A series of hefty clamps held the swords by their handles in clear tubes. He found the service in his link.

Just so I know how to get one, if I need it.

The left side of the closet held several military skinsuits and two medical robokits.

"What about the ship herself. Is she armed?"

"Nothing long-range," Arlin said a bit defensively. "We have disabler remoras. I think they'll come in handy if we find the smugglers in orbit. There are also four probes with modest defensive EM capabilities."

"Thanks for showing me. I'll put my stuff in my quarters."

"Of course."

Before Relachik left, he turned to Arlin again. "I'd like to inquire about takeoff procedures."

"Really?"

"As you said, I'm familiar with much larger Space Force vessels."

"Ah, yes. Well, if this were a hot landing zone, the ship would show you to the nearest crash pod. But as far as taking off on Malgur-Thame, no special precautions are needed. In fact, we're now underway."

"Excellent."

"Of course, exactly where we're underway to, I don't know. I'm taking us to the fringe, as you indicated."

"Yes, well, hopefully Cilreth can help us with that soon. But I'd let her do her job alone for a while. She knows the ball is in her court."

"Of course. As you wish."

Relachik found his small room and rattled around for a few minutes, placing his things into a few wall cabinets.

He had a sleeping web, a closet, and a shower tube that also worked as a toilet and a crash tube. It was much like the *Seeker*, only everything was smaller, and as Arlin had mentioned, all the gadgets seemed to serve more than one function. Relachik found that he could not guess many of them, though they all had link services full of explanations. He suppressed annoyance at the realization he would have to learn to use a lot of new equipment.

A different world.

He checked the outer sensor net and navigation. They were already leaving the atmosphere. The gravity spinner was amazing. Nothing had disturbed Relachik through the entire ascent. There was not even any vibration to speak of.

Sometimes I'm glad for bureaucracy. It slows things down.

The ship neared its first in-system checkpoint. Nothing more than a small satellite that scanned them and verified their credentials. But Relachik noted that many such checkpoints lay ahead—more than there should be. A network of satellites appeared in his personal view, embracing the planet. It took him a moment to realize what they were.

"Defenses," he said to himself.

The destruction of the *Seeker* had no doubt initiated such changes across most of the colonies. Relachik saw more activity over Malgur-Thame. Several construction facilities were on the display. He zoomed into the public view of one of them. A series of robots worked to construct a ship's hull. More machines unloaded a transport full of raw materials while another transport waited to dock.

Relachik made some inquiries about the schedule of the local industrial facilities. It felt strange to go through the public net for UNSF information. And, predictably, what he could find out with civilian clearance was very limited. Apparently every colony with a population greater than one million people had been tasked with fabricating ships for the cause. The class varied by the size of the colony. Malgur-Thame, being quite small, had received plans to fabricate a Space Force corvette.

The burden on such a small colony was fairly steep. Those resources were needed for other things. Yet the sentiment was largely positive in light of the news that Terrans were no longer alone on the galactic stage.

Relachik's pulse quickened a bit as he thought about humanity's situation. *We've finally encountered others out there, and they don't like us.*

***

For Relachik, the key to spending time in space was a routine. A daily regimen that included many glorified habits, all of which were productive, but none too efficient. If you had the time, you had to draw it out. Many would retreat into virtual worlds and spend their time there, but Relachik loved working more than anything. When he did create virtual worlds, he filled them with more work—training and planning.

It was all about what was going on in reality. He had invested too much time and effort in real life to let it rot by attending imaginary worlds for any length of time.

This philosophy had taken a hit when he left service. Now, his reality required considerably less work. *I have a crew, of sorts. At least one is woefully under trained to be on a ship. I should try and fix that.*

Relachik staked out the mess and waited. He set up a few VR scenarios to pass the time, creating situations he could foresee them encountering. In each case, the objective was the same: approach various hostiles holding Telisa captive and rescue her.

Eventually, Cilreth showed up to get something to eat.

"So, is the network setup here good enough for you?" he asked.

"Yes. It's adequate," Cilreth said, smiling slightly.

"I think we should train a bit while we're stuck in this tin can. I hope the smugglers won't turn out to be a problem, but maybe we should practice just in case..."

"Yes."

"...and I think the exercise—what?"

"I said yes, silly."

"Ah. Good. I guess I expected you would say you're busy looking for Telisa."

"I am, but the computers do most of the work. Though I like to tweak things often. Still, I have to take a break now and then, just like anyone."

"After lunch then?"

"Yes. Sure."

"Spend a lot of time in VR?"

"Doesn't everyone?"

"How about action?"

"Yes, I play a lot of action stuff. And I exercise in real life, too."

"You're a gem among the hacker crowd."

"I'm not a hacker. Don't mistake an investigator for a hacker. I know how to look for people. That's my specialty."

Relachik nodded. "Got it. Okay, I'll set some stuff up. See you soon."

He returned to his quarters and contacted Arlin to see if the mercenary would join their little exercise. Arlin agreed eagerly.

He needs something to do as well.

When Arlin and Cilreth showed up later, Relachik was ready. The first environment he had created looked like the *Vandivier*. Arlin and Cilreth appeared in the simulation. They appeared as copies of their incarnate selves.

"Okay, what's the drill?" Cilreth asked. She sounded genuinely curious and ready to go.

"We should practice using the disabler remoras and boarding another ship."

"Pirates now, are we?"

"Of course, he means to practice a boarding in case we find the smugglers on a ship or a space station," Arlin said.

"Exactly," Relachik said. "The ship is on our scanner now. Arlin will deploy the remoras. Cilreth, you watch my interface. I'll show you how to use these defensive probes to mask our approach."

"They can do that?"

"Yes. Their primary mission is, of course, to observe for us, but their EM capabilities include creating false images of the ship and obscuring the real one."

"Okay, I'm watching."

They worked for the next fifteen minutes to intercept the other ship. Cilreth watched as Relachik launched two probes and tried to cover their approach. The *Vandivier* launched a remora, a flat, plate-sized device that would attached itself to the target vessel. When it discharged, it would disrupt the target's control systems, temporarily disabling it unless it had military grade safeguards.

One side of his display showed his best guess of what the other side saw. At one point, a ghost of the *Vandivier* appeared on the other screen.

"I think I screwed that up," Relachik said. "Okay, if this happens, move to plan B. Make them think there's more than one of us. But let them think we're farther out."

"You could even say you're Space Force. Pretend that you're escorting them to the nearest planet. So they won't expect a boarding action."

"Yes. Anything to keep them from being ready to defend the lock."

"The remora is down. Arming it now," Arlin said.

The remora discharged. A timer started up to show them how much time had passed since the remora went off.

"Now what?" Cilreth asked.

"We'll need gas masks, small arms, and a couple of seeker grenades," Relachik said.

"Okay, I'm on it." Cilreth hurried to the virtual weapons locker. "Hrm. We have interesting stuff in here. Do we have swords for real or are they only here?"

"For real, too," Relachik said. "I'm told they're amazingly, unbelievably, super-dangerously sharp. Emergency only."

"Check," she said. "Okay, I have the grenades. One for each of us?"

"Yes. Three masks, right? One for Arlin, of course."

"Of course."

They met at the lock. Cilreth handed out stunners and soft slug pistols. Relachik and Arlin had utility belts to hold unused weapons, but Cilreth ended up with one in each hand.

At least she's not pointing either of them in our direction, Relachik thought. *If her weapon discipline is lax, she'll end up shooting us sooner or later. Hopefully in a simulation.*

"There's a bit of cover here," Cilreth said. "But only enough for one of us on each side."

"Arlin and I are Space Force," Relachik said. "We'll take this cover, you stand beyond, around that bulkhead."

"You got it," Cilreth said. "I wasn't looking forward to hitting the beach first anyway."

If this were the Seeker, we'd be readying the assault robots.

She handed her gas grenade to Arlin. He nodded his thanks and armed the grenade with his link. Relachik did the same with his.

"Give yours a low detonation threshold. I'll set mine higher, let it go farther into the ship," Relachik said. Arlin replied with a short digital chirp used by the Space Force as an efficient acknowledgment. The marines called such transmissions 'battle yah' and 'battle nah', for a positive and a negative, respectively.

The lock doors opened. A set of robotic arms folded up from the floor and started to pry the hatch of the other ship. If it were not for the disabler on the other ship, they would have to cut through. As it was, the arms, designed to open the hatch of a dead or disabled ship, would work fine.

As soon as a gap opened, they released their seeker grenades. The devices rolled through the lock and into the other ship.

"Masks on," Relachik reminded Cilreth.

Arlin's grenade reported its detonation. When the gap widened enough, Arlin jumped through. Relachik remained under cover.

"You can come forward," Relachik told Cilreth. He pointed his weapon into the opening to cover her as she moved into the lock and to the side. Then Relachik went in.

"At least one of them succumbed," Arlin said.

The other side had filled with translucent gas. Battery powered emergency lights illuminated the interior. A man lay on the floor, motionless. An awkwardly folded leg told Relachik that the man was not faking it.

Relachik's second grenade reported detonation, further into the ship.

"The main hall is clear, one more appears down," Arlin reported.

"Okay, cover the hall. We'll go door to door," Relachik said. He tried the first portal on his left. The chamber beyond looked like a power room.

Relachik sneaked out into the main corridor. He caught a glimpse on his right of Arlin covering him. In the middle of the corridor, another smuggler lay unconscious. The next chamber looked like a common room beside the mess.

"No one in the mess," Relachik said. He checked a food cabinet, but it only contained an electric storage belt that carried food in from a larger store. No room for anyone to hide.

Relachik returned to check the other side of the corridor. It was a private quarters, empty. He checked another room.

There, he found his daughter. Telisa lay inside on a divan, unconscious. She wore durable frontier clothing. He checked her pulse.

"I found her. She's okay," he transmitted.

He picked her up. Suddenly he was gripped in emotional turmoil: He had found his daughter.

It's just a simulation you idiot.

"That was straightforward. We're a good team," Cilreth said.

Relachik took a deep breath and cleared his head.

"Don't relax until we're out," Relachik said. "One of them may have found a gas mask."

"Okay. But I'm barely even in yet," she said. Cilreth backed out while Relachik carried Telisa out. Arlin was the last to leave.

"So far so good," Relachik said. "Of course, the settings will get harder. I'll challenge us a bit more next time."

"Sure," Cilreth said. "That was pretty tame."

"It went better than I thought. Of course, it gets a lot uglier than that if we screw up. Now, how about a planetside approach?" Relachik said. He brought up another of the scenarios he had prepared.

The three of them stood on an alien planet with surface breathers over their faces. Furry orange columns surrounded them. A quick glance upward revealed fern-like leaves spreading from the column tops in a dense canopy. These were likely sessile life forms generated by the program. Whatever star lit this world was either dim or fading for the evening.

"Are we restricted to this?" Cilreth asked, holding up a stunner.

"No. Outfit yourself from the ship," Relachik said. "We're making an approach before dark, so there's a bit of time. This planet rotates slowly."

Cilreth nodded. Her appearance instantly changed as she donned a military skinsuit for the simulation. Arlin added to his inventory as well. One of the sword tubes appeared at his belt.

"Should come in handy getting in," he said. "It can cut right through most locks."

Relachik nodded. "Ready then? You'll see the target on our maps now. To the north."

"Got it," Cilreth said. She cast a glance around the forest.

She's alert. That's good. I'll have add outside threats as well, to encourage that. And Arlin is thinking ahead, too, bringing the sword to cut in.

They moved out. The alien forest floor was strangely clean, devoid of anything that resembled dead leaves. Strange tracks of glistening goo crisscrossed the scene, as if the debris had been cleared by giant slugs. Whatever had done it was gone.

The target structure came into view. It was a primitive-looking two-story dwelling, made of local materials. The huge hulks of cut trees were visible in its walls. The roof was covered in rough ceramic tiles. What few windows it had emitted bright white light into the forest around it.

"Hey! This place is really out there," Cilreth said over their link channel.

"Yes, very isolated. We have to get in suddenly and hit them. The grenades won't work, the house isn't airtight, and they'll have breathers on in there."

"I can get us through that door," Arlin said.

"Let's see if there's a side door or a back door," Cilreth said.

"Out here, does it matter? There isn't really a front."

"But there's a deck. Psychologically, this is the front. Tradition dictates it will open into a wider common area than the back door."

"We don't know the local traditions, but I see a sensor module there, right above the entrance," Arlin said. Relachik could not spot it. He looked over and noticed Arlin wore a scope goggle across his left eye.

"Cilreth, do you know how to disable security systems?" Relachik asked.

"No. But I can look into it for next time," she said.

"You'll have time to learn the basics, most likely. But we'll have to work around not having an expert in that area."

The team slipped around the cleared perimeter of the homestead until a side door became visible. He did not see a sensor module there, but one could have been hidden nearby.

"That looks good," Relachik said. "If there were one more of us, I'd say we should break in at two places simultaneously. But with only three of us, it's a close call. Arlin and I will go in that door. Cilreth, see that window? It may open into the room we'll hit first. You can go up there and check if it's empty or not, and cover us once we're in."

"Okay," she agreed.

Arlin grasped the sword tube at his belt and prepared to draw the blade out.

They took their positions beside the house.

Cilreth reported immediately. "There's a woman in there. But it's not Telisa."

"Does she have armor? Weapons? Do you have a shot?" Relachik asked.

"No armor. She has a stunner, like me. I think I can hit her if I break the window. But how strong is it?"

"Probably very strong," Arlin said. "No one out this far would take any chances."

"I agree. Just tell us when she's facing away from the door."

"She's not looking in that direction," Cilreth said.

"Okay, go."

Arlin drew his sword and sliced it across the locking mechanism. The sword sliced through the lock and a large section of the door. Arlin kicked it in. He tossed the sword aside while Relachik charged in and shot the woman with his stunner. As she dropped, Relachik summed up the area and decided it was a kitchen. Arlin came in with a projectile pistol in his hands. There was only one way out, a set of swinging doors.

"Wait or go?"

"Go."

Arlin hurried through the doors and Relachik followed. He did not see Cilreth, but he figured she would be coming any second.

Relachik heard the retort of a gun. He saw Arlin still standing in a corridor and assumed he had beaten an enemy to the punch. A set of stairs rose to his right, so he swung around a bannister and headed up. He did not see anyone at the top. There was another hall, two open doors, and a closed one. When Cilreth appeared at the bottom, he waved her up.

Relachik crept over a carpeted floor. The two open doorways revealed rooms that appeared empty from his position. One was a bedroom and the other a den with an old-fashioned clothing fabricator. The hallway turned ninety degrees and ended in another closed door.

"We're clear downstairs," Arlin said. "No sign of Telisa."

He turned back and saw Cilreth in the hall.

"Either there's a basement, or she's right there," Relachik said, pointing.

"Where?" Cilreth asked.

"In the center room. There are two ways in. You go in that side at the same time I come in here. Ready?"

"Wait, almost... okay, ready."

"Go!"

Relachik burst into the room. It was big, maybe a master bedroom. He caught sight of two men and Telisa. He felt an impact through the armor of his suit. One of the men had already hit him. His stunner flew from his hands as he fell to one side. He drew his glue pistol.

A split second later, Cilreth came through the other door. Her stunner fired.

Relachik glued the second kidnapper with his pistol. The man at Cilreth's side dropped to his knees. Cilreth kicked him in the face.

I doubt her shin is hard enough for that in real life, Relachik thought. *Then again, a shin bruise would be worth getting Telisa back alive.*

"By Hastur, that hurt," Cilreth said, confirming his suspicion. He had set the pain thresholds for the sim fairly high.

The target raised her hands and stood patiently. Her face looked calm.

More passive than she'll be when she sees me for real, he thought.

"What now? Are we done?" asked Cilreth, limping toward him.

"Check the bathroom there," he said.

Relachik stared at the copy of Telisa standing before him. The simulation gave her a blank smile, indicating she was unharmed. He pretended she was real for a second. She looked familiar, yet he felt like she was a stranger. *There's one more thing I need to practice. What am I going to say to her when I find her?*

"Bathroom is clear," Cilreth said.

"Yeah, that's enough for now," Relachik said. *I have more work to do. But there's time. I think.*

"Has anyone ever been doing simulations of their ship like this, then they exit, and forget they're not in a simulation and blown themselves up, or walked out an airlock incarnate?" Cilreth asked.

"Not any more often than the same thing happens on Earth. What age were you linked?"

"Nine."

"Then you shouldn't be getting reality and VR mixed up," Relachik said. "Just don't turn off your link's exit simulation alert."

I wonder if she's telling the truth about nine years old.

Some people were linked at birth. Their parents wanted their child to take advantage of the plasticity of a young brain, for instance, to develop a wider visual cortex capability while the brain was still forming. Many disadvantages attacked these children, though, such as a lesser appreciation for the distinction between real and virtual. Kids linked too early occasionally ended up dead through their own negligence. Many said they would eventually learn how to infant-link safely. Whole societies had left Earth over the controversy and set up new colonies with different rules, ranging from required linking at birth to no linking at all, ever.

Relachik himself had not been linked until age ten. He had linked Telisa at age nine, knowing that was what her mother wanted. It had seemed to work out well for her.

Not that I was really around that much to know.

The practice session disbanded. Cilreth returned to her search algorithms. Relachik settled into his tiny cabin. At the first hint of boredom, he automatically countered it with work. But now he was merely a passenger on a small vessel instead of the captain of a Space Force ship.

The diagnostics made him feel a bit like he was back on the *Seeker*. He missed her a lot. He missed his men, the best in the Force. He missed the ship's artificial personalities, Observer, Mechanic, and Shooter. Leaving them all behind was painful, like saying goodbye to family.

I already said goodbye to my real family long ago. And I don't even really miss them anymore.

Commanding an advanced ship like the *Seeker* had been the pinnacle of his existence. If he still had her, he felt sure he could find his daughter quickly. The UNSF had amazing cyber-specialists, black-ops robots, and alien technology at its beck and call.

Relachik satisfied himself by conducting a virtual inspection of the vessel until an anomaly caught his eye. The ship's life support system was working for four people.

A wasteful oversight to set it manually, he thought.

Relachik inspected the settings. It was set to auto detect. He frowned and double-checked everything. Nothing seemed amiss, yet the scrubbers, oxygen monitors, and heating requirements were providing for more passengers than Arlin, Cilreth, and himself.

The conclusion was inescapable.

There are four people on this ship.

Chapter 6

The alien skittered on board, his golden legs a blur. At the top of the ramp he paused for a second to wave his mass-sensor bulb back and forth before continuing. Three huge containers floated along behind him. The airlock closed behind Shiny and his train of containers.

It's shocking to see him again, Magnus thought. *I had reached the point where my memories of him felt like a dream.*

Magnus eyed Shiny's luggage. "We don't have much room for all that. I'm using most of the bay to build a robot from your walker."

"Shiny help increase packing efficiency of your cargo bay," buzzed Shiny.

"What is all that stuff?" Telisa asked from behind Magnus.

"Useful materials. Supplies," Shiny said.

"Food?"

"No. Construction materials. Remote devices to build, construct, configure. Must mimic Terran designs."

"What are they going to be, Shiny? Why are you using our stuff? Isn't Terran technology way behind your own?"

"Destroyers, invaders, conquerors search for all that is part of Shiny's race."

One of Shiny's tiny spheres lazily floated between them.

There's more of them than last time, Magnus thought.

"I see you got resupplied," Magnus said, heading for the bay.

"Achieved limited inventory gains," Shiny agreed.

"What do those spheres around you do?"

"Defend, sense, scout. Many functions."

"One function per sphere? Or are they each capable of everything?" Telisa asked.

"Specialists and generalists both present. Many choices, possibilities, configurations."

Telisa tagged along and smiled when she saw the bay.

Magnus sighed. "I suppose I need to stow most of this for takeoff, anyway," he said. "The *Iridar* isn't what she used to be. We're getting a rattle or two in her when we maneuver."

"Primitive Terran vessel unstable in atmospheric acceleration and spaceflight," Shiny agreed. "This is optimal time to arrange cargo bay to receive, accommodate, house new materials."

"I wonder if he feels a sense of danger, traveling on an alien ship of more primitive design than his own," Magnus sent Telisa privately.

"If he's like us, then he's acclimated to a more dangerous life," she replied.

"Ha. Okay, drone-killer!"

"Make fun of me all you want. You know I can handle myself now."

Magnus shrugged. She was right. The matter-of-fact way she had said it made him respond with a poke. But she had faced real danger and made it through.

Magnus cleared a minimal space for Shiny's cargo. When he finished, he regarded the alien again. He reminded himself that what looked like a beak was its back end, and the round front with the growths underneath was the closest thing it had to a head, since the eyes were there, dozens of little growths, like a garden of crab eye stalks. Its golden exterior and many legs made it look like a fancy statue. He waited for the twitch, but it did not come.

Come to think of it...

"I see you have your two legs back. And your twitch is gone," Magnus observed aloud.

"Repaired, healed, restored."

"I'm happy you're whole again," Telisa said.

"Time to leave. So where are we going, exactly?" Magnus prompted.

Shiny gave Magnus's link the coordinates.

At least he's not taking over the ship again. Yet.

Magnus inspected the general area indicated. It was way past the limits of Space Force exploration, which he had half expected.

"Okay, here we go then."

"Are you comfortable here in the bay?" Magnus asked the alien.

"This area acceptable living space," Shiny said. "Shiny has work to perform. Currently in planning phase."

"Okay. I'll leave you to it then, but I need space to work on my project as well. As we said, I need to learn more about your walker."

"Acceptable arrangement."

Magnus walked back to the mess with Telisa. He smiled a contagious smile.

Telisa smiled back. "What?"

Magnus scooped her into his arms. "Nothing. We're on another adventure!"

She laughed. "I guess you were getting bored..."

He kissed her. "Not bored," he said. "It's good to be on the move again. C'mon, you're a danger junkie now, too."

"Me? No. I'm a student. Well, I mean, I sit around and study things..."

"Not anymore. That's the old you. I know you love the thrill of going places, even dangerous places, or you wouldn't have signed up for another go."

"Yes. But it's just that... well, Jack and Thomas, you know?"

They died right in front of us. Their blood sprayed over us.

He exuberance drained away. He sighed and kissed her forehead. "This time, Shiny's on our side from the beginning."

"Is he? I mean he's on our side *at* the beginning, whose side is he on at the end? His own?"

"There are no guarantees, but we have the robot this time, too."

"What are you going to call it?" she asked.

"I don't know. We could call it Scout I guess. I think we'll have it in the lead, checking out the situation ahead of us."

"Really? So much work you put into it. I figured it would have an impressive name."

"Destroyer of Worlds?"

"Uh, no. Why don't you stick to Scout," she said.

"I'm excited to have Shiny here to help me finally figure the walker out. With—whatever his race is called—with those parts, imagine how much better this robot could be. Truly singular."

"So let me get this straight. You're trying to build an alien machine, and Shiny's trying to build a Terran machine. I think you have a suboptimal arrangement."

"Not really. We're learning from each other. Besides, I feel sure whatever he's making, there's more than one," Magnus said. "And I feel better relying on a machine I made than one he made."

"I want to know what his project is about. I'm going to get to the bottom of it."

"Well, Shiny's better at this by far, whether he's making alien things or Terran things."

"He has better tools. I wonder how his raw intelligence stacks up against ours on the curve."

"We'll probably never know."

"Have you thought this through? If Scout is based on the walker, then these things that destroyed Shiny's world are going to come after it, right?"

Oh no.

"I didn't consider that."

"Then Scout's going to last about a second there," Telisa said. "And whatever takes him out might kill us as a side effect."

Magnus threw her a sour look. "I've been working on this thing for so long. I'll have to stick with my old design."

"Learn from him anyway. Next time, we could use the improved one."

"Yeah, next time."

Dammit!

*　　　　＊＊＊*

Telisa and Magnus fell into their old shipboard patterns. Magnus trained with Telisa in combat VR every day. She still had a lot to learn, but she excelled beyond his expectations in every aspect of the training. On their last adventure, he had thought she trained in combat simply to please the rest of the crew, but now he could tell she had genuine enthusiasm for it. He felt guilty for thinking before that she had only studied it to prove herself.

After every training session, Magnus went to the bay to work on Scout. Then, at the end of the ship's artificial day, he collapsed into his bunk webbing with Telisa nearby. They floated together with the gravity turned off and did things (both virtual and real) that made Magnus forget all about the real world until he woke the next day.

Four days into their trip, Magnus waited for Telisa to join him for training.

Telisa has turned out to be the best thing that ever happened to me, he thought. *She's strong and smart. Yet this can't go on forever. If we keep rolling the dice, we're going to die like Jack and Thomas.*

"You have that look on your face," she said.

"Heavy thoughts."

"You have a hard time staying positive, don't you?"

"You're young. You haven't learned to be cynical yet."

"Well, weren't you telling me just the other day that we have Shiny and Scout this time and the odds are slanted in our favor now?"

"Yes," he said.

"So what are we going to do? Fight androids? Robots?" Telisa asked. She had done especially well in their last firefight simulation. She had gotten good at hitting targets around gentle corners and timing the releases of seeker grenades.

"I think it's time to go to the next level."

Telisa looked surprised. "Next level?"

Magnus nodded. "You're still getting better, of course, but you know the basics of small arms combat. But I've never exposed you to squad tactics or the integration of your personal view into combat. Both of these would be logical next steps to train on. You can fight on your own, but you don't use your PV, and you don't work as part of a team."

"But we fight together all the time!" Telisa protested. "We link to each other to coordinate. I don't follow you."

"We fight as two separate entities. Yes, we talk to each other a bit, but a tight squad is much more integrated. Using your PV, you can see what your friends see. You can receive information from battle probes. It takes practice to integrate views coming in through your link with what you're seeing with your eyes."

"You should have told me about this earlier!" she said.

"We've been too busy. And I prefer to introduce one concept at a time. Besides, did you really think you reached the pinnacle of Terran combat on one long mission and a few months of hiding out? This takes years."

"Okay, I'm ready. What should I do?"

"First, the concept. Then we can try something fun."
Telisa smiled.

I love her energy, Magnus thought.

Magnus put her into VR. He watched from the outside, controlling the scenario.

Telisa held a powerful rifle. She stood on a wide balcony overlooking a road three floors below. Shrubs and parked cars obscured the approach. Behind her, a wide lounge was visible through floor-to-ceiling windows. It was filled with leather furniture and elegant tables. A fancy bar dominated the far wall, with revolving doors flanking it.

"Attackers are moving down the road toward you. From the woods on the left and the draw there on the right. Of course, they'll use cover to best advantage. You're sitting here behind a blackfield that covers this balcony. Take them out as they approach."

"Okay. Waiting for the hard part." Telisa knelt by the concrete lip of the balcony and rested her rifle across it, facing the road.

"Here is your battle module," Magnus said. He added the module to the simulation. A tiny sphere the size of a tennis ball floated up behind her. He hooked its output up to her link.

"Ah. Wow. I can see whatever it sees. Got it."

"Now, more attackers have flanked you. They'll filter through the building below you, though much more slowly than those from the road. Deploy the battle module to patrol behind you and watch its cameras in your PV. When an attacker approaches from behind, you turn, take cover or whatever is appropriate, and take him out. You have to be time-efficient to cover both front and back."

"Got it."

Magnus started the action and observed. Telisa started logging shots. Her rifle launched smart rounds that sought their targets, slicing through the cover below as the attackers tried to avoid detection. Telisa periodically checked the battle module to look for the flankers.

"Aha. I see them," she said.

She turned and scampered through an open doorway into the lounge behind her, keeping low. Then she fell prone and waited.

Two attackers emerged through a revolving door into the wide lounge. Telisa went to free fire and released two bursts on quick manual. Rounds skewered the bar in spectacular fashion, sending expensive liquor flying everywhere. The attackers were cut up and dropped in a second.

"I hope I saw them all," she said, turning back to the balcony.

"You're switching your attention back and forth. You need to watch both of them at once," Magnus said.

"My brain doesn't work that way."

"It'll come."

Telisa turned back to the road and launched more smart rounds. She brought down four more assailants at long distance. "It's difficult. I can't pay attention to both of them at once."

"You can. It just hasn't become smooth yet. I know you use your PV and shower at the same time."

"Well, that's different."

"Only a bit. We all have things we can do while concentrating on a news feed or a game in the PV. This is another one of those things."

Telisa dropped two more attackers from the road. Two enemies charged out from behind her. She had not spotted them. They brought up stubby weapons and fired at her through the windows. The massive windows shattered in a huge explosion of plastic shards.

"By the Five!" she exclaimed, rolling to one side. A grenade rolled toward her. More shots rang out. Telisa lost hold of her rifle as she scrambled over the balcony and jumped.

Would she do that in real life?

Magnus knew that even with real pain in a simulation, people often played it a bit fast and loose. That was all fine for training brave soldiers who would risk their lives, but it hurt him to watch Telisa being reckless.

"Ooooooouch!" she yelled, in anticipation of her impact with the street below. Magnus cut the sim before she hit.

"Thanks."

"You owe me one. Next time, I'm going to let you feel it."

"Don't get all soft on me," she said sarcastically.

"You know I won't."

"You mentioned something fun?"

"I'm going to join you."

Magnus changed the scene to the interior of a vast building. Telisa and Magnus perched on parallel walkways overlooking a series of warehouse rows. Containers of all sizes rose in stacks beneath them, forming a maze of twisty turns and cubbyholes.

"Okay, I've set it up. I'll see what you see in my PV and vice versa," he said.

"Ha. I hope you're good at it."

"I am, actually," Magnus bragged. He smiled. *Telisa knows better than to take me too seriously.*

She looked toward his walkway and smiled. He spun around and fired his weapon.

"What the—?" Telisa asked.

"I saw someone behind me in your view of me," Magnus explained.

"Uh oh!" Telisa replied. Another shot rang out. She dropped dead.

Magnus smiled. *She'll get the hang of it.*

***

Hours after their practice, Telisa and Magnus lay entwined in her sleeping net. Finally given a moment of boredom, Magnus wondered if they were making a mistake to head out with Shiny. Ironically, in the original conversation about the new mission he had tried to encourage her, but instead he had planted more doubts into his own head. *If I weren't here, would Telisa take such risks? Am I going to get her killed?*

"Now you're moody," she said.

"Sorry. I'm thinking about the future."

"You're worried about our new venture."

"Okay. I admit it. You had a point the other day. We've led charmed lives so far. I'm waiting for something bad to happen."

Telisa gave him a mock laugh. "Ha! Charmed? Is that what you call losing our friends, living as fugitives?"

"We're still alive, and we have each other."

"That's sweet in a grim sort of way," Telisa said.

"You sometimes mention the Five Entities. You're not into that stuff for real, are you?"

"No, it's something Mom used to say."

"I don't think Shiny is religious. But he was asking about it earlier," he said.

"Really? He's probably curious about our motivations and behavior."

"I got the feeling there was more to it than that. He asked me if our prayers were answered. I said I didn't think so. Then he asked me how long it had been since they were."

"How long? Since your prayers were answered?" Telisa asked.

"No. How long since humanity's prayers had been answered. I said I didn't know."

Telisa shrugged. "He's an alien, Magnus. Of course it's hard to get him completely. If I had to guess, I would say he sees the prayer behavior and assumes it must have worked at one time; otherwise we wouldn't be doing it."

"Yeah, you're right. Think, though. His people are so different, the idea of entreating a higher power to help, even when they were primitive, must never have occurred to them. No mysticism in their past? I wonder if he's trying to help us understand him, or if he's hiding stuff from us?"

"Probably both."

Michael McCloskey

Chapter 7

Kirizzo stood very still, but his mind raced through a long planning phase. His materials sat all around him in the cargo bay of the Terran vessel, the *Iridar*. The first goal: find a way to assist Telisa and Magnus in the retrieval of his artifact.

Openly opposing the Bel Klaven would require more time and resources than Kirizzo had available. It would be better to assist indirectly. He wanted to watch the enemy and learn. Kirizzo considered his inventory and that of the Terrans. He settled on a plan for forty small probes that could detect enemy movements and transmissions. Doubtless some of the probes would be lost, but anything he could learn would help the Terrans on their mission.

Kirizzo needed a suitable hiding mechanism for the drones. They were small, which would help when moving through the subterranean environment, but he needed something more. He believed the Terrans would be unopposed by the Bel Klaven. So his probes should be constructed as Terran devices.

His legs ached a bit. He settled his thorax down onto the deck. The lack of Gorgalan torso rests on the *Iridar* gave Kirizzo an idea. The homeworld was riddled with a huge number of the Gorgalan versions of chairs: two low columns of ceramic or plastic, spaced about a half meter apart. If the probes could take such a shape, then shut down, that should be sufficient to fool any Bel Klaven war machines that became suspicious.

The planning phase moved on to details of execution.

Kirizzo accessed the *Iridar*'s network to learn about Terran methods of automaton design and construction. Information came in, but something felt wrong, over and above the annoyance of using a primitive alien information source.

The *Iridar*'s network connections exhibited very poor latency characteristics, even for Terrans. Kirizzo compared it to his previous memories of access on the ship—yes, they had degraded considerably. The link was being maintained from a much smaller set of access points than before. In fact, the vessel was configured to ignore closer and faster connection opportunities. Kirizzo examined the current configuration of the ship's network access. He slowly came to the only obvious conclusion.

Telisa and Magnus were hiding from someone or something.

Kirizzo could reconfigure for optimal access. However, the possibility that whatever his Terrans hid from posed a danger to himself as well gave him pause. Also, if something found them, they could be killed. Then Kirizzo would have to negotiate new terms with other parties. Kirizzo decided not to tamper with the settings, but he had an idea to circumvent the obstacle.

There was a word for this condition among Gorgalans—the annoying state of being in a planning phase, dropping into a sub-planning phase, then realizing the sub-planning phase required an execution section before the original planning phase could continue. Kirizzo was there now—he had to speed up his connection in order to optimize the main planning phase. He thumped his last two legs forcefully in the Gorgalan equivalent of a curse. At least the execution of this sub-problem would not require physical action; that would have been an order of magnitude more frustrating and would have involved more cursing.

Kirizzo contacted his ship using his communications gear. It trailed the *Iridar* by many light minutes. It would never approach the home planet, for fear of attracting the attention of the Bel Klaven. But it could connect to the Terran networks and get him the superior network access he wanted. Kirizzo had to pause and add a planning phase for accessing the Terran network without any of the usual accounting infrastructure a normal citizen used for identification.

Finally, Kirizzo returned to his previous task of cataloging Terran methods of design and construction. He performed a review of materials commonly used, then expanded it to everything the Terrans could do regardless of expense. He moved on to design and control methods. Kirizzo entered all the information into storage and created a set of restrictions within which his design optimizer would have to work. The limitations did reduce the solution space, but it remained solvable. The laws of physics, his available resources, and his end-product goals already formed a complicated maze to work within, so more restrictions would reduce the quality of the result, but the computation load did not increase that much.

The main planning phase came to an end, and Kirizzo shot into action.

He constructed forty small devices, using methods and designs Terrans could have achieved. The devices lay before him in an organized grid as he proceeded component by component. He dared to improve performance only a bit—perhaps five percent here and there—so his devices would not attract the attention of his enemies. Kirizzo did not know exactly how the Bel Klaven detected Gorgalans and their machines, but he felt his approach was sound. Most likely his enemies had fairly sophisticated methods, but given time and knowledge of the challenge, it would be easy to circumvent the danger.

The Terran methods were so primitive compared to his own. Gorgalan technology was vastly superior, yet most of his race had been destroyed. Overwhelmed. They had not had time to devise countermeasures, even against machines as inflexible as the ones the Bel Klaven had sent. Kirizzo had learned much in his fight to survive the machines that hunted him. He knew the secret to defeating the Bel Klaven fighting constructs involved first understanding them, then outsmarting them. He believed the Bel Klaven made their war machines this way to prevent them from ever becoming a danger to their makers.

The devices grew before him in ordered spurts. He fabricated the same pieces for all of them in batches as he went, using his portable fabricator configured to emulate Terran materials and designs.

At some point, Magnus wandered into the cargo bay and watched Kirizzo work. Kirizzo noted the healthy curiosity exhibited by his ally. As he finished a phase of the construction, adding power units to each of the forty devices, one of Shiny's sensors routed an alert into his mind: it had detected the atmospheric vibrations of Terran speech. The message was diverted into the cognition layer which coated his long neural keel.

"So, Shiny, I could use your help with the walker here. I want to adapt its power plant and these ingenious legs to my machine over here. I can't interface with either of them, though. They use your generic computation blocks, but I can't even tell if these blocks are working or broken. For all I know, I burned them out or damaged them trying to scan the insides."

Kirizzo listened to the request carefully, yet he found the desired outcome to be largely unspecified. Kirizzo wondered how best to put power in the hands of Magnus to forge his own solution. That way, Kirizzo could not be blamed for any failure in the outcome. He pondered how to reply; the Terrans seemed to prefer verbal communication even though their link devices were more useful. Kirizzo replied by vibrating one of its guardian spheres.

"What is intended mission of the robot?"

"Telisa and I could use a safer way to scout ahead."

Kirizzo considered the oddity of the situation. He attempted to adapt Terran technology in his drones, and Magnus was busy doing the opposite. He could understand the motivation to improve the machine but, given the current objective, he had to discourage the plan.

"Potential disadvantage to using this technology: Homeworld destroyers will detect, notice, track, then neutralize. Optimal to avoid, refrain, defer usage of new technology for upcoming venture."

"Yes, Telisa already pointed that out. I'm still hoping to use these designs later, though."

Magnus breathed deeply and shook his head.

"Opposition, anger, disagreement?"

"I'm expressing irritation. And before you misinterpret that, I mean I've been working hard to integrate this walker. Now I know I can't use it on this mission. And I asked for help as part of the deal."

"Shiny suggest modular construction. Shiny-technology components could be swapped out for Terran ones as necessary."

"Very well. Help me out here. How should I interface with these legs? And this power source is amazing. How long will it last?"

"Please wait."

Kirizzo had just examined typical Terran methods of design and physical construction. He now accessed several Terran robot manuals and examined their iconic methods of presentation, interface, configuration, and control. This dovetailed nicely with his recent work on his probes. He simply had to expand his review into the area of manuals and protocols the Terrans had designed for themselves. Kirizzo created a model of the conventions used in the bulk of the manuals, fed it to a translator, and created a Terran style manual for the hardware of the walker.

The Gorgalan computing blocks were harder. Their capabilities were so far beyond the controller used by

Magnus, it would stretch the Terran's imagination to understand. Kirizzo provided a step-by-step guide for implementing the interface Magnus had created for the Terran machine on a generic Gorgalan computation cube. The cubes had 16 interface layers built at different levels of abstraction. Kirizzo exposed only one of the higher ones.

This took about fifty seconds. At the conclusion of the work, Kirizzo transferred the Terran manual and the guide over to Magnus.

The Terran stood up and froze. He did not communicate for a minute or so.

"Thanks, Shiny," he finally said. "This is exactly what I need. I have a lot of work to do, though."

"I will assist," Kirizzo said. He assessed the materials nearby and entered another long planning stage. Magnus stood by, doubtless confused by the alien's announcement in contrast to his sudden lack of activity. Some small segment of Kirizzo's long, thin brain noted that Terrans differed as much from Gorgalans as the Bel Klaven did. He considered the notion that maybe their relationship would end as tragically as the Bel Klaven one had. After a minute, Magnus stirred.

"Thanks for that, but you've given me what I need," Magnus said. "I'd rather fully understand what I create, so better if I take it from here. Besides, I have time to burn."

Kirizzo considered the words of the alien. The surface sentiment seemed reasonable; still, the possibility of a switch to competitive mode by either side required a model of concealed motives. Magnus probably feared the possibility that Kirizzo would install hidden control mechanisms if he had a direct hand in the construction of the device. But Terrans seemed to prefer extended periods of cooperation or competition over rapid switching; witness the continued cooperation between Telisa and Magnus. They were a mated pair, though; perhaps their race had optimized for slower switching within a family unit. If the Terrans did generally prefer extended periods of cooperation, why would Magnus fear the possibility that Kirizzo could be trying to get access to the robot? Probably because Kirizzo had revealed too much of his race's behavior patterns already. The Terrans saw the possibility that Kirizzo would switch to competitive mode very soon, so they guarded against it.

Could the Terrans have better models of Kirizzo's behavior than he had of theirs?

The one called Magnus worked a great deal on the scout robot. He seemed to follow the directions Kirizzo had provided, with a few modifications. The most notable deviation was in control software. This supported the hypothesis that Magnus kept his own software for the security of knowing more about how it would work—and hoping that Kirizzo would not have control of it.

If that was the Terran's plan, it was doomed. Kirizzo could easily commandeer any of the Gorgalan computation cubes by accessing a lower level interface, and Terran controllers were slower and simpler, if a bit unfamiliar. Every Gorgalan warlord was, by necessity, an expert hacker.

Kirizzo returned a line of thought to their long-term behavior. The Terrans still seemed to be mates. Kirizzo hoped they would not stop the mission to produce offspring, as he felt certain that would slow things down. As it was, it was already painful to wait around while the *Iridar* made its way back to his homeworld.

The Gorgalan tried to distract himself with entertainment from the Terran net. He participated in various virtual games and explored many artificial alien environments posing as a Terran participant. These activities only accentuated the loss of the Gorgalan network. He was able to spend time in artificial Gorgalan environments using his hardware, but it lacked the depth provided by the others of his race. He was very alone now.

He learned from their games and simulations that Terrans did have a concept of competition. However, perhaps like the Bel Klaven, their loyalties were more stable. The typical conditions causing a shift to competition were that one side or the other had feigned alliance in the first place, then initiated a shift when it was beneficial. These types were much more like Gorgalans. The shift was considered to be a bad thing to do before the other side did it, and there were dirty words for it: deceit and betrayal. It was clear that Terran mores demanded that loyalty remain in place long after it became detrimental to one party.

Kirizzo formed the hypothesis that Terrans had ritualized their competition and permanently relegated it to the realm of sports activities and games. This gave them an outlet for their natural aggression, yet allowed them to remain in cooperative mode in reality for longer periods of time. If such were the case, though, it could hardly be a stable configuration. If a few individuals chose competition in the real world against the others, they would enjoy huge advantages that would quickly slingshot them past the others. When Kirizzo considered the elite who controlled most of Terran society on their homeworld, he thought that perhaps this had already happened.

A key difference between the "evil" Terrans and typical Gorgalans was that the Terran betrayers often had never shifted to true cooperation at all: they had pretended alliance all along. Gorgalans usually truly wanted alliance when it was requested. They did not generally have any future betrayal in mind as a secret plan: it was just a given that the alliance would rapidly dissolve at some unknown time in the future when circumstances changed. A Gorgalan did not eagerly await or savor any switch to conflict, but when a situation changed, a Gorgalan changed fluidly with it and switched to competition more freely.

At first, Kirizzo thought this was favorable for him. Telisa and Magnus would very likely remain loyal to him until he decided the relationship should shift. That meant he could spend less time preparing for a harmful shift to competition and more time trying to get what he needed. But he could not be completely complacent: what if Telisa and Magnus were of the rarer, but deadly, "deceitful" variety? In that case, they might be feigning cooperation, even now secretly fostering an involved plan to switch to competition and seize a huge advantage. It was a risk-management situation, as with his own kind, but the likelihood of a switch was lower on average.

He concluded Gorgalan-alien interactions probably had different optimal switch points than Gorgalan-Gorgalan relations. It had all gone so wrong with the Bel Klaven...

Kirizzo remembered the beginning of the war. Several powerful Gorgalans, initially in opposition to each other, had sensed complacence in the Bel Klaven. Those Gorgalans switched to cooperative mode to form a new alliance. Working together, the suddenly aggressive Gorgalan alliance seized several resource-rich Bel Klaven planets.

The Bel Klaven had never experienced the rapid switch of behavior inherent in Gorgalans. Almost overnight, their greatest allies had turned into powerful aggressors. The Gorgalans had always remained vigilant, hedging against such a turn in the Bel Klaven, which had never come.

Instead, the Bel Klaven shored their defenses and bided their time. When the Gorgalans came back to offer cooperation again, they were rebuked. When other Gorgalans unrelated to the attackers offered friendship, they too were rejected. The Bel Klaven blamed all

Gorgalans for the actions of the powerful alliance. In fact, it had been a round of backstabbing back home by other powerful Gorgalans such as Kirizzo that had ended the offensive against the Bel Klaven and brought the alliance back home to protect its interests on the homeworld.

Kirizzo had not participated in the attack on the Bel Klaven, but he had profited greatly from it. The distraction had allowed him to storm and capture a lot of tunnels back home.

Those gains were obliterated when the Bel Klaven revenge fleet arrived and dismantled the planet by force of arms. If Kirizzo had not been far away, trapped in a Trilisk ruin, he probably would have died with millions of other Gorgalans.

Telisa shared his interest in the Trilisks and their technology. That was both good and bad. Though she might assist in procuring new technology, she would also be a competitor when it came time to split the spoils. Fortunately she had been easily satisfied by small items here and there. She did not have the grand designs Kirizzo did.

That was almost certainly because she was ignorant of exactly what the Trilisks were. Kirizzo had made it much further on that front, despite the fact that the Terran homeworld was itself a Trilisk outpost. After examining their history, he was sure of that. If Kirizzo had more of a sense of compassion, he would have felt sad for them. As it was, he considered it a study in failure, but whether it was a failure of the Trilisks' plan to help the Terrans, or a failure of the Trilisks to seize Terra for themselves, Kirizzo had not quite figured out yet.

Telisa and Magnus would have to venture into his house and retrieve the industrial seed. The odds of their success were hard to calculate, but it was easy to see that they would have a better chance than he ever could. The seed was key to Kirizzo's chances to start over again.

Without an industrial base, he would be doomed to spend the rest of his life wandering about in Trilisk ruins, hoping to get bootstrapped again to where he was before. It would be immensely frustrating.

The Gorgalan alliance's decision to attack the Bel Klaven had turned out to be a terrible one. Kirizzo decided to remain in cooperation with these aliens, at least until he could regain what he had lost.

Michael McCloskey

Chapter 8

"I assume you've started the search for them. Any ideas yet?" asked Arlin.

Relachik and Cilreth sat in the galley of the *Vandivier* as Arlin hovered in the doorway.

"It's too early to say. I don't think they came back to Earth, though."

"I agree, though I'm only speaking from the gut," Relachik said.

"It will take me a while longer. One thing I can tell you is, we'll know in a day or two if they're serious about hiding or not. If they're being sloppy, this will be quick and easy. Otherwise, we may have to wait for them to screw up."

"I heard the UNSF uses artificial intelligences to search for things," Arlin said from the doorway. He dodged in and grabbed a snack in the tight space before moving back out to the door.

Cilreth nodded. "Maybe so, but that's not as useful as you might think," she said.

"Are you flattering yourself or insulting the government?" Relachik asked.

"Neither. Just talking about diminishing returns in intelligence," Cilreth said.

"I've heard that many times, but I don't follow it exactly," Arlin said.

"We have artificial minds that do basic computations millions of times faster than we can. But that's still not enough because as the number of facts rise, meaningful interactions between them rises faster, forming a mountain of possibilities so steep that even something much faster than us still can't work through it all. The machines can make it farther up the curve than we can, to be sure, but they're only about a third smarter than the smartest of us."

"If it's so much faster, that means each second is a long time for it to think," Arlin said. "If you put me in a room for a million years, I could solve a lot of problems."

"Given a million years you could go through a lot with a small set of facts. But given a large set of facts, the permutations of all of them, their causes and effects, their associations... the number of possibilities explodes rapidly as the fact set grows. It's a combinatoric explosion. Considering the interactions of ten facts, possibilities, or events is much more than twice as hard as considering the interactions of five things. A mind with machine memory, incredibly fine senses, the ability to think about a hundred things at once, incredibly fast net connections, and everything else a large AI has, is confronted with millions of facts every microsecond it's alive. It has to wonder whether the third microbe from the left on the rightmost ceiling tile on the last row has anything to do with the murder of Mr. Mustard."

"Colonel Mustard. But we discard useless facts like that," Arlin pressed.

"It may be useless, or it may be the only remaining microbe of the disease that killed him. But yes, you're right, part of intelligence is about figuring out which facts to examine and which ones to discard. The only way to control that explosion is by aggressively culling facts that aren't important. Terrans do that all the time since we can only handle a few ideas at once. But care is needed: discard one fact necessary to solve the problem and you're stuck. And if an AI culls its fact inventory all the way down until it's aware of only the things a human is aware of, then it's only as smart as a sharp-minded human, though somewhat faster. It threw away all the extra facts that could have made it godlike. Somewhere in all those facts are chains that could be used to make amazing deductions, but the power it takes to analyze them rises exponentially with the number of facts."

"I guess I believe you. I find it hard to grasp intuitively," Arlin said.

"I can offer a more intuitive explanation, at the cost of over-abstracting. Take a five-year-old kid. When he considers a brand new problem, he sees it as black or white. He examines these problems from fewer angles, and he has a smaller grasp of the consequences. When an adult considers a new problem, she juggles more facts than a kid can. But does the answer always come more easily? No, sometimes you become aware of more and more of the what-ifs and the tradeoffs. Now remember, I said a new problem, so you aren't supposed to make use of canned answers kids don't know yet. Sometimes the more you know, the more confused you get. It all seemed so simple when you were a kid. Now you know enough to know you're partly guessing all the time. Are you a hundred times smarter than a kid? Not really. You pushed farther up the curve until the weight of a bunch of facts, consequences, and unknowns overwhelmed your ability to push farther. You considered all sorts of things the kid never even thought of, and all it got you was a swarm of what-ifs you can't really tie down. You may have achieved a key insight the kid couldn't see, but it wasn't easy. Now consider—kids are low on the curve, adults farther up, and a genius way up there, but it's getting steeper and steeper. Doubling the power of a genius's mind can't get twice as far anymore, it only gets you a little farther up the rising curve."

Arlin shook his head. "I'll take your word for it," he said.

Relachik laughed. "You think that's bad? Try talking with a physicist about the gravity spinner sometime," he said.

Time to make our play, Relachik thought.

"Now's as good a time as any," Relachik sent Cilreth privately. "We're only a few minutes away from Arbor Gellon Five."

Cilreth's face changed. She sat silent for a moment, sandwich in hand. Then she set her food down.

"Something up?" Arlin said.

"Yes. Looks like they're the sloppy type. We have a major lead from the nearby system, Arbor Gellon Five."

"Arbor Gellon? Crazy luck," Arlin said.

"Well, the reason I got the lead is partly because we're nearby. I concentrated my efforts there since we're passing by."

"So what's the lead? What's the plan?" Arlin asked.

"Someone there knows a lot about the ones we're searching for. A collaborator. This is the jackpot."

"Take us there now," Relachik said.

"Sure!" Arlin said. He got up and walked away from the mess toward the cargo bay.

Relachik rose after him. "I'm going to work up details for a meeting."

"Okay then, the plan is in motion," Cilreth sent on their private channel.

"Yes. Just stay calm," Relachik replied.

Arlin brought the ship into the Arbor Gellon system. He headed for the sole habitation there, a colony of about ten million souls on the fifth planet and a space habitat in orbit. Their spinner brought them into a reasonable range. Then Arlin used simpler thrusters to match orbit with the habitat. A complex series of bureaucratic handshakes took place, mostly automated procedures outside the typical realm of human attention. The *Violet Vandivier* proved itself a legitimate vessel.

This time there was a bit of extra scrutiny. The security had been tightened since the destruction of the *Seeker*. A ring of protective satellites was under construction in orbit of the planet, as well as a small Space

Force vessel. Once again Relachik took note of these developments and felt annoyance at his lack of clearance.

Relachik found Arlin in person and spoke aloud. "Arlin. We have a name. This guy is on the space habitat. I'm sending you the details." He sent the information Cilreth had provided about someone who lived on the habitat. "Check this out. Make sure it's not a trap. If the guy is alone, we'll arrange a meet at another spot."

Arlin nodded.

"Look," Relachik said. "You haven't done anything wrong. If it is a trap, they're either after me or Telisa."

"I wasn't complaining," Arlin said.

"Just letting you know I'm not putting you in harm's way... yet."

Arlin went to his weapons locker. He came back to the lock wearing a thick protective suit. Relachik saw his equipment and nodded.

"You got something better than a stunner?"

"Yes. A laser," he said, drawing the weapon.

At the cue 'laser,' Relachik activated the trap.

There was a loud snap and crackle to their left. The ship's lights winked as a humanoid form materialized from thin air. The stranger emitted a surprised curse.

Arlin shot the form in the shoulder without hesitation, then charged forward and bowled the intruder over. Relachik joined him, grabbing the spy's still-holstered weapon, a compact projectile weapon.

"So you made me," the person croaked. A visor covered half the face, open over the mouth. Goggled eyes locked onto Relachik.

"This is where you get off. Leave the suit behind."

"You're going to be in a—"

"Save the speech, or we'll space you instead," Relachik snapped.

The man stripped off the thick stealth suit. It had protected him from the majority of the laser's energy. He wore only a thin shirt and undersheers after shedding the suit. The laser burn was a round black hole on the edge of his pectoral. Pain dominated the spy's face.

Relachik covered him for a few tense minutes while the *Vandivier* detoured away from the habitat. The ship descended to the rugged planet below. Finally, Relachik extended the ramp. It revealed a remote location on a barren planet.

"Move it," Relachik prompted.

The man staggered down the ramp. Arlin closed the *Vandivier* back up and began the takeoff procedure.

"Even though you warned me, it still scared the crap out of me when he showed up out of thin air!" Cilreth said. "He's been here the whole time?"

"Yes."

"Who could have sent him? Maybe we need to interrogate him."

"He has to be Space Force. I guess they don't trust me very much."

They're covering all their bases because of the aliens. And they know I made unusual decisions in an encounter. How much do they know?

"What now?" Cilreth asked.

"We have to check all the systems and see what the remora broke," Relachik said.

He stole a glance at the remora. It was a thick disc stuck to the ceiling above the spot where the spy had been standing. A small green light winked on its surface as Relachik disarmed it.

"We used the lowest setting, so it shouldn't be too bad," Arlin said. "I have to admit, I'd never have thought of using a remora inside my own ship. But it sure did a number on his stealth suit."

Cilreth looked the suit over. "We don't have a key for it."

"Luckily, I have a computer expert in my employ."

"I'm a searcher, not a hacker."

"You can't do it?"

"I can do it. But it's going to cost you extra because you risked my life, just then."

"As long as we find Telisa."

Cilreth nodded and retreated with the gear. Relachik suspected she would head to the cargo bay, where she could find useful tools for her investigation. Or perhaps she would take the software angle first.

Relachik walked in circles through the tiny ship. His resolve to find his daughter remained firm, though now he saw a larger chance of failure. What if he led the Space Force to her? What if the Force planned to catch and arrest them both?

Dammit, Tel, you put us in a tight spot. I hope it was worth it.

He thought of Telisa's mother, a principled scientist, a woman who made great advances in understanding the first alien devices recovered by the Space Force, until her untimely death. He knew he was doing right by her memory to sacrifice everything to protect their daughter.

After a while, he decided to pester Cilreth. He knew she would not have made much progress yet, but he wanted to know if she would still participate in their training routines.

"Cilreth. Are you checking out that suit?"

"Of course. You think I could resist slavering over this treat?"

"Can we use it?"

"Too early to say. I'm still marveling over its design. Well, actually, I'm trying to figure out if it's one-hundred percent genuine Terran know-how, or modified alien tech, or reverse-engineered from alien tech. I may never know, though; some of these components have been shielded against probing."

"Of course. A lot of Space Force stuff is hardened against prying eyes."

"Well, I'm gonna keep prying."

"Good. Keep me informed. Shall we run a few more scenarios at fourteen hundred hours?"

"How about eighteen hundred? I prefer to work in longer spurts."

"Eighteen hundred it is."

Chapter 9

"What's up?" Telisa called from the entrance to the cargo bay.

"We've arrived," Magnus said.

"Where exactly?"

Magnus shrugged. "Shiny says it's his home."

Telisa accessed the *Iridar*'s sensor data. A light brown planet zoomed into her mind's eye. It was roughly Earth-sized. The atmosphere was thin. It was not a gorgeous blue and green planet filled with life. It looked rocky and dead.

"Shiny, has your planet always looked like that? Or was it the destroyers?"

"Planet appears normal from here," Shiny said. "Massive damage internally. Shiny civilization hidden, subterranean, submerged."

Telisa sifted through the details of the planetary data. There were indeed a few signs of life tucked away, even on the surface. Nothing big. In fact, much of what they had detected among the rocks were sessile creatures deriving sustenance from the star, creatures half plant, half animal. Hints of vast underground tunnels were there, as expected. Minimal volcanic activity. The air at the surface could barely sustain Terrans.

"What is it called? I don't think I should be calling you a Shinarian anymore."

Shiny stomped several of his feet in a quick pattern.

"Ah, right," Telisa said. "Say it again please?"

Shiny repeated the pattern. There seemed to be a duplicated preamble and a louder clack at the end.

"Sounds like... Vovok," Telisa said.

"Vovok it is, then," Magnus said.

"What algorithm provides translation?" Shiny asked.

"A whimsical one. No worries. The name doesn't translate. So I'm calling it Vovok. Which makes you a Vovokan. Be glad I didn't call it Klack Klack."

Before Shiny could inquire further, Telisa asked more questions.

"Where should we drop? What can we expect to find? Besides your target industrial seed, I mean. We have the specs you gave us for that."

Shiny downloaded an information module to *Iridar*'s storage. Telisa received a pointer.

"Study, learn, prepare," Shiny said.

"You do know where this seed is?" Telisa asked.

"Affirmative. Telisa, Magnus, dropped on planet surface nearby. Seed located deep underground."

"Makes sense. Your race is subterranean," Telisa said.

"Affirmative, correct, accurate statement of fact."

"You don't have to say that three times, you know," she said.

"Each word inaccurate, estimate, approximate. Utilization of multiple words helps to communicate lack of exact, perfect, aligned match. Defines approximate, estimated, local-meaning space."

"Amazing," Telisa said. "He's using the triple synonyms to tell us that there is no exact match."

"It's good to know. I thought he was still learning to use our language, but I guess this means there may never be a smooth match up."

Telisa noticed a series of low pillars, hourglass-shaped, lined up in the cargo bay.

"And these?" Telisa asked, pointing at the objects.

"Gift. Offer. Mutual benefit," Shiny said.

"Those are what you made on the way here, right? You said before they are remote drones."

"These gather information. They warn Telisa and Magnus of destroyer activity. Allow Shiny to monitor general, overall, long-range situation from remote location."

"Only us? Why aren't you coming?"

"Enemy. Danger."

"But you expect us to go in your place? This deal is getting worse."

"Robotic enemy sensitive to Shiny technological and biological footprint. Not sensitive to Telisa, Magnus. Safer, more likely success utilizing Terran agents."

Telisa accessed the information module. She saw a three-dimensional map of a Vovokan city in her PV. The complexity of the location sank in. The city he had shown them was a subterranean maze of epic proportions. The map contained many layers of various kinds of infrastructure. Telisa could only observe one of them at a time without overwhelming her senses. To look at all the tunnels, connections, and rooms at once was too confusing.

"That's a lot of tunnels and pipes," Magnus said, understating the obvious. "But I see no electronic networks."

"Power and information are transferred through electromagnetic fields," Shiny prompted.

"So they have broadcast power as well as wireless data transfer," Telisa summarized carefully.

"That is vague but right, correct, suitable as abstraction for elementary understanding of a thing very complex, complicated, confusing," Shiny said.

"The map can't be accurate anymore, if there's been a war," Magnus said. "I assume the city and your house were breached by destroyers."

"Also correct. Vast, wide, incalculable devastation."

Telisa searched for any sorrow in the artificial voice but found none.

"There's no way to tell how he really feels about it. If he feels," Telisa shared with Magnus over another channel.

"Shiny, how does the destruction of your home make you feel?" Magnus asked for her.

"Schadenfreude."

"What!?"

"Great opportunity created for personal advance, gain, profit, in absence of major, serious, heavy competition," Shiny elaborated.

"We're in league with the nastiest sort of space creature out there," Magnus transmitted to her.

"We can't expect an alien to stand up to our standards of moral behavior," Telisa replied, though she felt the same shock.

"So there will be dead Vovokans," she said to Shiny. "A lot of them. I don't know what this city was like, but—"

"City is poor, inaccurate, misleading term. Target location is inside my house, domicile, abode."

"Yes, a house in this city—"

"All information provided describes my house, abode, dwelling. Constructs outside the target area have not been provided."

"What?"

"Telisa, Magnus, enter from surface. Recommend remain within its confines."

Telisa checked to see if Magnus was catching the conversation. From his wide-eyed expression, she judged he was.

"Shiny, what are the approximate dimensions of your house?"

"All that is displayed, described, defined here. Twenty-five kilometers by fourteen kilometers at geometric center, extending from surface to an average depth of twelve kilometers."

"Five Holies. When am I ever going to learn to stop making assumptions about aliens? I'm supposed to be good at that!" *Still, such discoveries are exactly why I find xenos so amazing. I've been obsessing over the Trilisks, but Shiny's race is probably just as interesting.*

"Why is your house so large?" Magnus asked, beating Telisa to the next question.

"Safety. Productivity. Control. High number of reasons," Shiny said.

"So you want us to go in there and get you this seed. That's all you want out of this? We can take anything else that we want? We can steal from your house, right?"

"Affirmative, allowed, encouraged. Industrial seed is sole Shiny stake in operation."

"And it just happens to be full of enemy death machines?"

"Destroyers focused on controlling, suppressing, exterminating Shiny race."

His race is being killed off. At least here on their homeworld. I'd be so horrified for Shiny, except he himself seems only ready to take advantage of it.

Telisa looked at the data for a few minutes longer. Trying to familiarize herself with the complex maze made her mind feel fuzzy.

"I'm tired. We need to sleep before we start," Telisa said.

"Encouragement," Shiny said. He didn't move.

Telisa and Magnus left him alone in the bay and went to her quarters. Telisa lowered the lights and removed an outer layer of clothing to get comfortable. She noticed she already had Magnus's eye. She smiled. He never got tired of watching her. They were different, yet compatible in so many ways. They stretched out into her sleeping web and held each other close. Despite her fatigue, Telisa's mind still raced.

"If he decides to take the *Iridar* and leave..." Telisa whispered.

"He won't. He has his own ship; he doesn't need the *Iridar*. It's inferior. No, he needs the industrial seed, and he can't get it by himself. Now therein lies the real danger.

Once we've retrieved it, we have to hope he's not as bloodthirsty as we fear he may be."

"So, we're going to go down to Vovok and steal our next batch of artifacts," she said. "Vovokans. Hmm, I may need to revisit that name. It doesn't exactly slide off the tongue."

"I don't think the Vovokans need their stuff anymore," Magnus said. "Shiny offered it."

"It is basically looting a destroyed civilization—one being annihilated. Not exactly as honorable as being a true archaeologist."

"Does that bother you?"

"Well, the main difference here is that archaeologists have to recreate knowledge of a culture from long-buried clues. And that's what I studied for. In such a profession, progress comes slowly over years. But now we've found live aliens, and the information comes faster, easier. I don't feel bad about it; after all, the reason I would sift through a ruin is to learn about the extinct culture of the aliens. We don't have to do it the slow way anymore. A high-tech artifact tells you so much more about a culture than a shard of pottery. And a live alien should be even more informative. Though in Shiny's case, it's a bit hard to pump him for information."

"Yes, but we learn more every day." His hand caressed her cheek.

Telisa's mind slipped back to her last argument with Magnus. They had not broached the subject since.

The fact that he thinks we're not justified in the eyes of our own kind makes me doubt myself. I've always railed at the government for keeping the artifacts from me. They don't have our best interests in mind... do they?

"I'm sorry about the other day. Maybe your criticism hit too close to home," Telisa said.

"I never criticized you. I'm only saying, life is full of gray. I'm sorry I got so loud and angry. It's the pressures of our new life. We were blowing off steam at each other."

"To Shiny, the gray zone isn't a morally ambiguous area. It's a mixture of him gaining something and his competitors gaining something at the same time."

"Good guess. Either that, or the gray zone is a trade off of something gained for something lost. But unless Shiny is an aberration among his kind, these are Vovokan morals," he said.

"Wouldn't that be awful? If Shiny turned out to be a crazy Vovokan?"

Telisa was not sure who to be more scared of: the Core World government or the creature she had called an ally against them. She set her worries aside and turned her full attention to the man who held her. It was her favorite life-problem avoidance tactic.

Michael McCloskey

Chapter 10

The door to Cilreth's quarters announced a visitor. Startled, she sat up. She had been totally absorbed in her work. *Why drop by incarnate when they can call my link? Ah. Relachik just works that way. He's old fashioned.*

Cilreth let her door open. Beyond stood Relachik, exactly as she had surmised.

"I know you're good," he said from the doorway. "But I can't stand being in the dark anymore. So I'm asking, as your employer, what do you have so far?"

Cilreth's mouth twitched. She hated it when the drug did that at times when people could misinterpret it as annoyance or hesitation.

"Fair enough. Arlin, too?"

"Sure. Come to the mess and we'll have an FTF."

"Face to face? I think only the Space Force says it that way anymore."

"Oh excuse me. I meant to say, let's do it incarnate."

"No, that means we're going to have sex for real instead of virtually."

Relachik's face turned red. "Five Holies, do you understand me or not?"

Cilreth nodded and stood. Relachik liked to play the grumpy old man, but she had already picked up that he was not really irritated. It was just how he talked. She let her head clear for a moment, as she had been deep into her work. Then she followed Relachik to the mess.

Arlin had already arrived. He was eating a sandwich. Cilreth sat down and sliced herself a wedge of cheese.

"The way to find people is to trace their money and their links to the net," Cilreth said. "Unless Telisa and Magnus are completely off the grid, living in a cave on an alien planet, they have to use money. Of course, that encompasses various centrally controlled currencies like ESC as well as the dozens of peer-to-peer systems favored on the frontier. And they may need information, news, and entertainment. So they need access. Nowadays, anyone who can stay disconnected for long periods is a rare find. Most people, even wanted murderers, can't stand to stay off."

"But these two are determined," said Relachik.

"Yes. I believe Telisa could do it. However, she has a business to run. There will be connections for sales. I think she's online, which means we can find her."

"So they're operating with false identities. They've set up whole new lives."

"The fact that I haven't picked them up in the clean search means they've gone a step further than that. They're operating under the umbrella of a special organization."

"What?"

"The frontier has companies that specialize in masking operations from the government. They aggregate and shuffle data requests and money movements. When you access data through one of these illegal operations, they run huge caches, time shift your access requests, and wait for batches to accumulate. They process queries in large groups, then break them up into a new set of tiny requests that happen in other orders and on behalf of other entities, disguising all the patterns we'd be looking for. But knowing they're doing something like this is a step forward. There are only so many operations out there that are really good at it. I think I know who they're using, but I'm not absolutely sure."

Relachik had been listening with his face betraying growing concern. "How dangerous are these people they're working with?"

"As paying customers, your daughter and her friends are probably safe enough. But if anything goes wonky, then the outfit is capable of murder to clean up problems. Which makes our job harder. You see, if they find out what we're doing, the organization may try to eliminate us, or even eliminate your daughter to keep their exposure at a minimum. On the other hand, sometimes you can find the right person and simply bribe them to get what you want, as long as the repercussions are going to be clean and quiet."

"Why would they do that? All their customers would quit using them," Arlin said.

Cilreth nodded. "The smart, forward-looking ones wouldn't sell out their customers. But these criminals are only human. They're greedy and shortsighted. If the reward is large enough, they'll slip a name or two now and then. Not enough to get a lot of attention if they can help it. But sadly, almost any human can be tempted by short-term gain over long-term prosperity."

"What's this group called? Where are they located?" Relachik asked.

Cilreth sighed. "This isn't going to make you any happier. They were originally called the Enclave by the locals. Now, though, they're widely known as the 'F-clave.' The story goes, the leader was putting pressure on someone who said, 'Who are you guys?' and the leader said, 'We're the fucking Enclave!' and shot him dead, so now, they're the F-clave for short."

"And where are they located?"

He doesn't even bat an eye. He's going after them no matter who they are.

"I think on more than one world. For sure, on Brighter Walken. And that's probably where Telisa and Magnus would go. I've checked some spaceport information, and ships like the one you described have visited there. Of course, even those logs are subject to tampering. It's hard to estimate how connected her smuggler friends are."

"How many smugglers are we talking about?" Arlin asked.

"We know of at least five, but I wouldn't be surprised if they have more people out on the frontier. They're employees of a company that hired her back on Earth, Parker Interstellar Travels. It's a guide-and-scouting-company front to the smugglers. Apparently three of them are on Earth. I recently obtained video of them from several cameras that operate around their headquarters."

"I know Brighter Walken," Relachik said, and Cilreth believed him. If anyone knew something about almost all the inhabited worlds, it was probably a scout ship captain. Or an ex-scout ship captain.

"So that's where we need to go," Arlin said. "I'll set course for there immediately."

"Okay," Relachik said. "If this place is like Cilreth describes, it'll be a fortress. There will be muscle. We could disappear, walking into a place like that."

"So what now?"

"We go there. We find someone to pressure and force them to tell us what we need," Relachik said. He looked at Cilreth. "What do we need, exactly, to find Telisa?"

"The organization will have the data on their clients, locked up tight, of course. And they'll have tracking keys. No doubt it will be a super-secure location. Breaking in through the net won't be an option; I'm sorry, but they'll have top-notch hackers working for them. If the critical stuff is even connected to the net, it would be very dangerous to go snooping there. Most likely a death squad would show up out of nowhere and kill us."

"What do you mean tracking keys?" Arlin asked.

"I mentioned how they send all client's queries and data through the blender to mix them all together? Well, they can unblend it from the outside. In real time. Suppose gangster A is assigned to client C, who owes the organization money. Gangster A is supposed to keep track of C, and maybe drop in from time to time to pressure him. So gangster A is given C's tracking key. With the key, he can eventually find the client through his net usage, just as I would if the target weren't behind this obfuscation system. It's useless to decode information about any of the other clients, so giving gangster A this key is not too much of a security risk. But we need Telisa's key. Or the key those smugglers share."

"Then we should find the company member who has their key. The one assigned to them."

Cilreth shook her head. "I doubt there is one. If Telisa and crew are paying their bills and not causing a problem, there is no reason to send out a person to hassle them. Also, if someone has a tracking key and we pressure him, the first thing he'll do is wipe the key from his link with a thought. He knows he can always return to headquarters and get another copy once he's out of danger. We need to get access to the crime organization's most trusted storage."

"Maybe we could cause a huge debt to appear for them, one they couldn't pay off, then find the guy sent out to harass them, and follow him incarnate," Arlin suggested.

"I don't like that because it makes them hunted by the F-clave as well as the government," Relachik said. "For now, divide and conquer. Step one is finding out where that storage is."

"Finding it incarnate may be as dangerous as snooping around it through the network."

"Once I'm done with these guys, they're not going to be dangerous to anyone," Relachik said.

Cilreth wondered if she had signed on for the wrong job. Then she shrugged. *The twitch is already killing me anyway.*

***

Cilreth appeared beside Arlin and Relachik in the simulation. It was set up to present them with what they knew of the situation on Brighter Walken. This was their first practice session focused on the objective of finding the F-clave headquarters.

The star blazed overhead. Cilreth summoned up a pair of heavy shades. Just ahead lay the target building, a two-story frontier shack of plastic and metal.

"Okay, there's Frankie's club, the Vain Vothrile. Hadrian works in there. He's usually in the back," Relachik said, mostly for Arlin's benefit, since Cilreth had gathered most of the information.

It's probably good for me to hear it all again, too, Cilreth thought. *I didn't dig into the info very deeply. Relachik's a monster for detail; he probably learned a lot more from it than I did.*

"So let's go in there, close the club up, and have a little talk with Hadrian," Relachik said.

"How can we disable the club's defenses?" Arlin asked.

"Cilreth, can you do it?"

Before Cilreth could answer, Arlin snapped his fingers.

"Wait. Maybe this is another clever way to use our remoras!" he said.

"Maybe. Or maybe that's more attention than we want," Relachik said. "I was also going to have the club turn away new customers once we got in there. If everything's broken, it won't work."

"I can close it down. A place like this won't have top-notch security. Unless this is the F-clave headquarters, which I'm sure it's not. It's too small."

"I thought you said you were a searcher, not a hacker," Relachik said.

"I'm not a real hacker, but you hardly have to be a genius to shut a dive like this down," she said. "I got this one."

"Okay then, let's hit it."

They walked into the club. The place was decked out with augmented reality drink and drug ads, pictures of suave spacemen and women, and services offering lists of sporting-event feeds. It was an assault of sight and sound. There was an incarnate dance floor and a dozen virtual ones run as services from dozens of booths. A long bar dominated one wall, with doors beyond that opened into the back of the club.

Cilreth found it mildly interesting, having never been in such a frontier dive before. It smelled considerably worse than a virtual core world club. But the grittiness that came with its incarnate charm carried some dark, dirty appeal that surprised her. Perhaps it was the danger. A virtual club came with little or no risk, whether it was inhabited by bots or real cyber-visitors.

Relachik took one look at the busy bar, filled with people dancing, drinking, and making out. "Not gonna work. I'm taking us back to opening time."

The figures in the club flitted in high speed then disappeared. Now, only two patrons were inside, just arriving at the bar.

"Okay. Resume," Relachik said.

Cilreth started in on the club's controls. She hijacked Frankie's credentials then shut him out. Arlin and Relachik physically barred the front door, then stunned the patrons with their weapons. They charged into the back rooms to grab Hadrian while Cilreth finished up with the club security.

Oops. The cameras got Arlin and Relachik. I'll have to work on that.

Her allies emerged from the back with a short man in tow. Hadrian. They tied him to a chair.

"I can get it out of him," Cilreth said on a separate channel. She flashed a predatory smile.

"Do you really want to do the coercion when we're there for real?" asked Relachik.

"Oh. No, good point. You handle it."

"Do you have a plan to get him to tell us what he knows?" asked Arlin.

"I'll have to think on it," Relachik said. "For now, I'll wing it."

Relachik wound back and struck Hadrian savagely across the face. "The name of your boss. Now," he growled.

"You're a dead man," Hadrian mumbled, a stream of blood pouring from his mouth.

Cilreth got an alarm signal. "Dammit. The local constabulary is approaching."

"Exit strategy?"

"Uhm, that's TBD."

"Okay then. Let's run it again," Relachik said. "Or should we do the running firefight with the cops on the way back to the *Vandivier*?"

Cilreth sighed. "Run it again."

Chapter 11

The surface looked like teal-stained rock at first. As Magnus examined it, he decided the flat plates of greenish-blue material might actually be a type of plant life. They encrusted every boulder nearby. The rocks and growths were taller than Magnus, limiting his view in all directions. The sky, at least, reminded him of Earth. It was clear and blue.

Magnus immediately noticed the extreme isolation. His link picked up only a handful of services from items they carried. The environment was devoid of link traffic.

It's up to us now.

"Those are like mushrooms or lichens or something," Telisa said, kneeling to check the composition of the surface.

Magnus's link reported the *Iridar* as out of range as the ship lifted away from the planet, taking Shiny with it. They stood next to the cargo container they had unloaded from the *Iridar*. The landing had been tricky on the rocky landscape, made even more difficult by Shiny's insistence for a quick drop off.

"Maybe," he said. He walked toward the nearest growth and kicked it. It gave a bit under the blow.

"Wait. Is it safe?"

"We're going to go down into broken underground tunnels on an alien planet, and you're worried about kicking a giant... Okay, yeah, you're right. It could be dangerous. Especially if Shiny is used to living underground, he may not have thought to mention above-ground nasties."

"He said the entrance is over there," Telisa said.

"First things first," he said. He opened the cargo container. Shiny's probes nestled inside, sitting in hexagonal spaces like bee larvae. Each was about the size of a Terran head. As soon as the lid was clear, the

Michael McCloskey

cylindrical probes activated. One by one, they floated into the air. They emitted only a tenuous whine as they hovered off, each one in a different direction. The last one waited nearby.

"I guess that one's with us," Telisa said.

"Looks like it," Magnus said, lifting the empty holding tray out of the container. He discarded it to one side, exposing the contents underneath: Scout.

Magnus activated the machine with his link. Scout clambered out of the cargo container on long spider legs and stood ready. The body of the machine was almost rectangular, rather than the ovoid of an ant or spider, but its legs made it look very lifelike. Magnus felt frustration. It had to be all Terran technology this time. The walker machine had offered so much potential.

"Okay. Which way did you say? Just send him toward the entrance."

Telisa gave the command. Scout moved off through the tortuous landscape. Telisa and Magnus walked carefully over the rocks, keeping well behind Scout. Magnus routed Scout's sensors into his PV as they'd practiced on the ship.

The machine ahead walked up to a huge pipe rising from the ground. The entire thing was black and scarred. Pieces of debris lay all around among the rocks. The gaping opening was large enough to accept a car.

"There it is. Shiny's module describes how to open it," Telisa said. "But it looks like the destroyers made it here ahead of us."

"You must have spent a lot of time studying his house," Magnus said.

"Of course. Didn't you? I guess it's more up my alley."

"Well, I was putting the finishing touches on Scout here. You just watch."

The machine crept up to the ragged edge of the pipe and peered down. Magnus saw the tunnel in several different sections of the spectrum: infrared, visual, and an ultraviolet band. It looked cold and dead. There was wreckage lying about. Nothing caught his eye as valuable or dangerous.

Scout's tail grew a smart rope. The rope's end found a strong purchase point outside the entrance and wrapped itself around it. Then Scout jumped over the edge. The machine reeled down rapidly, dropping like a spider from a strand of webbing. Telisa and Magnus were arriving at the opening as Scout settled onto a surface thirty meters below. The smart rope released its hold above and reeled back into Scout's body. Then the machine scanned its new surroundings.

"Impressive!" Telisa said. Magnus could tell from her tone she was only a little impressed but hamming it up for him, so he played along.

"Of course! Who built it?"

"Now it's our turn."

Magnus scanned Scout's vision in his PV. "Looks clear enough. I agree."

"So nice to have him down there, and know we're not about to be ambushed. We need more robots!"

"Yeah. Next time," he said. He offered her a smart rope.

"I have my own, thanks," she said, digging into her pack. Magnus smiled. She wanted to prove she had come properly prepared. Of course he had not insinuated otherwise. It was just her way.

Magnus chose the same spot Scout had used to anchor his rope. He simultaneously monitored the feed from Scout, showing a wrecked chamber filled with dust and garbage. The machine caught a bit of movement to one side.

"What is it? Did I miss something?"

"Something down there," Magnus said. "It was small. Must be a critter."

"Great. A critter," she said flatly. They stood for a moment as Scout rooted about more, looking for the source of the movement.

"Should be fine. Keep practicing. Learn to watch both at once."

"While I'm climbing down a pit?"

"Gravity and the rope are doing all the work for us," Magnus pointed out. "Doesn't matter what you're doing, we need to see what it sees."

Magnus swung out over the pit on his line. The smart rope had controllers that responded to link commands. Each end had artificial muscles and retractable claws that could wrap around and latch onto objects, then release themselves at the top once a climber had slid down the rope. Magnus also had a launcher that could shoot the rope to high targets, and even a pair of climbing insect devices that could carry a rope up into areas where it could not be shot with the launcher.

Scout continued to patrol in a small circle as Magnus slid down his line. Telisa followed close behind. At the bottom, they told their ropes to release. The lines fell gently and rolled themselves back up.

"Sand everywhere," Magnus noted. The stood in a round tunnel with smooth sides. A large beam had smashed through the wall of the tunnel, sitting at an angle. The grit covered everything.

"Remember the Vovokan habitat in the Trilisk trap? The tunnels used sand as a self-cleaning carpet and transport system," she said.

"I doubt it's either anymore. This isn't a natural looking cavern like Shiny made in the trap. Whatever system was in place has probably been ruptured."

"What if the critter lives in the sand? There could be a hundred and we'd never know."

"Momma Veer will take care of you. I doubt it could bite through your suit."

Magnus took a deep breath. The air was dry. It smelled like metal. They had brought masks just in case, but the air was breathable as-is.

"Okay, I'm sending Scout in down this side passage," Telisa announced. "We have a long way to go through this, so..."

Magnus sent a short nonverbal acknowledgment. They had only taken a couple of steps down the new passage before Magnus got an alert through his link. It came from Shiny's probe network. He added a pane in his PV to see a map of the situation beside the feed from Scout.

A red dot moved toward their position. Magnus assessed what it meant.

"A destroyer's coming," he said.

"Oh no."

"Up against the wall!"

They curved their bodies to match the circular wall of the passage, facing each other from opposite sides of the narrow tube. Magnus halted Scout.

A light wind arose in the tunnel. The light from the opening above shifted erratically. Magnus caught a humming sound.

"What the hell?"

A humming noise rose in the distance as the wind picked up. Grains of sand whipped their legs and feet.

"By the Five," Telisa said, switching to link communication. "Either Shiny's right about these things not caring about Terrans, or we're dead."

The noise became louder. Magnus felt his heart accelerate. He breathed in quick, short bursts to avoid the sand in the air. He considered deploying his Veer suit's faceplate, but the wind abated. The light returned to normal.

"That's encouraging," Magnus sent.

They waited a few more moments. Magnus monitored the red dot. It moved away rapidly.

"Actually, it simply serves to remind me how dumb it is to go poking around on alien planets," Telisa said.

"We're okay. Shiny was right."

They came to an intact hatch at the end of the passageway. The hatch was circular, though it had thick bars of reinforcing metal or ceramic crisscrossing its surface.

"I know how to open this, though the sand may get in the way. I think you're right, the sand must have leaked from a damaged side system. This is supposed to be clean. We aren't in the natural-looking tunnels yet, where they lived."

"And died," Magnus added.

Telisa grabbed two struts along the surface of the hatch. The struts clicked and moved then the hatch clanged loudly. Telisa scraped the hatch open. A thick fog roiled out a bit at the edges.

"Great, like a house of horrors," Telisa said.

Magnus shrugged.

"Masks?" Telisa asked.

Magnus sent Scout in.

"Just watch," Magnus said.

Scout scampered through on its long legs. There was only a slight crunch of sand with each footfall. Magnus saw another dim passage filled with sand.

A message came from Scout. It showed an analysis of the air inside.

"Looks fine," Magnus said.

"It kind of smells," Telisa noted.

"There's most likely dead things in there."

Magnus heard a slight rustling noise through Scout's senses. The machine peered down a tunnel into a natural cavern. The entire inner surface of the tunnel spun clockwise. The noise came from a bit of sand Scout had knocked into the spinning tunnel, but it quickly abated.

"We have to go in there?" Telisa asked.

"You tell me. Isn't this Shiny's route?"

"Yes," Telisa said.

Magnus told Scout to wait until they caught up to look at the tunnel themselves. They slipped through the hatch. Magnus swept the cramped room beyond with his light, covering the illuminated areas with his weapon. Telisa seemed content to rely upon Scout's initial sweep. The walls became irregular, with a low ceiling. Magnus had to stoop a little.

The two advanced to Scout's position. Their lights revealed a long spinning tube, but they could not see the end of it. The tunnel was round, with a spiral depression winding down its length like a reverse screw.

"It carries things forward," Magnus surmised.

Telisa put out her hand. She touched the surface. "It's pretty slippery."

Magnus squatted to scoop up a handful of sand. He tossed it in the tube.

The sand scattered into the depression then moved away as the spiral carried it down the tunnel.

"It's a transport tube," Magnus said. "The ridges carry you along like an inside-out screw."

"This thing is still working somehow... shouldn't it have stopped? Everything else seems destroyed or dead from lack of power."

"It is strange," Magnus agreed, staring down the tunnel.

"It's probably great for Vovokans, but looks uncomfortable to me. Or dangerous. We'll be moving forward out of our control. Can we even walk in it? What if it dumps into...? Never mind, let me look at the map."

Magnus nodded. He gave the rest of the chamber a look while Telisa consulted the data from Shiny. The walls sloped like natural caverns, though they had a smooth surface, just like the ones he remembered from Thespera. These were the real thing, though, not the creation of a Trilisk machine emulating the preferred environment of its inhabitant. They glistened in the light with tiny pinpricks of reflective material. Other than sand, the only things on the floor were two ceramic columns about a foot tall.

"I think those ceramic things are Shiny chairs," he said. "Vovokan, I mean."

"This tube is about a quarter of a kilometer long. It should be okay to get into, I guess," Telisa said.

"We'll send Scout first, of course," Magnus reassured her. "We'll see any danger through it."

"Okay," she said.

Magnus sent Scout scuttling into the spiraling tunnel. The robot appeared confused. The spinning tube slid it up the right-hand side until it balanced the friction against the gravity. A couple of its legs caught against the depression, then it started sliding forward. At the same time, it took steps forward.

"It's not quite that smart," Magnus said. "I bet with the Vovokan walker's brain..."

Telisa laughed. "You can't let go of that, can you? We'll use the improved one soon enough. I think it's easier for Scout to get through than it will be for us. It has more legs to catch in the depression. I bet that's exactly how Shiny would move through there."

Scout emerged on the far side. Its feed showed more sandy ruin. A much larger tunnel ran perpendicular to the transport tube with dozens of doors or windows opening into it. Magnus did not see anything dangerous.

"I think I'm going on my stomach," Telisa said. "I don't trust myself to run or walk through it."

"Yeah, stomach sounds fine. You want to attach a line or just go for it?"

"Worked for Scout," Telisa said. She knelt forward, feeling the moving surface with her hands.

She's not afraid to take the lead, even after the close call with that destroyer-thing. A natural-born explorer.

Telisa hopped in. She moved slowly at first, then picked up speed as her boot tips fell into the depression and pushed her forward.

"Piece of cake," she said aloud.

Magnus pointed his rifle behind him and followed her. The ride was novel but uneventful. They emerged from the spiral tube in a minute or two.

On the other side, they could not see well. He became nervous. Telisa must have felt the same way because she switched to link communication. She preferred her link when she felt threatened.

"It's dark," Telisa said over her link.

"Scout to the rescue," Magnus answered.

The spider-legged machine returned to their location, flooding the area with light. The reflected illumination scattered through the space below, bringing it into view.

The scene revealed looked like a subway disaster. A long cylinder of metal ran overhead down the center of the tunnel, with no discernible supports. The ceiling was easily ten meters overhead. The light showed several openings in the walls of the tunnel, hinting at rooms beyond. Before them a huge hulk of a machine or vehicle lay partially covered by sand.

Magnus immediately got the feeling that, whatever it was, it had fallen from the metal rail above. He swept his light down the tunnel in both directions. It was a big wide open space, filled with sand. The openings in the wall continued as far as his light could reach.

Shiny's drone zipped from one side of the room to the other. It jerked about a bit, hovering around the debris in a corner.

"What's it doing?" Telisa transmitted.

The drone descended until it was a quarter of a meter above the sand. Then it started to change. Its shape divided into two bulky parts separated by a thinner span.

"I have no idea," Magnus said.

The drone dropped onto the floor. One of its ends had flattened into a base. Its middle thinned smoothly, then expanded again, forming a flat top like a little table.

"Wait. It looks exactly like all those other things. Like the chair-things."

"So… it's playing chair?"

"Wait a second… one of those red dots is getting closer."

A distant vibration carried through the air, barely detectable at first, but rising.

"Those are the destroyer machines! Something attracted one of them," Telisa said. "Now, the machine is coming so the drone is hiding. What about us?"

"Stay calm. Let's hide."

"Over here," Telisa said. "By that ruined... whatever it is. Train car, maybe."

They scrambled over toward the ruined husk. There was an opening under it, but it was too small to hide in. Once they were up against its surface, nestled beside the base, Magnus grabbed a large plate of metal debris and dragged it over. He leaned it against the hulk, forming a small space for them to crawl into.

"Scout? There's no room for him under here," Telisa sent over her link.

"I'll leave him out there. To distract this thing, just in case."

The humming noise became louder. Magnus crouched and waited. *We can't hope to fight these things... so just play rat and hope it goes away.*

White light washed over the room. Magnus shielded his eyes. Shadows danced as the bright machine moved to the far side of the room by Scout. The only sound was a steady hiss of moving air pushing sand around. Something moved to the far side of his cover, but the plate did not move. Neither did Magnus.

Magnus watched the view from Scout carefully. The ovoid destroyer machine emitted the bright white light across most of its surface. The illumination made it difficult to see details of the machine. It floated in the center of the wide-open passageway, inching toward the wreck they hid against. As it paused above Scout, Magnus saw several bulbous protrusions of equipment, including ominous-looking holes he imagined could emit projectiles or energy attacks of some kind.

Then it had moved over Scout and the wreck. It continued down the tunnel, picking up speed as it left them behind. After another minute, Magnus opened his eyes and pushed away the plate. They rose and stared down the tunnel after the receding white light.

"It must have come up on Vovokans just like that, then killed them," she said.

Telisa stood still with her arms wrapped around herself.

"Are you okay?" he asked. "It's gone. More evidence the destroyers don't care about us."

"I'd forgotten," she said. "Now I've been reminded twice."

He puzzled through her statement for a moment. "What it was like to be in danger?"

"Yeah. To think I was about to die. How could I forget that feeling?"

"It's good you forgot. Some people stay afraid. Even when they go home and they're safe, they can't shake it. It's good you can process it, live with it."

Telisa stared at the drone camouflaged as a chair. "It had to shut down. I wonder how it will wake back up?" she said.

"It could be a timer. Or the other drones might send it a signal when they see the hunter go away."

"Hunter. That's exactly what it was. Those things came here after Shiny's kind. And they killed millions, he said."

"It sounds horrible, and yet—" Magnus said.

"What?"

"And yet, I wonder if they deserved it."

"We sure are willing to trust him, despite the fact that we don't trust him," she said nonsensically.

"I know what you mean. But he saved us before. And he's offering us a lot now, even though he's after something himself. An industrial seed. I think he must plan to restore his civilization, but on his terms."

"Yes. In absence of 'heavy competition.'"

"So, what's this wide open road? And why the cylinder above us? It doesn't seem to attach to anything."

"It's a rail. A transport rail," she said.

Magnus nodded. "I agree. But why the open windows? Did it carry something worth seeing? Because in a Terran city—"

"In a Terran city they have to keep the noise out," Telisa finished for him.

"Oh. Of course. Yes, Vovokans might have a lot less trouble with the noise, since they're deaf. A bomb could have blown the windows out. But I meant, was something on this rail worth seeing?"

"Maybe. Scout is moving ahead. I see the next room."

They left the wreck behind and followed Scout. Shiny's odd probe revived and floated after them. Their robot took a right, disappearing into one of the dozens of passageways that opened onto the underground thoroughfare.

The machine sent back images of a big room with a low, irregular ceiling. One side of the room had caved in.

Rows of familiar golden creatures were arranged on small platforms of machinery.

"Something very interesting ahead," Magnus said.

"Looks... not good to me," Telisa said.

They entered the room. Scout had already moved around the circumference and identified a possible exit. Magnus told it to hang close until they could figure out where they were.

Telisa approached the first golden alien on its complicated throne. Tubes or wires ran around its body, often entering it. It was definitely a Vovokan.

"It's a body. Like Shiny."

"Well, we knew we would see this. Though I was expecting more of a them blown to pieces, rather than just sitting dead in these weird machines."

"I wonder, did Shiny know them? Were these his friends?"

"Ask him."

Telisa walked closer.

"Why are they hooked up?" she asked. "I thought everything was wireless here."

"These machines could keep them alive while they're in virtual realities until they lost power, maybe."

Telisa nodded. "A meat shack."

"Makes sense, right? They're advanced. Highly automated."

"Shiny barely seems to eat, though. This seems like a lot of hookups for something so self-sustaining."

"Maybe they stayed here for years at a time," Magnus said.

"I don't know. We're missing something."

"Hospital?"

"Maybe. I would expect something more advanced, less intrusive, from them in curing injury or sickness, but that may depend on how severe the problem was."

Telisa looked over the creature before her carefully. "I don't see any wounds. It must have died some other—ah!"

A small creature darted over the surface, then dodged into a hole in the outer husk. Telisa recoiled.

"Five Holies! Did you see it? Oh. It must be living in the body. Eating it."

"That's one theory," Magnus said.

Telisa smiled. "Point taken. Dangerous assumptions. Okay, what else could it be? Let's see. An infinitude of possibilities, such as... Vovokans reproduce by mating in threes, then the body of one fills with larvae and dies. The parent is eaten by the larvae, and I just saw a baby Vovokan."

Magnus shrugged. "It's totally possible."

"Another question for him. I felt like I was asking him a lot of questions on the voyage, but more keep coming up."

"Well, it's a little hard to talk with him. He speaks well enough, though not fast or with many details. Maybe he holds out on us. It's not fair that he learns huge amounts about us through the network, but we have to phrase each and every question carefully and still get a vague answer. It felt like I was imposing on him if I grilled him for more than ten minutes at a time. It was just, ask, get an answer, over and over; it's not a two way exchange."

"And the map he provided us of this place has a lot of physical detail, but it's lacking in background. Come to think of it, he must be holding out on us on purpose. He could have provided me with an encyclopedia on his house, but he didn't. He just gave me a 3D diagram."

"We need to ask him for data packages about whole subjects: his government, society, technology, history, things we can absorb offline. I half think he may refuse to tell us everything."

"A competitive advantage to keep us in the dark?"

"Yeah, I think so."

Magnus signaled Scout to move ahead. So far, they were on the course Shiny had provided. Magnus hoped their luck held out. The farther they could get on the planned route before coming across a collapsed section, the faster they would be able to get in and out with the seed.

Magnus noticed unusual movement in Scout's vision feed.

"Telisa. Heads up," he transmitted.

She gave him a curious look, then scanned around. She must have seen the input from Scout because she stopped looking frantically around and grew still.

Through the feed from Scout came the image of a large room filled with moving shapes and flickering lights in bright colors.

"Five Entities, it's beautiful," Telisa breathed.

Spheres floated through the room. They were metallic, shining, with lights of rapidly shifting colors of the rainbow.

Many similar spheres lay piled on the sandy floor.

"A lot of them have run out of juice."

"Let's go there now! I want to see those things, grab a couple of them."

Magnus stared at the moving spheres. They moved like schools of fish, carefully synchronized in groups of ten or twenty that flowed around the scene in complex patterns.

"Maybe we should figure out what they are first?"

"They aren't concerned about Scout."

"Yeah. Let's be ready, though."

"Of course."

Magnus picked his way through the sandy debris toward Scout. He swept his light over the dead Vovokans behind them one last time before they left. The golden corpses reflected his light brilliantly, utterly still and silent.

I hope they died quickly. Maybe they didn't even know anything was wrong.

Telisa walked eagerly ahead. Magnus considered warning her, but decided to just stay alert himself. Scout wandered in the room among the floating spheres.

When they saw the room with their own eyes, it was even more beautiful. The floating spheres went through the colors of the spectrum in four or five seconds before starting over. The tiny machines did not react to their presence, but neither did any of them collide with Scout or Telisa as she stepped out into the open area.

"I think I know what this is. It's very much like a dance club," Telisa said.

"Well, yeah..."

"Think about it. Bright lights. But Vovokans can't hear music. They sense moving mass. All those spheres, and the ones on the floor used to be moving the same way. It's an aesthetic display. It must be very pleasing to them."

"That's a better theory that I have."

"What were you thinking?"

"I thought maybe it was designed to confuse. So many moving bits of mass, so many lights... it might overwhelm a Vovokan's senses."

"For what purpose?"

"Obscure something. Hide something. I don't know. I said your theory was better."

Telisa's face compressed.

"Scout saw something warm," she said.

Damn, I missed it, Magnus thought. He watched Scout's feed and caught a glimpse of a long, thin signature of heat. It moved behind something and Scout lost it.

"Another critter, maybe," he said. Magnus checked his rifle. It was ready to shoot a lethal round. He turned in the direction of Scout.

"Don't shoot a Vovokan," Telisa said.

"We'd probably already be dead if it was one," Magnus said.

Remember Jack and Thomas?

Magnus caught sight of it—a large, ugly creature, like a cross between a giant worm and a scorpion. It was mottled brown with gold flecks. Magnus tracked it from about six meters away. The little spheres kept floating in and out of the way.

"I think it spotted us," Telisa transmitted. The creature moved straight for them.

"It's bigger than I thought. Bigger than the other thing," Magnus said quickly.

"Should we shoot?"

Magnus pointed his weapon but held his fire. He logged the creature as a target.

"Don't move. It probably detects mass like Shiny," Magnus said through his link.

"This place is like a horror VR."

Magnus got a better look through the spinning objects and their bright lights. He saw mandibles. They were unmistakable, even on an alien creature. Those were meant to apply huge pressure and break something up. Possibly something to eat. The mandibles opened and the creature moved the last couple of meters right toward him.

Magnus fired his weapon. The sound exploded through the tight space. The creature bucked upward in response, then it darted toward Magnus. He shot again. The mandibles snapped, but Magnus shuffled back, narrowly avoiding its jaws.

I wonder if Momma Veer would have saved me that time?

The creature slowed and stopped, its mandibles frozen open in death. Some of its many legs still twitched.

"There. Easy enough. It was just another critter. But bigger than the others," he said.

111

Telisa looked it over, then she seemed satisfied. There were no signs of any clothes or machine enhancements like Shiny had.

"I hope it was a Vovokan Rover and not a Vovokan teenager," she said.

"Rover?"

"You know. Like a pet?"

"A pet or wild, yeah. Vovokans have their mouths in back, remember?" he said.

"It almost bit you. How do you keep so calm? You're a machine."

Magnus did not answer at first. He did not have to say anything. He felt closer to Telisa than he had to anyone else before, and she risked her life alongside him.

I can share anything with her.

"The war against the UED. Those orbital attacks. For the first few weeks, I was constantly terrified. Then, slowly, something changed. My emotions dried up. Kind of like accepting death, but not giving up." He grimaced. "That's not exactly it. I haven't tried to say it before. Something inside me changed. Everyone who knew me before saw it when I got back, but they didn't say it out loud because they knew it was the war."

"An insane solution for an impossible situation," she said.

"It serves me well enough now," Magnus said. "I wish I could say it was a triumph of mind over fear, but I think it was probably more of a natural reaction to stress. Some kind of a shutdown of the part of my mind that was drowning in anxiety and taking the rest of me with it."

"I'm sorry you had to go through that. But you know what? I'm glad you're strong enough for both of us. I knew there was something different about you from the beginning. You were distant, but you trained me so well. I could tell you liked me, even though you never said it."

He nodded. She must have seen something on his face.

"Tell me more," she said.

"I'm starting to feel some of the old fear return. Not for me, though."

"For me?"

"Yes. I care about you, and I feel the anxiety returning, the fear that you'll die."

Telisa reached out and put her hand on his shoulder. "I'm an adult. I know this is dangerous. It's worth it, though. We'll explore this in depth when we get back to the *Iridar*," she said with a tentative smile.

Magnus laughed out loud at the unexpected reply. "Here I thought I was opening up to please you, but you don't want to hear about it any more than I want to talk about it!"

Telisa laughed too. "Just means we're a good couple. We can both keep our respective emotional messes canned up."

Michael McCloskey

Chapter 12

Relachik missed having a battalion of Space Force troopers at his command as he walked out of the spaceport on Brighter Walken. It was one thing to face danger at the helm of a ship and another to face it in the flesh. Here, every man and woman had to exude a sense of hardness to avoid being seen as prey. Relachik adapted himself quickly. He was fit, armed, and backed by two friends, one of whom was ex-military. His determination was high. So they marched out of the *Vandivier* and headed for the Vain Vothrile.

The surface was bright, as the name of the colony hinted. The white star was far away, but it still shone with a fierce intensity that made eye protection a must.

The spaceport looked fairly primitive. The gritty pavement resisted a few cleaning machines wandering about. It suited Relachik just fine. The frontier worlds felt frozen in time, but it was a time Relachik was familiar with. The Core Worlds believed in a glitz more virtual than real. They held billions of eccentrics who spent more time in imaginary worlds than in the real one.

The club was barely open when they arrived. Only a couple of people were inside. It looked similar to their simulation, though the wall decor was considerably more obscene. Half of the booths appeared to have active pornographic holos running. The images were not real but had been broadcast straight to links and overlaid onto reality. Relachik screened them out. The feeds were meant to allow other patrons to see who was interested in what. The feeds could be made private, but the social atmosphere was all about sharing while under the influence of your favorite mind-altering chemicals.

So far, so good.

"Ready?" Cilreth asked.

Relachik gave the go signal over his link. Cilreth got to work first. Relachik knew she would break into the club controls and mark the club as closed. They had concocted an excuse about a fire that morning which had damaged the club, to help draw off any suspicion. The announcement would go out to anyone seeking entrance, or to any queries over the net from people at home planning their evening.

Once Cilreth had closed the place down electronically, including bringing the internal cameras down for maintenance, Arlin and Relachik used their stunners. They broke a few glasses and knocked out the men inside, but it did not cause much of a stir.

"This one looks like Frankie. Supposed to be the owner," Relachik said over his link to Arlin and Cilreth.

"Hadrian better be back there somewhere," Arlin said.

As soon as Relachik knew they had the front under control, he hurried into the back, Arlin at his side. They found a short, broad-shouldered man sitting in a back room. The man was bald, yet his face was covered in stubble. The retro desk before him looked chipped and worn almost like the damn thing had been shipped from Earth itself.

"You go in the side door there," Arlin suggested. Relachik kept going, headed to the side.

Arlin walked in first.

"Hadrian?" Arlin asked.

"Yeah?" the man replied, already suspicious.

Got to give the guy credit. He's already arming his weapon. Probably wiping any tracking keys he's got, too.

Relachik shocked Hadrian with his stunner from the other side. The man collapsed. His weapon remained under the counter, untouched.

"In here," Relachik directed, finding his way toward the back. A private room beside the bar was empty.

Arlin threw a table aside to open up some space. They worked to tie Hadrian to a chair.

Cilreth hovered near the entrance of the private room.

"You don't want to be here. Maybe just make sure no one comes in?" Relachik suggested over his link.

"Copy that," Cilreth replied eagerly, disappearing.

Relachik broke out the robokit he had brought from *Vandivier*.

"Need anything else?" Arlin asked.

"Yeah. Get me a whiskey," Relachik said.

"Coming up."

Relachik had never tortured anyone before, though he had been directed his fair share of interrogations. Putting the subject into a virtual reality was pretty typical procedure, but he did not have that luxury. It would have to be the old-fashioned way. He took out an illegal tool he had rigged up to use on Hadrian. He activated it against the man's head, disabling his link.

Telisa, I hope I find you.

Relachik used the kit to give Hadrian a stimulant. The man stirred.

"So, who's our lucky man today?" Relachik said, feigning enthusiasm.

"His name is Hadrian," Arlin supplied.

"The club's all shut down, Hadrian," Relachik said. "We have plenty of time."

"Yah know I can't talk. Waste ah time," Hadrian said.

Relachik hooked up the *Vandivier*'s medical robokit to Hadrian.

"What yah doin' there?"

"I'm making sure you don't pass out. We want to make sure you're awake for the full experience." Relachik took out an injector and pressed it against Hadrian's shoulder.

"What is dat shit?"

"The Space Force has a wide selection of useful drugs," Relachik said. "This particular number intensifies pain in the subject."

Hadrian's breathing and heart rate increased. Actually Relachik had injected an alertness agent that did have a mild side effect of pain enhancement, but it was hardly the purpose of the drug.

"There. Now we're ready to have some fun," Relachik said.

"Iz ain't saying nuttin'. Yah'z tame compared to muh boss. I'm nuh afraid of yah at all," Hadrian claimed.

"Tell me Hadrian. Where does the F-clave keep its main storage? The important storage, with the client information on it, the one that can unscramble all the queries and give out tracking keys."

"Dunno, man."

"You're going to know where it is soon enough," Relachik said. He stabbed the needle into the man's leg and started to inject the contents.

Hadrian started to scream. A sizzling sound rose from his leg along with a bit of smoke. An awful smell filled the air.

Relachik sprayed some quickskin over the gaping wound to stanch the bleeding.

"I wouldn't want you to bleed out. We're just getting started," he said.

Hadrian shook his head.

"I can't tell yah nothin', man." Tears streamed down his face. "Iz not just me. Iz my family I'm protectin'."

"Your boss isn't going to get your family. We're the damn Space Force. We're going after them. Don't you see? They screwed up, got our attention. The F-clave is going down. The ones left alive, if we leave any alive, are going to be mining ore out of some asteroid until one of them screws up and depressurizes the whole thing. Then they'll be dead, too."

Hadrian hesitated. "I know dis ain't real," he said. "You blocked my link. Dis ain't real."

He's mine now. Relachik slowly filled another hypodermic as he talked. "You think you're not incarnate, Hadrian? You're dumber than you look. I shot you with Frankie's zapper when I walked in. You forget that already? Your link was fried the second I hit you with it."

Hadrian's eyes bulged for a moment.

"That's right, this is real-world shit. We aren't in a VR."

Hadrian deflated.

"You got four balls. Two in your eye sockets and two in your sack. This one's going into one of them," Relachik said.

The needle descended. The man recoiled, fighting against his restraints.

"No, no, Iz tell yah what yah wanna know."

"Then tell me where's the storage with your client info. The UNSF wants to get it intact before grabbing the F-clave leaders."

Hadrian vomited over himself.

The sound of breaking glass came from the other room. Arlin went to investigate.

"You'd better hope that's not a marshal. If I'm forced to run before I get what I need from you, I'm going to shoot you and take off."

"Okay, okay. Iz said I'd tell you. The storage is on Halthia Hyri Three."

"Say it again," Relachik ordered.

"Halthia Hyri Three. Storage izzon Halthia Hyri Three. Map callz it Natali Compound. It ain't gonna do yah no good, man. Dat place is a death palace. Real nice, real deadly. Yah'll never get in 'dere."

"Shut up and answer my questions," Relachik said.

Arlin walked back in. "There was another local in the bar. Cilreth took care of it," he said.

I like the way he implied Cilreth killed somebody.

"What are the defenses at Halthia?"

"Iz never been dere. Just a friend o' mine. Said dey have demselves some Space Force hydras."

Hydras... military robots. Damn.

"What else?"

"What else? Dat ain't enough? The whole place iz wired top to bottom. Booby trapped, yah know? An when somebody crosses dese guys—"

"Yeah, I get it. They're not afraid to frag someone."

"Dey'll do you, yah try to go dere."

"How many men there? How many hydras?"

"Who knows, man? At least three hydras. Gotta be dozen enforcers dere."

Relachik raised his stunner and shot it into Hadrian's face. Hadrian was out instantly. His head flopped to the side and his tongue lolled out.

"We're leaving now," Relachik announced to the others.

"What's the summary?" Cilreth asked.

Relachik marched out into the front and saw her. Dried blood crusted the side of her head. A lot of it.

"What the hell happened?"

"Some femme came out of the bathroom and smacked me with a bottle," Cilreth said. "I probably lost a lot of neural connections."

"Where is she?"

"I stunned her. Well, I had to stab her in the hand with a knife first. Look, I can fill you in later."

"We don't want to hurt anyone we don't have to," Relachik said.

"Preaching to the choir. Summary?"

"Basically, they have an opulent fortress on Halthia Hyri Three. Paid for with all their ill-gotten gains, no doubt."

"And?"

"Everything we need is there. Well protected, of course. We'll have to think through our options. Let's get out of here."

Michael McCloskey

Chapter 13

All the Bel Klaven capital machines were easy to see. They had nothing to hide from. The huge floating fortresses were interstellar vessels turned into military headquarters. They resupplied smaller hunting units under the ground and lent EM support as needed. Dozens of them hugged the planet, evenly spaced, hunting for and guarding against any Gorgalan activity.

The Bel Klaven themselves were soft, round liquid-dwellers who manipulated their environment electrically and chemically as much as with coarser physical tools. Kirizzo wondered what they thought of the Gorgalans now that they had struck back. Did their behavior call for continued competition or would they be satiated, having brought their revenge full course? They must blame all Gorgalans for the war since so many uninvolved Gorgalans had been killed.

Kirizzo considered the powerful enemy who had obliterated his homeworld. He had uncovered the story of the fall piece by piece. It had taken the Bel Klaven a few weeks to finish a planet that had endured a millennium of Gorgalan internal strife. First, their ships had destroyed or scattered the Gorgalan fleets. Then they had rained down bombs, but the Gorgalans lived deep underground. Some thought they had found respite from the assault, but then the Bel Klaven descended to the planet to hunt the Gorgalans in their subterranean homes. There had not been time to develop a coherent strategy or outsmart the Bel Klaven war machines, as Kirizzo had done with the small force that pursued him. The Gorgalans died, though they had used every robot at their disposal to fight back. They simply had not prepared defenses capable of repelling a huge attack from above. Most of their automated defenses were designed to defend their houses against other Gorgalans.

123

The few Bel Klaven who had come personally to lead their machines had taken a small Gorgalan house and turned it into a planetary headquarters by filling it with liquid and living inside. Few thoughts disturbed Kirizzo more than that of his house becoming a liquid-filled tomb. The water levels in that house had dropped considerably; Kirizzo took this as a clue that the Bel Klaven themselves had left, leaving behind only their war machines.

Kirizzo focused on the vessel nearest his home. He formed the hypothesis that the capital ship monitored the Gorgalan power and data frequencies to dispatch hunters whenever something became active. Kirizzo decided to test the theory and watch the enemy in action.

His probes linked into the Gorgalan infrastructure. As he had suspected, his familial domestics had turned most of the system off near the end to try and hide. In particular, the broadcast power grid had been deactivated once most of the systems had been damaged. Whoever had been in control at the time of the attack had decided to turn off the grid to preserve whatever assets they had left. If Kirizzo could reactivate those assets, he could distract the Bel Klaven, learn more about them, and help his Terran allies.

He connected to his house from a couple of the probes. His old access keys were intact. Kirizzo took stock of the damage. It was extensive. His house was a ruin. For a moment, Kirizzo felt rising frustration at the amount of work blocking him. He shook it off and started.

If he ordered machines back online and started repairs, that would attract an attack, so he needed something to throw away, a non-critical asset to activate and watch. Kirizzo selected a group of drilling machines scattered throughout the house. He found a power storage facility and broadcast the necessary energy. The drilling machines activated. He sent them on random paths through the house. The machines could cut through all manner of debris, making them mobile even in the aftermath. Kirizzo decided to alter the random paths in some meaningful ways to increase the benefits of the experiment. Telisa and Magnus might find a few new tunnels useful for making their way through the damaged regions toward the seed.

Not that they should need any more help. The seed itself would likely take care of them. Kirizzo wondered if he had made a mistake by keeping them completely in the dark. He could have suggested they pray as their ancestors had—hinted to them that they might once again find it useful. Such a shame their race had been cheated of the boon they once enjoyed, then struggled to recover for centuries in its absence.

Within four minutes, large hunters descended into the remains of Kirizzo's house. They, in turn, dispatched smaller destroyers, which penetrated the smaller tunnels and moved in on the Gorgalan machines drawing power. Kirizzo monitored what communications he could pick up for later analysis. Then he deactivated all the drilling machines, as the first two were destroyed in the upper levels of the house.

So what was it, exactly, that the Bel Klaven homed in on? The obvious answers were moving masses or electromagnetic emissions. He decided to work with these first.

Ironically, Kirizzo's house defenses were largely intact. The Bel Klaven had descended from above, not from the other tunnels where Kirizzo's old enemies had threatened attack. Less than ten percent of his automated forces were deployed to protect from surface incursion. There were famous instances in their history of Gorgalans attacking other houses unexpectedly from the surface, grand tales of daring which resulted in amazing success, but such risky attacks were rare.

Kirizzo still had a lot of assets at his entrance checkpoints deep underground. The Bel Klaven had not attacked through them. Each of the checkpoints included moving-mass systems of great complexity, designed to conceal the defenses and confuse attackers. The systems were also independently powered because the broadcast power systems could be blocked or tampered with in an assault.

Kirizzo was ready for the second test. He picked a checkpoint and activated it.

The system turned on. Kirizzo was unable to feel it himself, being so far away, nor could his probes report the readings to him since they were limited to Terran capabilities. Kirizzo calmly noted to himself that any conclusion based on the results could be flawed since he had only the station's self-diagnostics to rely upon. In all likelihood the obfuscation masses were in motion; he had no way to verify it externally.

No reaction came from the enemy machines. Given the lack of evidence to support the first theory, he decided to move on to the next test. He could always return to this one if other avenues dried up. Besides, it made sense once Kirizzo factored in the fact that the invaders were not Gorgalan. Tracking moving mass was inherently a Gorgalan-centric method. Neither the Bel Klaven nor the Terrans would naturally employ such a system.

The third test began. Kirizzo started with a flurry of communications to one of the drilling machines. It did not move or draw significant power. Its energy storage had already been filled by the first experiment. He simply exchanged an artificially high amount of information for a short time. He waited.

This time, the Bel Klaven reacted. A smaller hunter shot from a nearby patrol machine. It closed unerringly upon the drilling device. The hunter examined the driller carefully, then searched in an expanding spiral pattern.

Kirizzo wondered why it did not destroy the machine. Perhaps the weapons of the enemy were limited? Or was it left intact in hopes of pointing the way to more Gorgalans elsewhere?

The evidence so far suggested that the Bel Klaven monitored Gorgalan frequencies for communication and broadcast power. The theory could be flawed. Kirizzo's experiments may have resulted in a higher state of vigilance for the last experiment. Some of his readings could have been in error, especially given the extensive damage to his house systems and the primitive abilities of the probes he had constructed.

Kirizzo decided to work for the moment as if the theory was correct. What leverage did it offer? He knew the Bel Klaven machines were not flexible. Kirizzo doubted any Bel Klaven remained to oversee the machines now that the campaign had mostly been completed. The machines were left there to ensure that no Gorgalans survived—or that none who fled could ever come back.

He had at least one important piece of the puzzle, which might help him learn to avoid the Bel Klaven. His house was not what it used to be. His abilities to block and alter EM transmissions at a distance were mostly destroyed. Besides, if the Bel Klaven warships were as sophisticated as his machines, they could track the tampering to the sources and destroy his remaining assets.

Another possible use presented itself: distraction. The signals could be faked more easily than real ones could be hidden, which meant he might be able to distract the Bel Klaven machines when Telisa and Magnus were ready to bring the industrial seed to the surface. Or perhaps the distraction would best be saved for when the *Iridar* was ready to leave? Shiny himself would be at risk at that time. Yet if his new allies were killed, he would have to figure out how to sneak in himself.

Kirizzo had not been planning on contacting Telisa and Magnus, but this information was too valuable to withhold. They would have to be informed. Kirizzo set about planning how to pull it off without being noticed.

Chapter 14

Telisa had pocketed several of the dead spheres when she noticed that a school of the floating devices had broken away from the room to follow her.

"Hello?" she said, glancing at them. "Are you following me?"

The orbs simply coruscated in different colors and floated around lazily as a loose unit.

Telisa took the dead orbs out of her pocket and laid them back on the floor. Then she moved to the side. The school of coruscating devices followed her.

"You really are following me," Telisa said, gathering her prizes back up.

"Who are you talking to?" Magnus asked.

"These things are following me. They're the only ones that changed behavior."

"They may be confused. Or maybe a group is supposed to follow each visitor?"

"But when I move away, they follow me, always on that side. And there's a way out in that direction."

"It's different from Shiny's route," he said. "Scout already moved off in the other direction."

"What do they want? Do you think... could those tiny things be smart?" she asked.

"They could be smart, or they could be controlled by someone who's smart. I'd normally say we should trust Shiny's route over some unknown, but Scout is currently blocked."

Telisa checked Scout's feed and saw that a cave-in had blocked its route. The robot searched the dead end, looking for some tube or crevice that would allow it to continue, but the way was thoroughly blocked.

"Mysterious floating spheres it is," Telisa said.

"I hope they aren't controlled by destroyers... or attract them."

Magnus recalled Scout. They took a few lazy steps toward the exit indicated by the floating devices.

"Could be Shiny controlling them," Telisa suggested.

"That seems more likely than the invaders doing it. He could have hacked them through one of his machines."

Scout moved on by the scene and scurried out to see what lay beyond.

The school of glowing spheres meandered in circles out in the wide-open space of the 'dance club.' As Telisa watched, one of them went dark and dropped to its death.

"Oh, no. We'd better hurry after them. They're running out of energy."

"Okay. Scout is far enough ahead we can risk it."

They walked through a natural-looking cavern with a sand floor.

"This must be the equivalent of putting plants and birds into a Terran building," Telisa said. "They could have made the corridor any shape they wanted, but they preferred a natural look."

"I bet the sand isn't exactly like their primitive caves. It carries refuse away and moves things around. At least it did while this place was working."

"Yes. Very high-tech sand," Telisa agreed with a hint of amusement.

The cavern widened into a large chamber. A huge circular pit dominated the center of the floor. The colorful spheres moved over the opening.

"Do they really think we're that dumb? They want us to walk out to our death?"

"We have to head down," Telisa summarized.

"Are you sure?"

"Our target is over a kilometer below our current depth. We might as well head down here."

Scout went first. It anchored itself to the smooth metal rim at the edge of the pit and dropped into the darkness. The spheres remained near Telisa.

"That's a mild problem. We don't know where to send Scout because the spheres stay here with you," Magnus said.

"I think I can guess at the route, given Shiny's original. Or maybe not. This map is crazy complicated."

"Okay. When Scout gets to the bottom, if it's safe, we can join it and watch the spheres or whatever."

"We're not getting to the bottom of that shaft. Nowhere close. It goes down for kilometers. We're going to drop down four or five levels here, I think."

"If our links are disabled—"

"Then we'll get lost and die down here," she finished for him.

"We might find our way to the surface at least."

"We could from here. Not from much deeper, I think. Not without more food than we have in our packs."

"We could follow the probe."

"It follows us."

"Okay. Enough grim talk. Scout is down one level. Should he check it out?"

"Just for a minute. To make sure nothing is sitting there waiting to eat us."

Scout's feed showed an environment similar to their current surroundings: natural caverns with sandy floors. She tried to keep an eye on the feed as she removed climbing gear from her pack.

I think I'm getting better at watching everything simultaneously.

Telisa attached her smart rope and put her back to the pit. She let the rope twist its way through her equipment rings at the belt of the Veer skinsuit, then dropped over the edge. She descended smoothly, controlling the rope's friction through her link. As she reached the first level, she pushed away from the inside of the tunnel to swing into the entrance and land on the lip.

Her light revealed the side passage. She saw only sand and a gaping hole that led to another layer of the house. Everything was eerily quiet. Between the lack of link services, the darkness, and the almost total loneliness, there were only the sounds of Magnus's descent to interrupt the silence with a few soft foot impacts as he dropped.

"You think it's creepy too," Magnus said over his link as he dropped beside her.

"As creepy as the Tomb of the Third Entity," she said.

"They make that creepy on purpose. This is the real deal."

Telisa suppressed her discomfort and concentrated on the descent. They repeated the procedure, sending Scout ahead, then following on their smart ropes when the coast was clear. Magnus reported another scurrying "critter" in Scout's visual feed, but nothing threatened them directly.

They reached a level that looked special on Shiny's directions, where they had to jink over a ways before continuing the descent. Scout moved ahead to check for danger while Telisa and Magnus put their climbing gear away and shared a snack. The floating spheres still led them, though another had dropped dead.

"I would go crazy down here by myself," Telisa said. "When I imagined Shiny's homeworld, I didn't think it would be so... quiet and empty."

"Everything's dead and gone. At least the spheres' colors brighten it up a bit."

"Scout sees something," she said.

Scout's lights illuminated a machine the size of a big truck. The design confused her. Eight smooth treads ran along its length, two on each side, two on top, and two underneath. The treads were separated from the machine, mounted on arms that reminded her of land vehicle suspension systems.

Scout circled around to the front, revealing a massive drilling apparatus. Tunnels of the exact size of the machine's front drilling apparatus joined the room ahead and behind.

"Amazing. This is their equivalent of a road-paving machine back on Earth," Telisa said.

"Let's go check it out. Maybe we could drive it?"

"Probably automated," she said, but they both moved to join Scout. They walked to the end of their tunnel and slipped down a one-meter drop. Telisa found the drilling machine in her light. The machine stood over them, at least four meters tall.

"These treads can press out against a tunnel on all sides... I bet this thing can drill upward at a high angle," Magnus guessed.

Suddenly the machine hummed to life. Running lights activated across its surface. The entire tunnel lit up. Telisa and Magnus retreated.

"What—"

"This way!" Magnus yelled.

Telisa sprinted toward the tunnel he indicated. The drilling machine growled loudly and lurched forward. Telisa ran and did not look back. The noise behind her rose.

She ran recklessly after Magnus into the dark side tunnel. At first, the sound behind them was masked by the rock as they left the main tunnel. Then a terrifyingly loud grinding noise erupted behind them.

It's drilling after us, she realized.

"Is it trying to kill us?" she asked on their link connection.

"It's still coming! It'll crush us if it catches us!"

Telisa caught a glimpse of bright red and green darting ahead and down a passage on the left. She knew Magnus saw it too because he grabbed her hand and charged after the spheres.

"I wonder if they led us to that machine on purpose," he said over his link.

"Well, now they're leading us away. Just make sure they don't lead us over a cliff!"

They ran down the lit passage and took a left, following the colorful spheres. Once again the horrible sound grew more distant. They kept running, sweeping their lights to check the way ahead. They passed two side rooms. Telisa caught a glimpse of several glistening stalagmites rising from the floor with a mesh of white strings crisscrossing among them. The next room had a giant worm floating in a tube of dark fluid.

It's like a nightmare.

Finally, they stopped to catch their breath. Telisa's hands trembled.

"I never shake like this in the VRs."

"The animal part of you has learned the difference," he said. "Besides, how many times have you been chased by a giant drilling robot in our training sessions?"

"Yeah. But there were soldiers, monsters..."

"Your physical body shakes under adrenal overload. That may be an oversight of our VR software. I'll look into it," he said.

She flitted her light across his face. He smiled wildly at her.

She laughed out loud. "Ha! Oh, thank you so much! Haha! Hey, did we lose Shiny's probe?"

"No, it's over here. Scout got sidetracked but I think it'll be here soon."

Telisa caught sight of the probe. She felt relieved that they still had their main connection to Shiny.

"I wonder what we did to set that thing off," Telisa said.

"Why would it attack us?" Magnus asked.

"If the destroyers have machines under their control, they may have set them to attack the populace."

"But the destroyers don't care about us."

"Yes, but these are Vovokan machines. They might not be so good at discerning their targets. The Vovokans may have used their robots to defend themselves against the destroyers. And we are alien..."

"Okay, so they're hostile one way or the other. Except for our guides, there," Magnus said.

What if they're against us, too?

"Hmm. They may be leading us into traps." Telisa checked her map. So far, the course they suggested paralleled the course Shiny had wanted. "I think Shiny may be causing those spheres to do that. He probably saw our way was blocked with the probe here, and he's giving us a new way around."

"I thought that too, at first," Magnus said. "But the probe was with us the whole time. It didn't have a chance to see the way was blocked. The spheres redirected us immediately."

"That is weird. Could be another probe?"

"Turns out we can see the other probes' positions," Magnus said. "There's a service for that on this one."

"Oh?" Telisa hadn't bothered to check for new services since she assumed the Vovokan devices would be dead or unconnectable to human links. She used it to see the probes. They were dispersed about the house and above the surface.

"No doubt Shiny uses them to keep tabs on the destroyers."

"Where should we go from here? Keep following the spheres?"

"Let me take a look," Telisa said. She felt a bit suspicious of the spheres after their close call. She would feel better if her estimate of where to go matched the general direction urged by the tiny devices. She looked at the map and tried a few route programs. The most obvious way looked blocked by what she saw of Scout's most recent explorations.

"Yes. Let's get Scout back here and send him in that direction from right here."

Magnus nodded.

Scout was in a long tunnel with a rail on the ceiling. It moved in their general direction, crawling along under the rail.

"I guess Vovokans wouldn't walk down that type of tunnel. It's probably for faster transport."

"We can take it if it gets us closer to the seed. I doubt there will be fast vehicles moving around anymore."

"There was the drill machine."

"Hmm, good point. What do you say?"

"It seems to be the best way to get where we're going."

They followed the spheres through an empty cavern that adjoined the railway.

Telisa stepped out into the tunnel. She looked at the rail. "No supports, just like the other rail, but smaller. How does it stay there in the air?"

She lifted her hand toward it. Magnus intercepted her arm and brought it down.

"I know the power is supposed to be out, but please don't complete any circuits."

"Okay," she agreed.

The spheres floated down the tunnel. Scout walked by and took the lead, opening the distance between them. Telisa and Magnus started after it.

They traveled the better part of a kilometer through the tunnel. Telisa felt trapped there. She kept thinking about the massive drill machine. If something was trying to hurt them, would it send a vehicle down the tunnel after them?

They came to a long series of open platforms adjoining the tunnel.

"This used to be a major stop, I think," Telisa said.

"I wonder what it was for."

Telisa referred to their maps in her PV.

"We're over a huge chamber. Some kind of coliseum, I think. There's a lot of structural damage. It could be dangerous to descend into it, but the good news is, there are dozens of passages connected to it. We could get back on track from there. I don't think all the exits could be blocked."

"Coliseum? Isn't that a bit archaic for a race as advanced as Shiny's?"

"Damned if I know, but they are alien, after all."

"They must have perfected virtual reality, unless they had a religious objection to virtual worlds. And automated manufacturing, robotics, everything. I wonder if they moved around much at all."

"We Terrans still get around, don't we?"

"Some of us more than others, yeah," Magnus said.

They stepped onto the platform toward a series of holes. Scout was already descending into one of the portals. Telisa saw handholds in the narrow shaft.

"I think this is the Vovokan equivalent of stairs or ladders," Telisa said. "Maybe there are so many to allow a lot of them in or out of the chamber quickly."

"My guess too," Magnus said.

Scout's searchlights struck distant walls in the huge space under their feet. Here and there, mysterious structures rose from the sand.

It looks like yet another world. A dead world. Or a high-tech cemetery.

"Looks like a cemetery with huge headstones," Magnus said, echoing her thoughts.

"Yes. I'm tying off and heading down."

"I'll head down this tube right here. See you inside."

Telisa slipped down her smart rope with ease, telling it to drop her the last foot. It released itself above and wound back into a tight bundle.

Sand was everywhere. The foot coverings of her Veer suit sank into it.

Somehow more of it must have poured in from above and pooled here.

"The sand may have buried the exits," Telisa noted.

"Scout can dig, I think," Magnus said.

Telisa walked up to one of the structures. It was the size of a small house. Her light washed over it. The gray surface could have been stone or metal or plastic. Tiny pockmarks crisscrossed the surface like alien writing. A panel made of little hexagons dominated the center. Sand shifted from above, cascading down the side of the building.

That's weird. Is Scout up there? I thought he was—A dark shape rose up before her.

"What the hell is that?" Telisa screamed over her link. She had her stunner in her hand and leveled in an instant, one of the benefits of her training.

"There's more than one," came Magnus's only answer.

The shape was an alien. It stood as tall as a Great Dane on dozens of legs. Filth obscured Its golden surface. It scuttled toward her. Telisa stepped back, but it accelerated in response. Telisa fired her stunner at the attacker as it lunged at her. Telisa skipped back, tripped, then rolled away in a continuous disaster of movement. More shapes moved in the swaths of light.

Vovokans? Like Shiny?

She shot her stunner at another Vovokan. The creature kept shuffling forward. Magnus's rifle boomed. Dampers in the neck section of her Veer suit kept the sound from harming her ears.

They're slower than Shiny! And uglier!

A sound caused Telisa to whirl around, her light seeking the source. Another Vovokan shuffled out of the sand before her. Patches of its golden integument were visible through holes in a black plastic covering that looked tangled-on more than worn. The legs on its left side were missing. It surged forward at an angle, unable to move correctly.

Telisa keened. She aimed her stunner, gave it an override code, and shot twice without missing a beat. The alien did not seem to mind the sonics much, though it thrashed harder.

They can't hear. The sonics are much less effective.

Telisa dropped her stunner and unsheathed her long dagger. Instead of attacking, she stood fast, holding the weapon before her. The creature swam closer to her in the sand, wiggling its long body like a dying worm.

Another Vovokan advanced from her flank. Telisa switched her attention just in time. She stabbed the creature with her knife. Its mass sensor bulb buckled with a dry crackling sound like a hollow gourd. Telisa kicked at its trunk, crumpling several of its legs. The thing clawed at her with its other legs, trying to run over her. She stabbed it again in the trunk, once, twice. She rolled away, her knife dripping gore. Her light whipped around frantically as she tried to identify the next danger.

I just killed an alien!

Her light settled on a new Vovokan. Another loud crack sounded in the wide space. It echoed crazily. A puncture wound appeared on one side of the thing before her and gooey body parts erupted from the other side. The thing slowed but kept coming. Telisa stabbed it in the forward hump. The outside was crunchy, but after initial penetration, her knife cut easily into its flesh.

"Magnus! How many are there?"

Telisa heard the sound of a grenade launcher.

Scout. Help!

"Just keep fighting," Magnus transmitted. She heard his rifle firing again.

Scout rushed toward her. It lit the scene without blinding her, automatically turning down the lights whenever they pointed directly at her or Magnus. Three more shapes ran toward them. One tried to land on Scout, but the machine scooted away, its legs flipping sand up in its wake.

Two Vovokans lunged for Telisa at once. She did not try to fight both of them. She ran to her right until one blocked the other, then sank her knife into the top hump of the closest one. It reared up and wrapped her in dozens of thin legs. Telisa screamed.

The legs clasped her, might have tried to pinch her, but she could not feel much through the Veer suit until something grabbed her leg. Telisa stabbed upward furiously. Her light was not pointed in the right direction. A splatter of ichor fell across her face. She brought her knees up, screaming in anger this time, rather than fear.

The creature flipped off her. Her shin was in its mouth. She kicked its abdomen away with her other leg, detaching herself. She looked up and saw Magnus standing over her. His rifle shot again, hitting her attacker.

"Thank you," Telisa whimpered.

The Vovokan before her twitched again, causing her to jump back. Magnus stitched two more rounds through the creature.

"Five Holy Entities," Telisa gasped. "Alien zombies? This is insane. It can't be happening." Her voice trembled. She still held the gory dagger in an iron grip.

"They were just Vovokans. Maybe they decided any aliens must be with the destroyers."

"They were dead! Did you see that one? Half its legs had been blown off, and the other one had a gaping hole in its side!"

"Calm down. Just calm down. They aren't zombies, okay? We don't know that much about Vovokan physiology. They may be under the control of the destroyers. They may have some way of taking over the populace. It may have been part of the attack."

"But they were dead," she repeated with less certainty.

"Probably they just injure differently than we do. I think they've probably evolved to lose limbs without dying. Hell, they have so many. And we don't know where their vital organs are. Besides, if they were turned into the invaders' puppets, maybe they're a sort of automaton. Could be controlled by nanomachines or something. Don't read anything extra-scary into it. They were easy to kill. And if it's a contagion, we're not going to get it, we're too different."

Telisa nodded as Magnus spoke, drinking in his logic. She sighed. "Yes. Yes, I agree," she said, struggling to stand. "If the invaders did this, it was probably to terrify the populace. It sure as hell worked on me."

"I wanted to ask them to stop, but there's no way they would understand us, not after all we had to go through to talk with Shiny," Magnus said.

"We should find an exit now."

"They're dead or gone. Take your time, catch your breath," he said.

"Telisa, Magnus. Shiny initiates communication," Shiny's voice interrupted.

"Shiny? I didn't think we would be in contact, though I'm glad to hear from you." Telisa tried to wipe the sand-filled fluids off her suit. It did not work well but she kept trying.

"Destroyer machines not in close proximity. Query about search: proceeding, developing, shaping up?"

"It's very difficult. I'm sorry, but your homeworld is a mess. There are a bunch of creatures like you here. Vovokans, maybe. But they're injured, or sick, or... dead. They attacked us."

"Those are not like me. They are duplicates, replicas, facsimiles. They are artificial."

"Well, they fooled us. That explains a bit, though. Some of them looked like they ought to be dead."

"Shiny studying destroyers further. Learned detection mechanisms. Identified signals used by destroyers to detect, mark, share presence of enemies."

"Well, that's something. Can we jam it?"

"Possibly. Distraction easier. Hiding difficult."

"Ah. You can mimic the signals?"

"Can cause emissions, radiation, noise, that will attract the machines, mark a target as Vovokan."

"Great work! That should be useful when it's time to take the seed out. That, and anything else I can find. So far I only have a few dead spheres. Oh. Are you controlling these colorful spheres that've been guiding us?"

"Negative. But they can be trusted."

"Okay, but who controls them?"

"Some devices, machines, computers, still working. I may repair further."

Magnus finally spoke up. "Shiny. Please share control of the drones. It will increase our chances of success."

"They perform automatically, autonomously, self-controlled."

"Just in case. Look, we're the ones down here risking our lives, so grant us this, okay? Emergency-only control."

"Acceptable. Done."

"One more thing," Magnus added. "Telisa and I have placed data packages that will be sent if we do not periodically check in. We made sure our deaths are suboptimal for you. If we die, the UNSF gets information about you, your technology, your methods, everything. Your optimal course is to keep us alive and keep working with us. We're very beneficial to you alive. Even after we get you the seed."

"Acknowledged, understood, accepted."

"Which is exactly what you'd say if you were planning to betray us."

"True, correct, accurate."

"Terrans prefer cooperative mode," Telisa said. "We can continue to be of use to you for a long time."

"Acknowledged, understood, accepted."

Michael McCloskey

Chapter 15

"I hate to be blunt, but is our employment about to terminate?" asked Cilreth. "I won't be able to find Telisa as long as she's hiding behind the F-clave. And we're not going to get in there, not without a small army. Even your stealth suit would only get you so far, I suspect."

Relachik sat with his employees in the mess. He thought over Cilreth's sentiment.

I didn't get to be a captain in the Force by giving up.

"Let's consider it a bit further before throwing in the towel," Relachik said. "What do we have? Some inside info about a deadly compound on Halthia Hyri that may have an expiration date on it. A stealth suit. A spacecraft. A couple of grunts and a savvy investigator."

"We could hit the F-clave with a meteorite," Arlin suggested.

"To what end?" asked Cilreth.

"If we destroy the F-clave's complex, it might shut them down for a while. It might flush Telisa out."

"That's good thinking," Relachik said. "What else can we come up with?"

"We could bribe someone else with access. They are, after all, greedy criminals," Cilreth said.

"Criminals? Kind of. Here on the frontier, just call them entrepreneurs," Arlin said.

"That may work. It would be hard, though," Relachik said. "We're complete strangers and haven't worked with them before. And you said the F-clave is notoriously brutal with traitors. Kill your whole family kind of brutal."

"Then we can finger someone who's worked with them before. Get them to purchase the information we want."

Relachik sighed. "I don't want to go spending months hanging out with lowlifes and building up a criminal record to find the right guy and buy our way in. Besides, I have a large sum of money, but it's finite."

"I get the feeling you have an alternative of your own."

"I may," Relachik said. "I just wanted to feel out some other ideas. Keep thinking on it, send me other approaches if you have them. I'm going to work on my idea and see if I can get it to work. If not, then we're back to meteorites and lowlifes."

Relachik walked back to his quarters. He knew he was going to contact someone in the Space Force, but the question was who and how. He thought of his secret contact, Nick. He might be able to get something done that way, but he didn't want to burn that particular bridge. This was going to require deception. Once they found out he had lied, whoever he chose might not listen again. Nick could remain a source of information, as long as he handled the relationship correctly.

"No, I think I'll go above board with this one," he told himself. Even an ex-captain dropped for incompetence would be able to get more attention than a random citizen.

After all, he thought, *the days of my open credit with the Space Force are over. I should burn the remainder of that up first, and keep my surreptitious connections alive.*

Relachik finished making his decision. He used his link to contact Commander Gaines. The other side accepted the connection immediately.

"Relachik! I wasn't expecting to hear from you."

"Hello to you too, Gaines. I have a tip for you."

"What? You working for the Space Force from a private eye's desk now?" Gaines said.

"Funny. You want the tip or not?"

"Not. If anyone finds out—"

"I'm not begging for a handout, from you or the Force. The info is free and you can use me as the source or fabricate your own."

"Then go."

"There's a group on Halthia Hyri Three. Commonly called the F-clave by the locals. I happen to know they're a danger to Earth and the Space Force."

Moments ticked by with no answer.

Then Gaines replied. "A known issue. But they're low priority. You *did* hear the news about the *Seeker*, right?"

"Of course I heard. What kind of dumbass question is that?" Relachik snapped. *Keep that up, Leonard, and you won't get anywhere with him.*

"The Space Force knows about them. Those guys are smart enough to stay off the radar."

"Well maybe they oughta be put on the radar. They have their hands into more than you realize."

"We know they front corporations out on the frontier. That's okay. It helps grow the frontier without as much red tape, gets it prepped for steady colonist migrations."

Relachik knew the migrations were an important part of the stability of the Core Worlds. With fully automated industry in place, the idle billions had little to do but cause trouble for the government when they could not afford to stay ensconced in virtual realities all day every day. The UN's solution to this upheaval was to ship people out of the central systems to the frontier, where they would have real-world work to occupy their attention. At least then they were not the Core Worlds' problem any longer.

"Then I guess you're okay with the alien weapons they've figured out? The next step is manufacturing, you know."

Gaines perked up.

"What the—?"

"Yeah, you heard me. They have their hands on some of the heavy stuff. And it's gone to their heads. Another few weeks and they're going to be ready to step out of the shadows and carve out a small empire for themselves. This is more than a handful of local marshals can handle."

"We'll see. The big guns are for aliens now, not shitty little gangs."

"Whatever. It's out of our hands. But it's more than a gang. They're well organized and well equipped."

"And their storage?"

"On site. I think they'll wipe it before you get there if you send a human team. But you have a shot at it."

"Okay, thanks for the tip. Take care of yourself."

"I intend to."

* * *

"As soon as we notice anything amiss we'll have to make our move," Relachik said, face to face with Arlin and Cilreth in their ship's galley.

"I don't see how it could be safe to go in there during an attack," Arlin said.

"It's safer than busting down the blast door ourselves," Relachik said. "Trust me, I know the navy. They're concerned with collateral damage. It'll be as safe as taking a stroll back on Malgur-Thame. We just don't want to attract attention before the attack happens. We were talking about AIs earlier? If they send in what I think they will—an Avatar-class battle module—then the attack will be AI-controlled."

"Okay so we're more or less safe. How do we just walk in there and get what we need? Won't they want it?"

"They do, but the pick-up team will come in to get prisoners and storage modules after the job's finished. We have a window. A slender window."

"I might ask why their hackers don't come in with the soldiers, if the navy is so squeaky-clean with their surgical strikes," Arlin said. "But I'm in as long as you're footing the bill."

Seeing Arlin was shored up, Relachik turned to Cilreth.

"I wouldn't ask you to go in there..."

"I know. I'm your computer expert. I'll follow your lead."

Relachik smiled. "Good. The suit's yours. For this one, anyway."

"What? The stealth suit?"

"Of course."

"Will it even fit me?"

"Yes. It will."

"Well if I'm going to be invisible, then why aren't I going in there alone? You two will be visible enough."

"I can't ask you to go in there alone."

"Dammit. Five Entities, just stay here then."

"Are you sure?"

"Shit. I'm a twitch addict, remember? I'm not looking forward to old age."

Relachik nodded.

As I thought. She's tough.

"We might not be able to back you up. If the criminals won't be jamming civilian link frequencies, the Space Force will. Once you get into the compound, you should be able to get anything."

"Just make sure the suit has the juice. I'll do it."

No harder than leading a bunch of green recruits into an alien ruin.

His internal monologue answered him: *And you know what happened that time.*

"I think they'll use the battle module. It just depends on what resources are within range. There's a chance—call it five percent—that they'll send in infantry instead. If that happens, the suit will need some software modifications," Relachik said. "It's designed to be used either solo or as part of a team. There may be a team of operatives in the strike wearing stealth suits just like this one, which means there will be a handler coordinating with them. And it's going to notice your suit."

"So they'll know I'm there? Suddenly the stealth suit isn't sounding as comfy as before."

"The Space Force will notice you. The F-clave probably won't. My idea is, we could try and make you look like a software glitch, or maybe a legitimate wearer who's misconfigured."

"Well, how do they manage them?"

"I don't know many details. There's a system there that uses frequencies banned for civilian use. We could turn it off completely. But then I'm wondering if you would be classified as a non-combatant. I mean, an unarmed civilian is a lot different than someone creeping around in a stealth suit in a firefight. I'm not sure if that would make it more dangerous."

"If we turn it on, then I need to join their team? And we won't be authorized to do it."

"Suppose their team was called WarFalcons. Then what if you weren't on the team but you called yourself SpyFalcon? Or Observer? They would be less likely to shoot you dead. As you say, we wouldn't be authorized to join their link channels, but you could imagine they might think someone screwed up somewhere and didn't add you correctly."

"The name might give them pause," Cilreth said. "Okay. I'll get on this configuration. Maybe ObserverDrone or UNDrone?"

"Could backfire," Arlin said. "If they think you're just a mechanical, they might be less concerned about friendly fire incidents. Heck, if I were special forces, I'd love to take out the government spy drone trying to report back on all my mistakes."

"Oh. Yeah," Cilreth said.

"I wouldn't be surprised if they try to deactivate the suit remotely," Relachik said. "But it's an officer's call. If you turned out to be on their team, or even a UN monitor, and they got you killed by deactivating the suit, it would be bad. So they might not take that chance."

"Better and better. I'll see if I can figure out how that would be done and disable that feature."

"Then we're back to them deciding she's a combatant if they can't turn it off," Arlin said. "Maybe we should all go in."

"If I figure out how to keep it from being turned off, I'll make sure the suit reports that it *was* turned off."

"We might have a week," Relachik said.

"Then I'll get on it."

"I'm curious about the battle module," Arlin said. "What kind of a thing is it? What's the plan for that one?"

"Its exact nature and specs are need-to-know," Relachik said. "But the plan in that case is simple. You'll sit there and hug a big rock about a kilometer away with the stealth functions on. The lights at the F-clave complex will go out. You wait three minutes, then go in and get what you need. Hurry out before the cleanup crew shows up."

"The F-clave has internal power," Cilreth pointed out.

Relachik shook his head. "Doesn't matter. The power will go out."

"Doesn't the Avatar thing hang around for the cleanup crew?"

"No. It will be gone. In three minutes, it will be long gone."

"I'll prepare for the less likely contingency, then," Cilreth said.

"Yes, that would be smart. I can lay out some scenarios for the case where they send in a human team. We can drill those a bit."

"I'll be waiting." She got up and walked out. Arlin and Relachik sat in silence for a moment.

"Did you get me to buy in first just so she would too?" Arlin asked.

"No. I was prepared to go with her. It just makes so damn much more sense for someone with the stealth suit to go alone."

"She might not come back," Arlin said. "I mean, I think she will, but..."

"I've led people to their deaths before," Relachik said. "But there was always a lot on the line. I go to sleep every night knowing that I did more good in the world by doing that than if I had sat back and refused to give the orders."

"What's on the line this time is personal. It's important to you, maybe not to her."

"But that's another thing, isn't it? She volunteered. She knows it's a little dangerous."

"Fair enough," Arlin said. "Can you tell me anything else about the Avatar battle module?"

"Let's see. Should I say 'I've already said too much' or should I go with 'If I tell you, I'll have to kill you'?"

"Ha. Okay. Let me know if you need help with the sim, then."

"Will do."

Relachik linked in with Cilreth and started to set up the parameters of the simulation.

***

Cilreth stood in the desert-like environment of undeveloped Brighter Walken. It was only a simulation but looked and felt real enough. She activated the suit's stealth function. She checked her arm. It appeared as if she could see through her flesh, though it had a ghostly glowing outline.

"Do I glow like that? I hope not."

"That's just for you. No one else can see it. It's not just the sim. The suit can overlay your limbs for you for real, just like that. Helps to keep you from shooting yourself or chopping off an arm or whatever."

"Nice."

She spotted the rock formation ahead that they had named Station One.

"I can only guess as to the location of the storage," Relachik said. "And chances are, the F-clave has modified its compound without notifying anyone. So I'm deviating from the floor plans of record."

"Got it."

"If the Avatar goes in ahead of you, there'll be nothing in your way. You just have to hurry. Find the storage and get out before the retrieval team shows up to capture the gang members and the storage. This simulation is for the worst-case scenario: a special team goes in backed up by local marshals. In that case, you have to get in behind the team, avoid the fighting, and grab what you can."

"Can I count on your support?"

The answer was delayed.

"Best if you can do it in silence. But if you get hung up on something, you can ask for help. Remote or otherwise. The suit's link frequencies may or may not be jammed, as I mentioned earlier."

He doesn't want me to talk. But he can't bring himself to forbid it, either.

"Okay. No noise then. Whenever you're ready."

"You're at Station One. Arlin and I will be watching. Here we go."

A tactical map came up in her PV. She saw the objective and her own position, as well as several guard drones patrolling the area.

"Relachik. Over on the west side," said Arlin's simulated link.

Cilreth got a surveillance feed. She saw that a drone had stopped.

"I see it," Relachik transmitted back.

"Has it seen something?"

"No. They neutralized it. Okay, Cilreth. Probably about a minute or two now."

"I'm ready," she sent back.

Everything happened at once. Two missile trails shot forth from the desert, only a couple of feet above the ground. The front and rear gates of the compound exploded. The drones on patrol around the perimeter were all dead in their tracks.

"Here come the robots," Relachik noted.

"There's two at the front gate and one at the back," Arlin added.

Cilreth watched two light combat robots charge the front.

"Do you hear any chatter?" Relachik asked.

"No. Nothing."

"Good. Maybe you're the only stealth suit out there. Go on in. Silence from here on out unless you get in a real mess. Good luck."

"Got it," Cilreth said.

She checked the suit diagnostics one last time. Everything looked good. She sprinted out from the rocks, watching the entrance as she approached. Soldiers in light armor prepared to enter after their machines. She counted eight of them. *And hopefully there are no invisible ones.*

The squad ran inside the gate.

Cilreth tried to calm her breathing as she walked out of the last cover toward the compound wall. Loud cracks of weapons fire erupted from within. She glanced back. Her footprints appeared lazily behind her, eerily trailing her by several feet.

If someone shoots at the head of the footprint trail, they'll miss.

The entrance yard was a mess. She saw scattered robot fragments and three men in glue. She did not know what side they were on, so she ignored them.

Her eyes scanned the main building. Two doors had been forced. She ran for the wide double doors straight ahead. A camera bubble or weapons turret had been melted above the doorway. The ruin belched black smoke. Cilreth stopped beside the door before bolting in. She heard the sharp snap of launchers and the whine of a stunner.

She took a peek. The door opened into a smoke-filled atrium. More people in glue struggled on the floor. Cilreth ran inside, keeping a wall on her right side. The room had once been luxurious, filled with low tables and faux-leather couches. She took the first corridor that offered itself and looked down its length. A black scar from some explosion marred the floor. She looked at the doors and summed them up: several small ones and a big metal one that had been forced open.

The small doors are too close to the entrance. They can't be important. Go deeper into the complex. She ran through the ruined metal doorway. A short mirrored hallway split right and left.

Cilreth experienced a moment of near-panic. *Which way should I go? There's going to be so many hallways, so many doors. I can't count on the map being any good.*

She chose the left. People chose the left less often. Then it struck her that might mean the soldiers went right and the criminals still awaited a fight on the left, but she did not turn back.

No time for second-guessing myself. Besides, the soldiers probably split up.

A commotion rose ahead. An opulent archway guarded by a beautiful but functional metal mesh had been forced. Cilreth ran up beside the doorway and dropped to a knee to peek around the corner.

She caught a glimpse of robots fighting more machines. The robots looked like Space Force hydras, a commonly used light assault robot. But the room was large. She should be able to sneak through. She stayed low and darted inside.

It was like a scene from robot hell. The room was filled with car-sized programmable fabricators and a series of raw material vats. A giant, many-armed industrial robot held two Space Force hydras aloft in the center of the room. Projectile holes had been scattered across its surface. As Cilreth took in the scene, the industrial robot dropped a large circular-saw-tipped arm onto one of the hydras. The hydra was ripped in half in the space of a second. Some part of Cilreth expected the lifelike hydra to scream in its death throes, but she heard only the squeal of metal and plastic being sundered. A soldier or marshal crouched behind cover in the corner to her left, looking at his puny nonlethal weapon, probably wondering what he was going to do next if the giant machine proved unstoppable.

Cilreth skipped to her right amid a rain of hot debris launched by the saw blade. Sparks and metal showered over the stealth suit. She ran for the right corner, next to an exit. She accelerated directly toward a desk and vaulted over it. As she dropped to the ground, a metal sphere rolled up beside her.

Oh, that's what he was doing.

The world went black.

"Was that what I think it was?"

"You bought the farm. Smart grenade. Look, you took a risk by running through that fight. You might make it, you might not. This time you didn't. Remember, you don't have to be detected to get killed in combat."

"Whatever happened to super-accurate smart weapons?"

"It was super-accurate, and aimed at that industrial robot's power spine. You also happened to be super-stealthy, and super-in-the-way."

Cilreth swore. *I wanted to do better than that the very first time.*

"Okay, let's run it again."

Michael McCloskey

Chapter 16

Magnus awakened with Telisa curled up beside him. He checked the feed from Scout. The situation appeared to be good. He accessed Shiny's probe and saw that none of the destroyer machines wandered nearby.

Their sleep had been light and brief. They gathered their equipment while Scout kept patrolling around them.

"Thank the Entities for that thing. How could I sleep with those alien monst... creatures around if it weren't for Scout?" Telisa said.

"Just change your perspective. We're hunting for those things. Not the other way around. We're deadlier than they are."

Telisa took a deep breath. "True enough, I suppose."

"Of course. We do have a growing problem, though. Scout needs power. If only—"

"I know, I know, if only you could have incorporated the Vovokan walker's power source, it would have plenty of power left."

Magnus smiled. "I have harped on that a bit, haven't I?"

"I know most things seem dead around here, but maybe there are some storage cells that we could tap for power. Do you have what you need to charge Scout from various voltages?"

"No. However, Scout, being designed to wander about on alien planets, has a wide range of acceptable inputs for charging."

"Aha."

"Yes."

"Well, what about that artifact Scout is looking at now?"

"Not sure," he said.

Scout had found some piece of equipment that stood out. It was roughly square, taller than Scout but perhaps no taller than Magnus. It emitted greenish light from a panel on the front. Thick ropes or wires hung from both of its flat sides.

"He's this way," Magnus said, checking his rifle and heading out. They walked through the sandy tunnel where they had taken a nap. It was a cul-de-sac, the result of a cave-in. Telisa grabbed her pack and followed.

They found Scout two caverns over, waiting near the device. Magnus looked over the find in person. It looked new. Everything else had been covered in sand.

He took out a heat charger he had brought for Scout. He had hoped they might be able to find a source of heat that could be used to provide energy. It had a multimeter on its side which he used to check the leads.

Magnus hesitated.

How convenient.

"Do you find it a bit odd that we've come this far so quickly?" he asked.

"No. I don't follow you."

"Well, we were led here by these mysterious colorful objects that float around. After we fought our way through the coliseum, we made it to the door which looked sealed, but it just opened for us, even though two others right next to it were melted shut. Now we're here, deeper in the house than we have any right to be, and we find this new piece of equipment and it just happens to be great for charging Scout."

"Coincidence? Or the reason the spheres led us this way is they knew ahead of time this door still worked. The charger, I don't know," Telisa said. "You did just make a big deal about how flexible Scout is."

"This source is almost optimal. It looks like it's been cleaned up and prepared for us."

"Maybe Shiny is helping us remotely."

"Maybe. But he said he couldn't risk attracting any attention," Magnus pointed out.

"With a Vovokan ship, I bet he couldn't. Maybe he's figured out how to influence things down here using only the *Iridar*."

"That I could believe," he said. "But how did he keep that door from being melted by the destroyers, however long ago that was? Or how could he have known it still worked?"

"Some sensors may still work. Minor stuff that doesn't attract the destroyers. You have a better theory, I can tell," she said.

"Maybe some of the Vovokans are still alive, and they need our help."

"They're leading us to them with these floating decorations. Devices so small and harmless, the destroyers can't or won't track them."

"That seems like a very real possibility," Magnus said. "What are we going to do if we find them? And what if Shiny thinks of them as more 'competition'?"

"We'll cooperate with them and encourage Shiny to cooperate. Explain that competition isn't a valid option now that his race has been culled down so severely. They need to work together just to survive. I think if we find survivors, though, they'll work together, because this is his house."

"His house may have suffered a mutiny in the face of the destroyer attack," Magnus said. "But you're right; no need to invent more problems until we know they're real."

"I'll say."

Magnus set up Scout to charge from the odd power station. It did not take long to draw the power it needed, so they had a light snack from their supplies and kept close. When Scout was ready to go, they sent it ahead to check out the next few rooms. Magnus watched the feed carefully. He did not see any new threats.

"Where to, navigator?" he asked.

"We'll head over to where Scout is now, then it's farther down."

Magnus shook his head. "Always down. This place is crazy." He hefted his pack and adjusted the light mounted on his rifle. He checked the spare flashlights at his belt.

"We're lucky to be comfortable here at all," Telisa said. "The air isn't bad. And the passageways are a bit low, but more or less our size. Imagine if the Vovokans had been worm-things that crawled through thin tubes the width of our heads. How hard would it be then?"

Magnus laughed. "Okay, I'm not complaining anymore."

Telisa shot him a smile. "Good. Let's go."

They walked down a tunnel toward Scout's position. They came upon a dead sphere lying on the sand. It had been one of their colorful guides.

"Another dead one. I hope they can make it."

The tunnel ended in a long room filled with debris. There were colored wrappers, shattered pieces of equipment, and Vovokan bodies. Telisa drew her knife and her stunner.

She's terrified of the bodies. I guess I can't blame her, and I'd rather she have her weapons ready than otherwise.

"Anything here for us to kill?" Magnus said.

"I know you're just trying to encourage that change of attitude you mentioned," Telisa said. "But yeah, if anything threatens us, I'm ready."

"All these bodies. If this is Shiny's house, what are they all doing here?"

"I don't know. We don't have knowledge of his race's living arrangements."

"Were these Vovokans related to him? Were they employees? Slaves?" Magnus asked.

"He said those others were fake. Or something similar. But I can't tell. These sure look just like him, only injured or dead."

The colorful spheres danced over to a rough hole in the floor. Telisa cautiously approached it and glanced down with her light.

"We have to go through that?"

"You're the navigator. Our little guides seem to think it's the way to go," Magnus said. He heard a crackling noise and spun around. His eyes caught movement— something small.

"What is it?" Telisa demanded.

"Small critter," Magnus said. "Probably attracted by all the bodies, or maybe some of this was their food, too."

Telisa knelt by the hole and picked something up.

"I think this is one of those little guardian spheres that Shiny uses."

"Makes sense. I wonder if he needs more."

"I'm going to pocket a few of them, of course," Telisa said. She sifted through some of the wrappers and garbage on the floor. She picked up a few more items.

Magnus sent Scout down the partially blocked shaft. As usual, the floating spheres stayed with the Terrans. Magnus resisted the urge to bat one aside with the end of his rifle. He released a smart rope and told it to prepare for the descent. It snaked down the shaft after Scout.

When Telisa was satisfied, she anchored her rope and they headed down. Magnus watched Scout's feed. They were headed into a twisting, partially-collapsed well. The route was cluttered by fallen beams, boulders, and sand. There were also bodies and debris of Vovokan make, though Magnus did not see anything salvageable.

Magnus descended about two meters ahead of Telisa. They flicked their lights in all directions, watching the debris and bodies.

"There's a critter on my rope!" Telisa called aloud.

Magnus looked over. Telisa had trained her flashlight on something. He swung himself slightly to the side to get a clear view. A long, many-legged creature scampered down toward her. It was red and gold. The golden parts of its integument sparkled in her light.

"Don't shoot the rope," he said. "We don't have many extras."

"I only have a stunner," she said.

"I don't know, you might damage its controllers with that," he thought aloud. "I see it. It's small. Stay calm and use your knife."

Telisa drew her knife and waited bravely. Magnus looked around to see if he could get over to help her. A ledge covered with debris was nearby, but he could not tell if it would hold. Whatever supported the ledge was not visible beneath the piles of rock, sand, and fragments of a machine. He ordered his rope to retract a bit and started himself swinging so he could join her.

The creature descended within range of Telisa's knife. It was considerably longer than her twenty-five-centimeter blade. She allowed it to scamper halfway onto the blade then flicked it away forcibly. The creature went flying away into the darkness.

"Ug!" she said.

"That was good," he said.

"I swear that thing scares me as much as anything else down here. It's small, I know, just too creepy."

"It was like a tiny Shiny. Hopefully not actually a young Vovokan," he said.

"I don't think it was. Who knows, though?"

They resumed their descent. They wove back and forth around obstructions in the shaft. The debris also made it difficult to see very far. Magnus thoroughly scanned each short descent with his lights. Telisa did not complain at the lack of progress. He thought she was probably still worried about the "zombie" Vovokans.

They descended on smart ropes to another level and paused in a small cavern adjoining the shaft. A pile of dead bodies partially covered in sand lay in a corner where an exit had collapsed.

"Magnus!" Telisa sent the urgent call silently over her link.

"What's going on?" Magnus transmitted.

"Big gold centipede-things scurrying around here. No idea how many. By the Five, they scare me."

"Stay calm."

Three long, golden shapes scampered out of the bodies. Then another. They had red bands like Telisa's previous visitor.

"One of them is coming—*it's biting me*!" Telisa cried out.

Magnus leaped over. He was ready with his flashlight, but Telisa already had hers on her lower leg.

"Thank Momma Veer," she said. "It couldn't get through."

Magnus assumed it had tried to bite her on the leg. He concentrated on finding the critters in the dark space while mentally configuring his rifle. Telisa raised her hand to fire her stunner as Magnus turned to scan for more enemies.

"The stunner's no use. I only have a knife," she said.

Magnus concentrated on the creatures he could spot. His rifle thundered in the closed environment. Once his weapon had collected enough data to form a target signature, he started firing with less accurate aim. The weapon and his smart rounds took care of the rest.

He was just about to turn around and check how Telisa fared when the sounds of another weapon boomed out. Telisa had a compact assault weapon in her hands. The muzzle flashed as she shot again and again.

I didn't know she had that!

Magnus looked away to take more shots. His light scanned left, then right, looking for targets. He could still hear things scampering in the sand, so he turned his light downward. Something landed on his back.

Dammit, should have looked up.

He rammed his frame against the irregular cavern wall, hard. He tucked his chin forward to his chest. The Veer skinsuit distributed the impact evenly across his back, even though the wall was not smooth. He felt a wet pop where something died against his back. He stomped his feet, trying to smash anything that might be readying to scamper up his legs.

Telisa squealed. Magnus was next to her in an instant, searching. One of the creatures dangled from her wrist. Telisa shook her hand violently but it remained affixed to her. Magnus sliced it off with his dagger, leaving only about an inch of the thing on her. He sheathed the blade, dripping with alien gore. He grabbed her wrist to remove the rest of it. "Let me see."

"It fell off. It fell off after you cut it," she said. Her eyes were wide. She breathed in long gasps.

"Keep shooting!" he urged.

His rifle sounded twice more as his light swept over the golden creatures. There were more of them now. He could hear them crawling all around in the shaft. He told Scout, now fifty meters below them, to climb back up to their position.

His light swept the floor of the ledge before him. He kicked savagely at two of the things, sending them flopping away down the shaft. His light revealed more of them crawling across a garbage-encrusted beam toward the ledge. He shot three of them off the beam. Telisa kept shooting as well.

One of the things made it up Magnus's leg. He felt it attacking him, but it could not hurt him anywhere the Veer armor protected him. He disarmed his weapon and slammed the rifle butt against his quadricep, smashing the critter.

"I'm out of ammo," Telisa said.

"You still have your knife?"

"Yes, I got one with it already. But they keep coming!"

Magnus had noticed that. Every time his light swept across the area, he saw more. Another one crawled up his leg. Telisa emitted an angry noise that told him there were creatures on her, too. He swept his light over her.

Damn, there's two or three on her back! We're in trouble.

Magnus ripped the creatures off her back with his bare hands, tossing them away before they could bite or sting him.

"I don't know if I can keep going. So tired," she said. Her knife descended into two more of the things on the nearest cavern wall.

Poison? Or just fatigue from the fighting?

Magnus reactivated his rifle. He fired three more rounds in as many seconds. His ammunition supply was running low. *This is exactly why we have lasers and stunners. But you had to stick with old faithful, here.*

"Wait," Telisa transmitted through her link. "I think we're stirring them up. Let's get back on our ropes and be still."

Magnus had five rounds left. He was ready to embrace any alternate plan. He contacted his abandoned rope. The free end snaked over toward him so he could grab it. He swung out and asked it to retract a bit, carrying him away from the ledge.

"Now just be still," she said. "Maybe these things have mass sensors like Shiny. We move too much, and our bullets move a lot, maybe it attracts them."

The creatures did look a little like Shiny, or at least as much as a small monkey resembled a Terran.

"It could be our lights attracting them, too. Let's turn them off."

"Scary, but a good idea."

They turned off their lights, allowing darkness to envelop them. After a few seconds, Magnus's eyes adjusted enough to see Scout's lights down below. The robot had almost reached them.

"I think some of them are chewing on Scout. Let him attract them a bit longer, then I'll shut him down, too," Magnus said.

A swarm of the creatures attacked Scout, but its surface was too hard to be harmed by creatures so small. Magnus brought Scout to a halt ten meters below.

Telisa flicked a few crawlers off her rope as they came, but otherwise she had frozen. Magnus hung next to her and did the same.

"I'm leaving Scout's lights on. He's still now; we can see if it's the motion."

"I think it is," Telisa said. "On Earth, so many life forms have a lot in common. Heck, even a lobster has a head with eyes and a mouth. These creatures may all have the mass sense like Shiny. If these things are similar to him, those knobs at the end of their bodies are probably their mass sense organs."

"It has to be in relative motion, right?"

"Yes. And his clearest picture is when he stands still and uses that weaving motion to move his sensor back and forth in a regular pattern. These things don't do that. I bet their sense is inferior to Shiny's."

A quick check with Scout's light revealed that the creatures around Magnus and Telisa were already moving away. Telisa's suggestions were working.

They hung for five minutes in the darkness. Magnus used the light to check again. It did not seem to attract attention. He did not see any of the creatures. Magnus shifted slowly toward Telisa and reached out to grasp her arm. Blood poured out of her wrist. He wrapped his mouth around her wound and sucked blood out. He spat it out and sucked on it again.

"You think it was venomous?" Her rising voice told him she had not yet considered the possibility.

"It should be okay," he said. "It's bleeding, which is good. It'll wash out the wound."

Magnus pulled his pack around from his back and took out their medical kit.

"Why did you suck the blood out? You think it's venomous?" she persisted.

"I don't know. I saw some kind of sacs on the side of its head. It reminded me of a snake."

"Not exactly what I envisioned for a romantic interlude on an alien planet," Telisa said.

Magnus nodded, then spat again. He put a small light in his mouth, aimed it at her wrist, and sprayed artificial skin over the puncture.

"It's only a little red," he said.

"It just scared me more than anything else," Telisa said. "What are the chances a Vovokan critter's venom will work on a Terran?" She said it dismissively.

"Very low," Magnus agreed. "Especially judging by how different Shiny is. At this point, if you feel anything, it's likely you're just having a psychological reaction to the imagined danger."

He watched Telisa. She seemed to be calming down, but she was not fully recovered yet. His eyes caught the weapon at her side.

"I didn't know you packed that. I don't even *recognize* it."

Telisa stared back at him with an odd look on her face.

"It's from over there. I don't know who put it there."

Sweat glinted on her face in the reflected illumination of their utility flashlights. Telisa turned her light toward an alcove in the wall. Magnus followed the light and saw a square cabinet against the wall. The cabinet had clear doors, behind which weapons were visible, sitting vertically on a rack.

"That is—"

"Yes. It's a Terran weapons cabinet."

"Five Holies," he said, using Telisa's favorite exclamation without thinking about it. He walked over to the case. There was no doubt it was of Terran design. The case stood out as anomalous in the smooth natural curves of the Vovokan cavern. It had square corners and a smooth metal surface in sharp angles. The clear windows and weapons rack looked like the weapons rack back on the *Iridar*.

How is that possible? Has Shiny's race met Terrans before?

"So what are these weapons doing here?" Telisa asked, voicing the question Magnus struggled with.

Magnus took the weapon from Telisa. It felt good. He examined it with his light.

Oh, no.

"It says 'Meer,' like a screwed-up Veer logo. Like a blend of Momma and Veer."

Magnus handed it back to Telisa. She replaced it in the cabinet and took out another. Then she robbed the third of its ammunition. She slung the rifle over her back and packed away the extra clip.

"Does that remind you of anything?" he asked.

"Hell yes, it does! It reminds me of a certain crappy Trilisk trap we got stuck in. Are we in one now? If we're in one now I'm going to scream. What if we never left?" she asked.

"No point in assuming that. Even though it's possible, we can't really change our actions just on the possibility. At least the weapon actually works. It may be screwy on the details, but your link activated it and it killed several of whatever those ugly buggers are."

"Yes. It's quite effective."

Magnus looked at Telisa in the reflected light. His vision blurred for a second.

"What's wrong? Magnus!" Telisa's voice rose quickly.

Magnus felt a stab of pain in his stomach.

"Uhm. Maybe I should have used the extractor from the kit on your wrist," he said, kneeling.

"I don't understand. How could whatever is making you sick not be hurting me too? It's already in my blood."

Another wave of pain came from Magnus's stomach.

"Get an emetic from the pack," he grunted.

Telisa paused to access the inventory with her link, then plucked out a small vial. She handed it over. Magnus bit open the soft top seal of the vial and downed it. The pain in his stomach flowered. Then he bent over and vomited violently. When he opened his eyes, there was blood in the pool before him.

"By the Five," Telisa said. "Does it feel better now?"

"A bit," Magnus said. He sat heavily. "Our romantic interlude continues."

Telisa smiled weakly.

Michael McCloskey

Chapter 17

"Okay, Cilreth. Turn the suit on and proceed another hundred meters to Station One," Relachik transmitted.

Cilreth activated the suit. It was only the second time she had done so in real life. She looked down. Her body faded into a ghost with glowing outlines as it had in the simulations. She stopped reflecting light in the visible spectrum and replaced it with light from the outside environment. The infrared emissions were pretty clean, too.

She spotted the rock formation ahead that they marked Station One. It was clearly visible in the low illumination that was night on Brighter Walken. Enough natural light reflected from the planet's beautiful ring to see a hundred meters.

This was their selected spot to hide until the attack arrived. Cilreth wondered again if the attack would be spectacular. Relachik had assured her the distance would be adequate. Yet he had told her to hide among the rocks and leave the stealth suit activated "just in case."

He's probably being extra safe because he knows I'm not Space Force material. But pulling this off should show him I'm capable of handling whatever he's got.

She waited, watching the compound from her position as well as the feeds from Relachik and Arlin. The ground outside had been cleared of large rocks and other cover for fifty meters around the entire perimeter. The area inside the wall was big enough for a sprawling building over one hundred meters on a side. For the thousandth time, Cilreth wondered what was inside that compound. Stockpiles of drugs? Booby traps? Illegal robots? A small army of drug dealers?

"Someone is leaving," Arlin said. Cilreth caught sight of a group of men leaving the compound in Arlin's feed.

She stayed put and watched the compound for signs of attack.

"Cilreth, stay sharp," Relachik sent her. "We can't back you up for a while. If I'm right about the Avatar, though, this should be a piece of cake for you."

"Got it," she said.

Damn, having them nearby was really helping me stay calm.

She watched in silence for another ten or fifteen minutes. The wait was pure agony. She stretched her neck to release a bit of the tension. Suddenly the compound lights went off. Cilreth held her breath. A few blue sparks erupted from two spots around the perimeter. Then there was nothing but the glow from the planet's ring above.

She started her timer. Cilreth waited for three minutes without seeing anything else.

That was it? I'm underwhelmed.

"I'm headed in. Talk at you when I'm done."

The answer was delayed by five seconds.

"Good luck."

What they hell are they doing?

Cilreth tried to calm her breathing as she crept out of her cover toward the compound wall. The lack of lights became so creepy she almost stopped.

No! I can't chicken out now.

Cilreth started to breathe faster. She ignored the panic in her gut and kept advancing.

I'm invisible, goddammit.

The gate of the compound wall was gone without a trace. Cilreth did not see wreckage or burn marks. The edge of the wall had been cleaved perfectly. The metallic support beams were cut cleanly where they emerged from the stony ground. She looked left and right for any debris. She saw none.

Okay, that's a bit more impressive. The gate was vaporized within a certain radius.

The guards lay strewn about. They looked as though they had simply dropped in place. Cilreth approached one and stared. The man breathed very slowly.

Alive.

Cilreth shrugged and moved on. The compound had one entrance. It was a perfectly cut gaping hole where the front doors used to be. The new edges gleamed. Despite the apparent lack of any defense, Cilreth slinked into the building, hugging the edge of the hole and slipping carefully inside. She kept close to the wall and remained alert.

The basic layout looked similar to the simulations. A major corridor ran past the entrance, so she headed off to the right. Then she took a left to head deeper into the complex. The next room she found was large. It looked like some kind of small lab or factory. Two dead security robots lay on the floor. They each had a three-centimeter hole, edges gleaming, drilled completely through the main body.

Looks like the F-clave actually did get their hands on some hydras, for all the good that did them.

Her personal sensor suite detected a network storage unit in the floor. She walked over to the corner and pried open an access panel. She kneeled in front of the first storage unit. It had a white outer casing. Cilreth took out her cutter.

Looks standard enough. High quality, but normal. Here goes nothing.

She cut through the outer casing to remove a corner. The inside was constructed of three simple modules: a network controller, a processor block, and a storage block. Most of each block was neutral insulator. The actual componentry inside each one was very small: they were only hand-size for convenience. The insulator allowed the components to run at very high frequencies without being affected by outside noise or emitting noise of their own.

Cilreth cut away more of the casing. She unplugged the storage component and slipped it into her suit. Though it could not be accessed stand-alone, she could set it up for extraction later, after she had escaped with her life intact.

One down.

As she stood, she noticed a hole in the ceiling for the first time. Something had been cut away or vaporized there, too.

A laser emplacement? This place has been cleaned from top to bottom in three minutes. Kinda creepy, actually. So quiet in here.

Cilreth continued her sweep. The corridors were flawless, clean, and opulent. The plastic and carbon shone. Each room had a clear color theme as if professionally decorated. She walked through a wide room set up as a tropical paradise, with bright lights, bamboo furniture, parasols, and a video feed of the ocean playing across one wide wall.

· *Damn. High class criminals, I guess!*

The sensor found another storage unit to her right. She let herself through a door manually and found a vast suite. The walls were black, the ceiling a deep blue. Blue zetta ferns grew in two corners, a diatomic plant structure from one of the first alien ruins ever discovered. They were insanely expensive.

Must be the leader's quarters, or someone high up, at least.

A huge, low desk sat in the center of the main room. An alcove to the left held a bar, another to the right housed a bed with giant maroon pillows.

A naked woman sprawled across the desk on her back. Her body was magnificently sculpted, even in an age of toning pills and sleep-scheduled exercise. A man behind the desk had collapsed forward onto her breasts. He was bald with a long, black beard stylishly cut into two long spikes of hair. Saliva ran out of his mouth over her stomach. Another nude woman with short black hair and heavy makeup lay curled up on the bed, unconscious. A small doorway in the back revealed a pair of smooth, probably female legs sprawled on the floor.

Party much?

A silver cylinder with a screw top lay open next to the man, with a dozen pills spilled out of it. The pills were tiny red spheres. Cilreth fixated on the pills immediately.

Want. I can take these and no one will ever know. There must be five hundred of them!

Cilreth reached out to pick up the silver flask. Then she hesitated; her fingers retracted.

Dammit. I'd better not. I don't want to screw up this job and get Relachik's kid killed.

Cilreth struggled with the decision. She stood paralyzed over the treasure. *I could take them with me. But I won't be able to resist using them. DAMMIT!*

Her sensor suite demanded her attention, so she went to retrieve the storage unit from inside the desk. She had the second module in hand when her stealth suit picked up link traffic nearby. She did not dare respond or connect to any services, but it was clear from a passive scan that she was no longer alone in the building.

Here comes the Space Force to pick up their mess. Screw the pills. She sighed. *I'll regret this later when I'm bored out of my mind.*

Cilreth left the suite. She had walked to the right and through most of the building, so she figured she had covered most of the right side. She wanted to hit the left section on the way out, so she found a cross-corridor heading in the correct direction and followed it.

Something moved ahead. A man and a woman in smooth black uniforms that covered their hands and part of their faces were loading a sleeping person onto a carrier.

Cilreth avoided them. She circled around the side of the building, looking for an empty route. She emerged into an atrium with a security checkpoint. Another laser emplacement had been vaporized there. She froze as a couple of Space Force people walked through the other side of the atrium. They did not appear to be especially alert.

Why should they be? They're probably used to walking through the graveyards left behind by whatever that was. An Avatar-class battle module?

Her sensors located another storage unit. Cilreth found a panel in the wall to pry open which revealed her next target. A few seconds later she had the outer casing open.

Another pair of Space Force people entered the atrium. Cilreth cupped the storage block and told her suit to include it in the camouflage zone. The color of the block became transparent to Cilreth's view, visible only with a glowing outline. That meant it was invisible from the outside.

The new people headed toward her. She could see they were both women. Cilreth calmly walked aside and let them approach the open panel.

"We're missing at least one storage module. They must have pulled it."

"How could they know?"

"Keep looking. It's bound to be on one of them."

You're not going to find them, ever.

Cilreth managed to keep from sprinting as she headed down the last hallway toward the exit. In the front courtyard, more Space Force people worked to load the unconscious victims into a large white vehicle. Its side opened up to reveal dozens of slots for storing people horizontally.

The criminals aren't dead, but that's still kinda macabre.

She headed for the hole in the compound wall where the gate had been. She let her footprints blend in with those of the Space Force retrieval group.

A man in a skinsuit with a rifle in his hands stepped out from behind a building, heading toward the gate. Cilreth stopped in her tracks. *Would he notice the footprints?*

The man walked to the compound wall and took a look around. Cilreth took a few steps every time his back was to her. *Patience. Patience.*

Suddenly the man turned and looked toward her. Cilreth's breath caught in her throat.

I'm invisible, dammit.

Something had obviously alerted him. The rifle swung around. Cilreth drew her stunner.

But the man pointed the rifle at the entrance. He scanned the outside of the main building with his eyes.

Oh, I get it. They've told him things are missing in there and he's supposed to stay sharp. I'm outta here.

As soon as the man got a few meters past her position, she resumed her careful steps. As the distance grew, she increased her speed until she was loping past the compound wall.

She took one last look back. The soldier was examining the ground in front of the entrance.

Cilreth turned and tried to brush the sand in her wake. Since her closest footsteps were invisible, she did not do such a great job. As she retreated she saw her brushing had left a discernible pattern.

Screw it. I'll be gone by the time they figure it out.

She turned and ran, trying to stick to rocky ground as much as possible as she loped back toward Station One.

***

"Someone is leaving," Arlin said. They stood next to a storage shed well beyond the perimeter of the compound. Relachik and Arlin had found it on their initial scan of the defenses. It was so far out, they were not even sure it belonged to the F-clave. But the shed was deserted, filled with only food, water, and spare parts.

Relachik checked the perimeter. It was as Arlin said. Three men came out and ran toward two electric all-terrain vehicles. The men hopped in, two in the first and the last in another of his own. Relachik saw that they held several silver cylinders with rounded tops.

"They're in a hurry," Relachik said.

"Coincidence?"

"I would like to say yes. But dammit, there is no such thing."

"Those could be network storage modules they're carrying," Arlin pointed out.

"Damn. Damn! We have to go after them. How could they know?"

"There's a leak somewhere," Arlin said.

Or they have other clues. What could it be? Supply movements? Sensors in orbit? Maybe they hacked into the new planetary defense network.

"We don't have a jeep! We need to follow them."

"Yes, we do," Arlin said. "Out back!" Relachik and Arlin left the shed and ran around behind it. The criminals drove out of the compound. They left the back gate open.

"Could it be a trap?"

"If they're this far ahead of us what hope do we have?" Relachik asked, but he was already getting into the electric jeep.

"Cilreth, stay sharp," Relachik sent to their other team member. "We can't back you up for a while. If I'm right about the Avatar, though, this should be a piece of cake for you."

"Got it," she said, though she sounded slightly put off. Relachik did not blame her. She did not deserve to be left on her own. But they had no choice, and besides, she had the best hardware. The stealth suit counted for a lot.

The jeep was old. It might have been one of the first vehicles on the planet.

"It'll take a while to disable the—"

"Use an emergency override. Let it complain; we'll be gone before anyone can get out here."

"The Space Force team may respond to it."

"What choice do we have? Hurry," Relachik said.

Arlin brought the vehicle to life.

"Attempting to notify authorities of your emergency," the jeep told them. Relachik took the passenger seat and they started forward.

"Battery is at twenty-two percent," Arlin noted. He headed for the rough dirt road the men had taken.

They veered onto the road at top speed. Relachik set his link to process what he saw to enhance his low-light vision. In his mind's eye he saw another feed of the view, with more details. He could see a thin dust trail in the evening light.

"The authorities are temporarily out of range," the jeep said.

"I doubt they've spotted us," Arlin said over his link.

Relachik readied his rifle by selecting the human target profile. *Haven't done that in a long time*, he thought.

"It'll be most effective if we both shoot at once, and soon, before they see us," Arlin said.

"Yes. Lead vehicle. Use a lethal targeting option. If we only wound them they'll shoot back and kill us. Besides, you don't want one of them showing up for revenge someday."

"Yes, sir."

Arlin flopped his rifle beside the manual controls of the jeep. No doubt he was controlling it through his link, or he'd simply set it to follow the lead vehicle. Relachik saw they had the vehicles in sight. Somehow Relachik and Arlin gained on them.

"As soon as we come off this light curve... three, two, one, fire," Relachik said with cold precision.

The weapons obliterated the calm of the dry night air. Blood sprayed across the lead vehicle with two men in it. The jeep detected a problem and slowed to a halt. The driver behind allowed his jeep to remain slaved to the leader for a moment, then he took control of it and steered around the first jeep. The vehicle headed back out on the road, gaining speed.

Relachik lost sight of the man. Presumably he had taken cover behind the front seats.

Arlin shot the rear tire. The vehicle detected a malfunction and slowed to a halt beside the road. They arced around the blood-spattered vehicle to pursue. There was still no sign of any passenger in the front jeep. The vehicle was fairly open, like their own; there was little space to hide.

Relachik realized it was a trick. He scanned the side of the road. He saw the man, already fifty meters away from the road, sprinting through the sand.

"He bailed! He's going for cover!" Relachik said, pointing him out. Arlin brought their jeep to a halt.

He must have jumped out as he passed the other jeep.

"I'm headed in. Talk at you when I'm done," Cilreth's voice came through his link.

Relachik brought up his rifle and accessed its advanced optics. He could see the trail of footprints leading toward a group of rocks. He scanned the rocks from end to end. He spotted a foot. It shifted. Then the man was running for another nearby rock formation.

Relachik shot him. The round took the man down cleanly.

"Good luck," he sent Cilreth.

"We have all three. Should be simple cleanup now," Arlin said. "Should we take the vehicles off the road?"

"No. Let's take the storage and get out of here in case the Space Force team got that emergency override notification. Cilreth might need us, too."

***

Back at the *Vandivier*, Cilreth became visible at the top of the cargo ramp to greet Arlin and Relachik.

"You're back in one piece, I see," Arlin said.

"Mission accomplished," she said. "And I'm telling you straight: I've never been more terrified of the UNSF in my life."

Relachik nodded. "All nice and clean when you got there?"

"Yes. Whatever that Avatar thing was, it got in there and did a number on those guys."

"It didn't go inside."

"Sure it did! Every gate, every security mount, all gone, everyone knocked out. I mean, it could have knocked them out with gas or something, but there were laser emplacements missing from corridors—"

"It never went inside. The Avatar just flew over in orbit. No doubt it's already left the system on its way to the next mission."

Cilreth started to reply, but when she saw the serious look on Relachik's face, nothing came out. Arlin traded looks with her.

"They carted away the criminals like so much meat," she said, but her voice was quieter.

Relachik smiled. "Excellent work. Keep in mind, the UNSF is what's standing between you and the aliens. Here, Arlin and I got some more of their storage that may help. These are complete: storage and network modules, the full units."

"Really? Where from?"

"We found a supply shed outside the perimeter. You never know, these may have something. Add them to the ones you got and analyze all of them carefully."

Cilreth noticed a bonus drop into her company account. Relachik had been very generous.

Damn well ought to be for sneaking around out there with no backup.

Chapter 18

Magnus breathed loudly beside Telisa as they walked down a glittering tunnel. She looked at him repeatedly, though she knew better than to ask about his condition yet again. She had already started to get on his nerves with her attention, but his stubborn refusal to confess to his pain was not team player behavior.

If he's compromised, he should share that with me, to protect both of us.

As if reading her mind, he spoke up. "My stomach hurts, but I've taken a painkiller and a stomach-settling agent. I should be at about eighty percent."

"Got it," she said. "The good news is, we're almost there. Very close. There's an unusual area ahead on the map. At the center, there's a special structure, a kind of vault, holding the seed."

"A vault? Interesting. I didn't envision an industrial seed being held in a vault. It must not have been active at the time. Maybe it's a backup of some kind?"

"Your guess is as good as mine. If we could talk to Shiny while we're down here..."

"Then we'd risk more destroyer attention. Our communications equipment could do it, though. We'd need some relays planted in the right spots."

"He already talked to us once. I don't see how it could be such a big risk."

Magnus shrugged. "The destroyers may pay special attention to transmissions to and from the surface. I don't know. He knows better than either of us I suspect. He's been watching them with those probes. I bet he's learned a lot."

The tunnel widened. Telisa saw a vast chamber ahead. Some kind of passive lighting system still gave off a dull glow in a few areas, making the place look surreal, like a rendition of an eerie landscape under a full moon. They risked a couple of steps into the room. Magnus and Telisa swept their lights around.

Telisa checked Scout's feed. The machine was somewhere slightly above them. Telisa aimed her light higher. A balcony ran around the entire room, allowing access from the level above them.

In the center was the vault. Magnus kept his light pointed toward it. The vault was a huge, segmented object the size of a small house. Its curved surface looked like someone had taken a Viking ship, turned it upside down, and painted it silver.

Telisa swept her light along the ground, looking for the critters. Her light settled on a burn mark on the sandy floor. Fragments of metal or ceramic lay all about the mark.

"What's this?" Magnus wondered aloud.

"My guess is a robot was blasted here. By a destroyer."

"A robot or a cyborg."

Telisa's eyes looked over the rest of the platform. "There's another over there," she pointed.

"And Scout's vision above shows a couple more. There was a fight here. I hope—"

"The industrial seed is still here? Me too. But the destroyers came to kill everything, right? Not to steal things?"

"Could someone else have made it here first?" he asked.

"How many other Vovokans are likely to be out there conning aliens into coming back down and grabbing stuff? Don't answer that. Let's get in and take the seed."

They walked to their right toward a ramp at one end of the vault. It sat on a platform about a meter above the floor they walked on. Magnus ascended the ramp first. He idly kicked away some debris.

"Those pieces are... they look odd. They don't remind me of Vovokan technology. I think maybe there was a fight and some destroyers died here."

Telisa joined him at the top of the ramp. The smooth hull of the vault ended abruptly before them. There was obviously some kind of door, a wide, low rectangle on the end, but it had no visible means of ingress. Three spheres rested at the base of the door: the colorful spheres that led them here.

"I hope you know how to get in there," Magnus said.

"The map he gave us has an annotation on how to open it."

"Ah. I knew Shiny wouldn't forget such an obvious detail."

Telisa's mood dropped sharply as she read on. "It says we have to... it shows what legs we have to raise to open it. Magnus, it involves over eighteen legs in a sequence of five moves. In the space of less than a second!"

"Unbelievable. Don't panic. We can figure it out. We could create our own sound file."

"No. Vovokans are deaf, remember? They watch the legs move. Or use their mass sense. What are the chances the vault sensor uses sound input to check the password?"

"We can wait until he contacts us again," Magnus offered.

No. That's reaching.

"Tell me this isn't happening," Telisa said. She looked over the vault on the map again and again. She looked for more metadata attached to the map. There was a section on the vault.

"Oh, thank the Entities," Telisa said. "We have a digital access code."

"There you go. We got all upset for nothing."

"Not so fast. Our links can't talk to the vault," Telisa said.

"Shiny's probe here can talk to anything Vovokan," Magnus pointed out. "Send me the code. I can pass it along."

Telisa laughed. "Yes! I can't believe it. For a minute there I was imagining us hopping around like crazy people trying to speak with our limbs like a Vovokan. And even with Scout's eight legs, we'd be short a couple dozen. Of course, the vault probably wouldn't accept the code from anything but a Vovokan anyway."

Magnus smiled. Telisa passed him the code, and the door slid open a moment later.

The inside lit up. Telisa walked in onto a smooth, clean metal floor.

No sand. So sometimes they forego the sandy floor. Why here?

The left-hand wall was obscured by ten or fifteen stacked cubes over a meter long on each edge. Their sides had tiny rails with a row of small holes. Telisa imagined a Vovokan picking up the cube: several of its arms went on each side and its tiny stubby fingers fit into the holes.

On the right, a set of gray shelves held a collection of items.

"Five Holies," Telisa breathed. "Look at those..." she wandered over, mesmerized by the items.

These have to be valuable to Shiny to be in the vault. They must all be useful.

Telisa examined a cone-shaped spiral of metal with three small rods emerging from the top. She had no idea what it could be. The next item was a deep green rectangle. Its exterior was smooth except for three buttons on the front. She wondered if it was actually only a carrying case for the real item.

And they're not all Vovokan in origin. These over here are too different.

"Yes! Shiny and I share a passion," she said.

"How's that?" Magnus asked, his voice skeptical.

"He likes alien things, too. These aren't all Vovokan, I'd bet on it."

Another item caught her eye. It was a black bowl. It looked like it had a miniature turbofan over the top opening. The surface was chipped, crusted. Everything on the shelves looked shiny and new except for this piece.

It must be ancient. Amazing. Shiny is nothing if not practical. I doubt it's just for show. It almost has to be functional. Okay, maybe it is. He might keep it if it were somehow an investment.

"Parker Interstellar Travels to Telisa Relachik. Telisa Relachik, come in, over?" Magnus said. She ripped her eyes from the trove.

"Magnus, these are—these are all amazing. They could be priceless! Shiny obviously thought they were valuable, too. And he said we could take anything we want!"

"Whoa, whoa, calm down, please. How are we going to carry them all the way up?"

"Scout could carry one. Maybe two or three," Telisa said absentmindedly.

Her eyes danced over the items again and settled on an artifact that looked vaguely like a projectile weapon. It had a central hollow shaft ending in two handles placed sixty degrees apart on the left and right sides.

"And the seed? No doubt that information says what it looks like?"

Telisa forced herself to glance back at the other wall. The cube farthest from the entrance was obviously different. It held a blue sphere of a diameter slightly less than the cube's edge, making it look like the sphere had partially melted into the cube.

"That's it over there," Telisa said. She turned back to look at the items before her.

"Maybe you could take a look at it too, at some point. Tell me what you think. It looks heavy."

Telisa tore her attention away from the shelves and walked over to the device they thought was the seed. She looked over the odd cube-sphere fusion. It emitted a weak blue light.

"Yes, this is what Shiny wants," she said, double-checking through the map module Shiny had given her. "At least we found it. Now we need a plan to move it. It has a power source. I think the destroyers would notice it."

Magnus nodded. His brows came together as he contemplated the problem.

"I can't believe we have all these artifacts and we're basically stuck down here," Telisa said. "How can we get out?"

"Let's look at all our choices," Magnus said. "We could destroy the local invader machines. That option seems impossible on the surface of it. Or we could distract them and move the container while they're out of range. What other options do we have?"

"Somehow cloak the container. Or disguise it. If we could disguise it as Terran technology, they wouldn't care about it."

"How?"

"I don't know. Just brainstorming ideas at this point."

"I wonder why he didn't have us power it down somehow. We could look into how to do that. What else?" asked Magnus.

"Clear a shaft out of the planet. Put the container on a rocket, and shoot it out so fast the destroyer machines can't stop it."

"That's an interesting idea," Magnus said. "But they just fought a war. Most likely they have ways of stopping a missile."

"Yes. Yes, of course. How about the distraction?"

"Maybe our invisible friends can help us with that one."

"We don't know how to talk to them," Telisa pointed out. "And the last of the spheres died outside the vault, I think."

"It's going to have to be a pretty damn big distraction."

"We can do it."

"What's your idea?"

"The power grid. We could reactivate parts of it like Shiny did."

"Ah, yes," Magnus said. "And when thousands of powered-down Vovokan machines come back online, we have our distraction. Not bad, but the downside is, a minute later we'll have destroyers shooting the crap out of everything that moves. The entire house could collapse on us."

"Their weaponry is advanced, and that means well-targeted. I think they'll hunt down and kill the Vovokan targets efficiently."

"Then why is half this place trashed?" Magnus asked.

"It was full of Vovokans before. And there must have been infrastructure they wanted taken out. I don't know. You're right. We'll have to be careful to activate machines in different areas of the house, far away. We can switch areas from time to time, send the destroyers scrambling all around."

"I'll see if I can set up some crude controls or schedules for that."

"Keep thinking. I need to figure out what to take, and how to carry it," Telisa said.

Magnus nodded.

He thinks I'm being short-sighted. Putting the cart before the horse.

Telisa walked over to the shelves. "I need to figure out what to take. How the hell am I going to do that?"

"You know more than I do. Just guess at their functions and weigh their relative values. Either to us as tools, or to potential buyers when we get back."

Telisa pulled a silver cylinder from her pack. "Look at this. To us, it's a powered thermos/cooler. It purifies water and brings it to the temperature we set. But what is it to an alien? It opens up, it's hollow inside. But all the functions are visible only through our links. It's only a hunk of metal until you rip it apart. The construction is such that you destroy it by opening it. It isn't designed to be repaired. It's not until you scan it that you see a battery, a heat source, and sink. If you scan it with the wrong frequency or energy you can damage the link block."

Magnus nodded. "Yes, a difficult problem. But Shiny put all these in the vault. Or at least some Vovokan did. For all we know, Shiny is a post-apocalyptic bank robber and we're doing his dirty work for him. But these items are probably all quite valuable."

Telisa nodded. He had a point. It made her feel a bit better about the decision. Yet it took her the next two hours to unpack her equipment, examine each one and pick out two for her to carry, two more for Magnus, and two for Scout to bring back.

Magnus worked on something in his mind as she chose. He seemed to sense she was nearing readiness and approached her. "I think I have a sequence of distractions ready. How's it coming here?"

"Ready. If you can carry these two." Telisa handed him a heavy sphere and a metal rod over a meter long.

"Okay. A bomb and a pool stick. No problem."

She growled and he winked at her.

"The sphere is heavy, but it looks sophisticated under my passive scanner. It doesn't appear to be Vovokan. The rod might be Vovokan. I found it by accident. It actually created a hologram that hid itself on the shelf."

"Oh, nice. Yes, that would intrigue me too. Okay, I'm not questioning your choices," he said. "Looks like you have a weapon there."

"Maybe so," Telisa said. She had chosen the tube with the two handles as one of her items. The other device she carried looked like a triple-bladed marine propeller. She was not certain of its origin; perhaps she had selected it for no other reason than its trilateral symmetry.

Magnus called Scout in and helped Telisa load more items onto him. The machine had no useful interior holding space, but Magnus had a tough backpack designed to fit Scout. Telisa's appreciation of the machine went up a notch.

"We need to bring more of these next time," she said.

"You're telling me? We need an army of them!"

She laughed. Then she stood up to watch Scout move around, adjusting to the weight of the pack. She found herself staring at the shelves.

"We're leaving most of them behind," Telisa lamented.

"We could come back someday," Magnus said. "I mean, if we don't have a better opportunity."

Telisa sighed. "Okay, let's hit it."

Magnus grasped the seed. She could tell it had significant mass.

"Starting up the first distraction," he said. They waited for a few seconds. Telisa watched the probe network display in her PV. Destroyer machines were scrambled from the surface capital ship and started to descend into Shiny's house.

"Okay, here we go."

Telisa and Magnus headed out with Scout only twenty meters in the lead. Soon they arrived at the first long shaft upward. Scout clambered up, using smart cables and its many clawed legs to climb up quickly. It seemed a bit more clumsy than before carrying the pack, but it compensated for the new load fairly well.

"I hope we don't have another problem with those critters. We can't afford to be sitting around."

"I was thinking the same thing," Magnus said. "If they show again, we'll send Scout off to distract them and slip by."

They worked up the refuse-filled shaft with their smart ropes. Their machines and ropes did all the work, moving them up each leg quickly, but because of the fallen beams and cave-ins, they had to move in smaller leaps, constantly adjusting to find ways around the obstacles.

"Something's coming," Magnus said.

Telisa checked the probe network. A destroyer advanced toward them.

"I wonder how big it is," she said. "Probably the size of that one that flew over us before?"

"I don't think we can fight it, if that's what you're wondering."

"Is it coming down from above?"

"No. It's in an adjoining level," Magnus said. "About thirty meters above. It's getting too close."

"What can we do?"

Telisa became aware of holes in the side of the shaft as light emanated from them. She had not realized the holes led anywhere before, as they had been utterly dark. Now the light from the destroyer machine was leaking through.

Five Entities. It's too close!

The machine glowed. It was hard to look at after the dim light of the tunnels. By unspoken agreement Telisa and Magnus turned off their lights at the same time.

The light shifted for a few moments. Telisa thought the machine was too large to fit through the debris and into the tunnel where they hid.

More lights started filtering in from above.

"It's dispatched smaller machines," Magnus said over his link.

Telisa almost grabbed her stunner, but she immediately knew it was futile. She took hold of the artifact she had taken from the vault instead.

I don't even know if this is a weapon. I don't even know if that hole is the business end.

Telisa brought up the tube and aimed it. She found the actuators, which were presumably manual backups to an alien control system that would not interface with her link. Just in case, she made sure the opposite end of the device was pointed under her right arm, away from herself and Magnus.

Glowing machines floated down toward them. The nearest two were already less than twenty meters above, though there was still debris between them and the destroyers. Magnus dropped the seed down on its own smart rope, trying to make space between them and the destroyer's target.

Telisa pressed the triggers.

A loud hiss assaulted her ears as a vibration erupted in her hands. Something flew out of the weapon in a blur. The glowing drones closest to her burst in tiny explosions, then three or four drones farther away, then finally a split second later, another five or six drones just entering the tunnels. A second later the light was gone, as if the drone incursion had never happened. The sounds of debris and sand falling down the shaft dominated the pit.

"Five Entities!" Telisa breathed. "What was that?"

"It must have launched a dozen guided projectiles at once. Although it looked almost like they split in mid-air, or maybe they impacted the target and then split, if that's... well, it is possible, I guess."

"We'd better save this one. Emergencies only. Who knows how many shots—"

"We're going back down," Magnus said. "More destroyers are coming!"

"But we—"

"Turn around *now*! This isn't working, we're going to be dead soon, or at least the seed will be destroyed. If these next machines don't get us, another one will."

Telisa reluctantly agreed. She checked the Shiny's probe grid and saw destroyer machines moving all about the gigantic house. At least two more were headed their way.

"Back to the vault. Somehow it screens the emissions," she said.

They dropped down dangerously fast. Scout followed after. When they reached the bottom, they sprinted through the last caverns toward the wide open vault room.

As Telisa entered the vault room, she saw silver structures placed around the vault she did not remember.

Something looks different.

"What are—"

"Defenses," Magnus said.

"Shiny must have deployed them."

"I'm glad they're there. Destroyers incoming!"

They ran into the vault. Scout was close behind. Telisa and Magnus barreled into the interior, then turned around and regarded the door stupidly for a moment. Scout skittered in and stood to the left of the entrance.

"Close it," Magnus urged.

"I don't know how!" Telisa replied frantically. A roar erupted from outside. The floor shook.

Concentrate. The map has to say how to close it, right?

A small destroyer drone hovered into the vault. Its light played over the interior. Telisa hit the floor. Magnus fired his rifle. The drone fell, destroyed. Telisa's suit protected her ears.

Holy Entities, that's so loud in here!

Telisa tried to link in through Shiny's probe, but it did not respond. She looked over and saw it had folded up into a Vovokan chair again.

"Dammit, the probe has gone belly up on us."

"Coward piece of crap," Magnus transmitted. His rifle boomed again. Shrapnel sprayed over Telisa. "Hey, I found more ammunition!"

Could there be a manual switch? What would a Vovokan manual door switch look like?

Telisa scanned the walls by the entrance. The sides of the vault were featureless. She scanned the floor. She saw a minor imperfection in the floor, a line in the metal.

Are those scratches from the shrapnel?

Telisa crawled over toward the door.

"Stop. Don't go over there," Magnus urged.

Telisa scrabbled on, sliding on her belly across to the scratch. As her point of view changed, the scratch elongated into an oval and finally a tiny circle as she looked down on it.

A button on the floor? Crazy.

If it was a button, it was perfectly flush with the floor. She pressed it. Nothing happened other than another explosion outside the vault. The debris from the dead drone rattled across the floor. The shaking reminded her of a horror vid she had watched as a child of a giant monster so tall it shook the floor with every step.

"Telisa," he said, his voice laced with irritation.

I hope the destroyers don't have anything like that.

Telisa started to retreat, then she saw another circle a meter to the left. *Another button?*

The rifle boomed again. Hot metal sprayed over her skinsuit. She felt a nick on her ear and an itching flow of blood there. *Those buttons are about the right distance for a Vovokan standing facing the door to have a leg over each one.*

Magnus grabbed her leg. Telisa reached out with both arms, pressing both the buttons simultaneously. As Magnus dragged her back, the vault door started to shut.

"You did it! Thank you!"

Telisa laughed, more a release of tension than a genuine appreciation of his outburst of gratitude. "You almost stopped me," she said, though she felt little annoyance at this point. She was glad to see the door finish closing in front of them.

"I had no idea what the hell you were doing. Next you can figure out how to open them back up."

She laughed again.

"That might be a problem, but for now, I'm calling this a victory."

Magnus dragged her the rest of the way toward him and embraced her.

The vault rang with the sounds of battle. The floor shook.

"Do you think they're trying to get in?"

"I hope not. It can't hold. At least I don't think it can."

"Should we be doing something?"

He kissed her. "If they don't get in, we're good, if they do, we're dead," he told her over his link without interrupting the kiss.

"Good point," she transmitted back. "We're sleeping in here tonight."

Chapter 19

Cilreth worked alone in her quarters. She had practically threatened Relachik not to bother her, telling him to do so would risk the whole operation.

This was a critical juncture in her work in finding Relachik's daughter. Somewhere on the storage modules were the keys and smart filters she needed to track down the smugglers. Along with booby-traps and misinformation. All packed up and encrypted.

This is going to be a lot harder for me than it would have been for the Space Force. They captured all the criminals, and can interrogate them.

Cilreth copied the contents of each module carefully and set extras aside. But as she started into her task, she realized its magnitude was such that she faced weeks of work. Relachik would wait if he had to, but there were other possible courses of action.

There's more than one way to chip a cat, as her grandfather used to say. Cilreth wondered about the origin of that phrase. *How many ways could there be to put a link into a feline, anyway?*

Cilreth asked for a link connection to an acquaintance. It went through immediately.

"GoliathFive?"

"Hello, Cilreth."

Cilreth suppressed a mild shudder. She suspected her white-hat contact was not human. Or maybe he was, but he must have access to an AI.

"I need a package opened and cleaned."

"I see. What's in it for me?" The question was cheerful. It did not sound greedy, somehow. Strange turns of phrase delivered off tempo were part of the mystique.

"You might like to see it, too."

"More details?"

"I have the storage of the F-clave here," she said.

Information that could be useful to you, and a lot of other parties, I imagine.

"I might like to see that. What stake do you have in that organization's secret files?"

"I only need a particular smart filter to find a couple of smugglers. People working with Telisa Relachik. Though she may have used an alias. She's out on the frontier, finding artifacts and selling them on the black market. Someone hired me to find her. I don't need to know—don't *want* to know—anything else."

"Satisfactory. Send the data and I'll get you what you need."

"There's a lot—"

"I have a Z-class bandwidth priority. I'll cover the tab for this one."

"Of course. Sending it now."

Even at the top transmission capability of the *Vandivier,* it took a few minutes to make the transfer.

"I like this deal. Here's what you wanted."

A file came back to her link.

"What? I don't understand."

"The smart filter you asked for. I believe you now have it?"

"You decrypted it just like that? Why does the universe scare me more each day?"

"You make too many assumptions. As for the universe, the more you learn, the scarier it gets."

The connection broke off.

Make too many assumptions?

How could the smart filter be obtained without cracking the encryption on the modules?

It already had the filter? Oh. Or it already had the encryption key. Or I don't know what.

Cilreth sat back and duplicated her contact's results into several storage modules and disconnected them. She brought up a workpane in her PV on one of the modules, isolated from everything else.

Got it. Look on the bright side. Relachik will be impressed by my quick results. Not that I'm going to tell him what happened. Oh, crap. He may find that transmission log. Hard to overlook a transfer of that bandwidth and time.

Cilreth took the smart filter and ran it through several threat detection suites. It came out clean. She stashed it in her link and shut the module down. She reconnected with the net and searched. When she came up against the F-clave wall, she started to use her smart filter. The mass of queries and traces fell away to a much more manageable trace. Exactly what she would expect to see from a couple of people exiled far from Earth. A brief history, a lot of new accounts, and traceable access points at F-clave long-range receivers.

She opened a link to Relachik. "I've got their trail. I'll tell Arlin where to head from here."

"How far?"

"There's not much Terran territory in this direction, so if they're on the frontier, not far. A day or two. If they're beyond the frontier, then who knows?"

"Great job. Thanks for letting me know."

***

Relachik sat in his tiny quarters on a chair that folded out of the wall. He had not been able to resist chatting with Arlin now that they were underway again.

"How far out can this ship take us?" Relachik asked.

"A long way. Though I'm not sure I'm looking forward to heading out of Terran-controlled space when we've just been attacked by aliens."

"The *Seeker* met its doom in a completely different direction."

"I certainly wouldn't call it a *completely* different direction. It was destroyed on this frontier. We don't know how much territory the aliens have."

"If the smugglers left the frontier, they had a good reason to go."

"You're probably right about that. The rogues of the frontier have proved to be a well-informed lot."

"I can't believe those criminals knew the Space Force was coming," Relachik said.

"It's not surprising. They have connections."

"But the Avatars' very existence is secret. Only the top people work with those outfits. Yet they leaked it. Or else the criminals have ways of tracking things we never guessed they had."

"They probably didn't know what was coming. Only that the Space Force was headed their way."

He doesn't get it. The Avatars operate in their own branch. Even regular Space Force personnel don't know about them or where they are.

"If a few petty criminals can do that, how can we hope to fight against aliens?"

"Those criminals are human," Arlin pointed out. "They can worm their way into places aliens won't. Though you're right that our chances against more advanced civilizations are low. We'll fight to survive and hope the aliens have other problems to deal with besides us. Like a big predator that can finish a smaller one, but doesn't want to get hurt while doing it because then it wouldn't be able to deal with other threats."

Arlin's simplification didn't lend Relachik much ease.

"I hope so," Relachik said.

"Shall we put in a little more practice with boarding exercises? I assume Cilreth is out for now."

"No, she might be up for it. But give me a couple of hours. See if she wants to join us."

"Will do. See you in a while."

Relachik disconnected from the channel with Arlin and looked over his work list. But it was just a formality. He knew exactly what he had to work on next.

I've been putting this off too long. Relachik opened a new file in his PV. He started to record some thoughts there.

Telisa.

He stared at her name for a long time. He tried to remember the few years they had spent together. Vacations and the occasional event he had actually managed to attend.

I'm so happy to see you again.

But she won't be happy to see me. He started again.

Telisa, I'm sorry I wasn't there for you. I know I'm a bad father, but I'm here to help now.

Relachik sighed. He should have started this earlier. Anything he could say would sound lame. But if she was in trouble, he could speak through action. He could save her. Maybe that would be a start. He skipped down and tried another entry.

Telisa, are you okay? Really okay? Do you need help? Do you want to go back home?

He stared at the words and imagined himself uttering them.

Shit.

Michael McCloskey

Chapter 20

Telisa opened her eyes. Her head lay across the plane of Magnus's armored chest. His breathing was steady. She remembered they slept inside the vault. Everything looked calm in the pale blue light emitted by the industrial seed. She enjoyed the moment.

Magnus has a magical ability to make me feel safe.

She stretched a bit. Magnus awakened. He swept the hair from the side of her face and kissed her.

"Ready?" he asked.

"Yes. I'm anxious to get what we can and get out. How *are* we going to get out?"

"I don't know. We need a faster way up. Maybe find a Vovokan conveyance down here to take us? Maybe one of those drilling machines."

"Yeah, but the drilling machine itself is a huge target that's sure to get attention."

Telisa stood and walked back over to the shelves in the vault. She replaced the weapon that had killed the smaller destroyers and reexamined the other items there.

"What are you doing?" Magnus asked.

"This is too heavy. It slowed me down before. I need to figure something else out. If we're getting out of here, we have to be fast. Besides, how many shots like that could it have left?"

"Too bad. I was hoping for a powerful weapon. We might be able to reverse engineer it. Or maybe Shiny could."

"Any of these could be weapons. They all could be weapons."

"We need a new plan—"

"I agree. Give me a minute."

Magnus tolerated her delay. He paced.

Her eye caught a smaller, more complicated object in the back on the left side. She leaned down and retrieved it from the end. The response was immediate. The remaining artifacts started to slide down their shelves, moving smoothly toward the center.

"Oh no," she said. She watched in alarm.

"What's happening! Where are they going?" Magnus demanded.

"No idea. Wait."

The objects slid smoothly into the central shelf, which folded from the top and bottom. The shelf compressed into a container of less than half a cubic meter of volume. The container floated up to Telisa's side.

"Five Entities!" she said. "Can you believe it? They pack up. All of them. Just like that. I guess Shiny wanted them ready to move, too!"

Telisa could not contain her excitement. She pumped her fist and stomped a foot. Magnus smiled.

"To think, we almost left most of them sitting here!" she said. "Now we have all of them! Do you know what this means?"

"If we can get out alive, this mother lode is ours," Magnus said.

Telisa beamed back at him.

"We should figure out how to open the vault first," Magnus said. "According to Shiny's probe network, the destroyers are gone."

The probe that had followed them had resumed its normal shape. It sat in one corner, waiting.

"Okay. Let's try the obvious."

Telisa shrugged and walked over to the door. She lay across the cold, smooth metal and pressed the buttons. The door started to open.

"If only all our problems were that easy," Magnus said.

A gory Vovokan scrambled through the doorway in an instant. Telisa yelped, but her jiu-jitsu training took over. She automatically spun onto her back and presented the attacker with her booted feet, kicking it back. Several of its tiny pincer hands grasped her legs as it reared up over her. For a second it seemed like a stalemate, but then its mouth-end curled underneath the body like an upside down scorpion, allowing the beak to snap at her.

Magnus's rifle sounded in the tight space. The round had been well aimed. It went into the front of the trunk and traveled down its length, blowing shrapnel and gore out the far side of the alien body.

The creature spasmed but did not let go. Telisa fought harder with her legs.

I should use my hands. Oh, my knife.

Telisa grabbed for her knife but discovered it was not in its sheath. Magnus appeared over her, stabbing the Vovokan thing several times. It kept thrashing, so Magnus started to cleave the legs holding Telisa.

The alien finally slowed and weakened as Magnus carved away at it. Telisa freed a leg and kicked the trunk away from her. Then she rolled to her feet and kicked the Vovokan savagely several times, breaking off more legs on its left side. Magnus stopped before she did. He stood back while she kicked the corpse several more times.

"Are you injured?" he said.

Telisa was breathing heavily. "I'm angry," she said, ignoring her adrenal tremors. "How could that catch me by surprise? We should have had all our weapons out and ready."

"Yes. It was sloppy. I was only thinking of the destroyers. We should gather our stuff."

"I don't know why my knife isn't back where it should be. Damn those creepy things!"

They unloaded Scout and organized the equipment. They each had a big meal; in all the excitement they had neglected to eat. Telisa opened the Vovokan carrier and reloaded the artifacts she had selected earlier before allowing the device to repack them. Now she felt relatively light: no new artifacts and less food and water to carry. She found her knife sitting near where they had slept and slipped it back into its sheath.

Yet I can't outrun the destroyers.

Telisa took out the rifle she had found and checked its load. "Meer. That would be funny if it weren't so creepy. And if we hadn't seen those crappy copies of stuff before."

Still, the weapon made her feel better, especially after the close call. She leveled the rifle and walked down the ramp out of the vault. The floating case followed in her wake. "We could leave the seed here and go back without it," Telisa said.

"I think that would be dangerous. I think that would give Shiny an excuse to decide we weren't useful anymore," Magnus said.

"So what? You think he's going to kill us just like that? Out of the blue and with no warning?"

"I think that's how his race operates... operated."

"They would have destroyed each other long ago. The whole race would have become extinct."

"Well they are now, right?"

Telisa made a frustrated noise. "Okay, it's time to think things through again," she said.

"Okay. We killed a few, but they can still see the seed. And it's hard to hide," Magnus said.

"We've been doing it backwards. It's hard to hide stuff, as you say. The machines are focused on finding any survivors. They've been in that mode a long time."

"You say backwards—so instead of hiding stuff, we're going to find it?"

"Find it for them," she said. "Shiny has shown us how. We can fake the signatures."

"Yes, but they come in and blow stuff up."

"Then we fake the other destroyer machines as being Vovokan. They'll shoot at each other."

"Sounds too easy," he said.

"These are only battle machines. They were designed for one swift, crushing campaign against this planet. They aren't actually very smart. Probably on purpose. Who wants a huge army of machines that can think really well on their own?"

"It's worth a try."

Magnus sat on the ramp to concentrate. Telisa looked around at the recent battle damage. As far as she could tell, all the defenses had been crushed. The outside of the vault was scorched in several places.

I'm lucky the destroyer machines didn't kill me after that weapon destroyed the small ones. I think they didn't have a clear view of what hit them. They might learn next time; then I'd be stuck in here forever.

Telisa pocketed another of the tiny spheres that had led them down to the vault.

Too bad you guys died off, we were getting quite an entourage going here.

She thought about going to look for more even more artifacts but decided it would not be wise to leave Magnus far behind.

"Okay. This is what I've set up," Magnus said. "I'm going to add a bunch of fake signatures near where we activated a lot of the machines last time with the broadcast power. But this time, once, they've engaged, I'm going to add signatures to a third of the destroyer machines themselves. Let's see if we can start a party."

Telisa took a last scan around the chamber, then sat next to Magnus. Scout moved around the vault in lazy circles. She accessed the probe network data in her PV.

She watched Magnus activate several robots in the house. Predictably, the red dots of the destroyers came from above to hunt the Vovokan targets down. Magnus waited for the right moment. He allowed one Vovokan machine to be killed. But then when two destroyers came at another machine from two directions, he put down fake

Vovokan signatures on both machines. The destroyers both altered course immediately, spiraling closer in the tight corridors, hunting each other.

"Look at that! They're going for it!"

Telisa watched as two destroyer heavies closed on each other. A bright exchange of energies played across the spy network.

"I think two of those larger machines destroyed each other! This is great!"

More machines were scrambled from the capital ship above the surface. The number of destroyers in the house increased. Magnus activated another set of signatures over a couple of them, causing their fellow machines to turn and attack.

"Hurry. Make more, before they figure it out," Telisa said.

Magnus put false signatures on half the destroyers. More combat broke out in several sections of the house. Telisa watched several of the destroyers die in friendly fire.

"This is going to be easy. I never thought it would work so well!"

"They're catching on now, actually," he noted. "They're firing more slowly. And getting closer before shooting."

"That's good for us. Some of them are dead and the others are less effective."

"Yeah, yeah, it is a step in the right direction." Magnus's voice lacked enthusiasm.

"See what else you can do," Telisa said. She stood up. The artifacts were all packed away, so she decided to check on the seed. Telisa walked over and examined it again.

The blue sphere part was made quite differently than the rest of it. The components of the square that embraced it were obviously Vovokan. They looked like the silver rods and bulbs on Shiny's personal gear. Telisa took out a passive scanner and gave the seed a run-over as she had with many of the artifacts on the shelves.

"Wait a minute," Telisa said aloud.

She took out a field mapper and pointed the sensor at the device. The mapper interface opened in her PV. The electromagnetic fields around the device were immensely complex. Impossibly so. The EM fields pulsing in thin air before her looked like the inside of a computation block.

She fumbled through her pack for her spectrometer and took a reading from the surface of the sphere. Her tool showed her the exterior had a known absorption signature: a Trilisk compound no civilian human knew how to replicate.

Her excitement rose again. "Five Holy Entities!" she sent over her link. "Magnus. This center part isn't Vovokan. It's Trilisk."

He walked into the vault to join her. "How? You sure?"

"Sure. It has a known absorption pattern. Trilisk only. The fields are amazing!" Telisa was still watching through her mapper. She moved her hand close to the seed. Her hand created a safe zone wherever she moved it.

"Magnus, these fields surrounding it are as complex as the inside of a processor. But when I move my hand here, they all dynamically clear for me. Wherever I move it—just like that."

"What's inside? A power source? All its computational power is in the fields?"

"I can't scan into it. There are no controls. This outer part is nothing but a glorified holder. Actually, maybe it interfaces with it somehow. Could Vovokans actually know how to interface with Trilisk technology?"

"Once again our companion proves to be less than forthcoming. To the edge of betrayal, really."

"Shiny? Yes. He has to know what this really is."

"He has to know all about the Trilisks. He has this artifact in his house, and it's important enough to come back for. Or to send *us* back for. And don't forget where we first found him—trapped in a Trilisk ruin."

Telisa shook her head. "Damn him. All I asked for was a bunch of ruin locations. But he knows a lot more than that."

"Why did Shiny send us down to his house to get a Trilisk artifact?"

"It must be valuable. It must be the most valuable thing on the planet!"

"Maybe. Maybe it's just the most valuable thing left after the destruction," Magnus said.

"I do wonder about what you said."

"What?"

"The Vovokans. Their planet has been destroyed. Maybe they deserved it. Maybe the destroyers are the good guys. Shiny's people might have switched into competitive mode. Maybe they even attacked the destroyers first."

"It wouldn't surprise me," Magnus said. "I hope they don't come for us because Terra can't fight either of these races."

"Did we kill enough destroyers to give us a chance at making it out?"

"I don't think so. Not yet. They're becoming less responsive as this goes on."

"Then our basic situation hasn't changed much. We're still stuck down here with the seed hidden in the vault."

"We could try and rip it apart. We could take back the Trilisk part, if the destroyer machines aren't scanning for Trilisk stuff. I wonder if Shiny would consider that good enough or if he needs all of it. What else?" asked Magnus.

"Back to the drawing board. Figure something out."

Chapter 21

The *Vandivier* shot through interstellar space. The crew waited inside the tiny shell as it traveled farther and farther from home. For the thousandth time, Relachik's patience was tested.

"Is there some chance this is a deception?" he asked Cilreth.

"Yes," Cilreth said. "Do you want to turn back?"

Relachik almost screamed at her.

No, I don't want to turn back!

"I think we have them," Arlin transmitted from his quarters.

Relachik checked the ship's sensors yet again. There was a contact at the edge of their range. He closed his eyes and initiated several actions. The ship slowed relative to the target. A probe launched and moved between the *Vandivier* and the contact. It began to screen out all traces of the approach of their ship.

"I doubt they saw us, unless they've significantly upgraded their ship since the war," Arlin said.

"They may easily have done so, given their mission and also their success at Thespera," Relachik said. But he believed they had to proceed.

We can do this. Finally.

The *Vandivier* began its stealth approach. Relachik handled everything smoothly due to all his practice. He was not nervous; he had always been rock solid under pressure. If anything, his focus improved when it really counted. He felt the approach of the *Vandivier* was well executed.

Relachik took a moment during the process and called up his document. He had been working on it steadily. He looked at the last entry.

If you can forgive me, I think we could work together. We're no longer at odds. You want to learn

about the aliens. Especially the Trilisks. It's no longer my duty to uphold the law, but I'm still a Terran and I have a duty to help protect Terrans. The Seeker was destroyed by aliens. We have to give the Space Force all the help we can. But that doesn't stand in the way of what you want. You can learn about the aliens. I can pass along what we learn to the Space Force anonymously.

Relachik set his link to transmit it directly to Telisa if she ever came into range. Just in case. He had not dared send it to her earlier using the key, for fear of interception by the government, the F-clave, or her fellow smugglers. He still wondered if Telisa was free to do what she wanted, or if she had fallen in with a crowd that had trapped her. It was also possible her captors had brainwashed her into joining them.

"Shouldn't we attempt communication?" Cilreth asked.

"Yes, if we want them to fire on us, or ambush us once we board. Don't worry, once we're on the ship, I intend to announce our presence and intentions. Until then, we're not going to give them any chance to slip away. We'll use the gas grenades as we practiced."

"Very well. And what of the pirate's option?"

"Unlikely," Relachik said.

"What's that?" Cilreth asked.

Arlin and Relachik gave her a look, then Relachik said, "I'll explain it to her. You get ready."

Arlin nodded and left them.

Relachik took a deep breath. "When two powered-up gravity spinners near each other, they have to cancel each other out more the closer they get to each other," he said.

"That sounds familiar. But what's the pirate's option?"

"It usually doesn't come up in combat because our weapons are useful at longer ranges. But this effect starts about a third of a light second out and becomes more pronounced as you get closer. By the time you're close enough to board, the spinners have to be in perfect balance, or else both ships are torn apart. The pirate's option is to choose mutual destruction over capture. You can violently misalign your spinner and destroy both ships."

"Oh," Cilreth said.

"This has been a problem for the Space Force from time to time, which is why we use robotic capture devices that shut the spinner down in the target. The pirate's option remains there, but it's more of a death-instead-of-capture rather than a mutual-destruction thing."

"So we're risking all our lives to do this. Maybe we'd better follow them to a planet."

"If they spot us, then it'll get more dangerous. I doubt they'll even consider the option. It's to our advantage that this is obviously not a Space Force cruiser."

"Not the way I see it. At least they know the Space Force would treat them according to rules. If they think we're another group of pirates, then they may fear capture more than death."

"But they'd have a fighting chance against us."

"Okay, there is that."

"If I do the approach right, and you know I can, they'll have minimal time to react before the gas takes effect. And the remora Arlin will deploy will eventually power down their spinner. Ours will come down with it, then back up. There might be a few seconds of weightlessness."

"Yes. Okay, let's get this over with. I hope we get your daughter back safe and sound."

"So do I."

As they approached, maintaining stealth got trickier, so Arlin moved in on the other ship while Relachik managed the probes. The target remained quiescent.

If we can make it the next few seconds, then it should be disabled, Relachik thought.

Arlin fired the remora. Relachik thought he could feel it launch, a small vibration through the ship, but it might have been his imagination. It ate up the distance between the ships rapidly as it approached the target. Then it slowed and latched onto the skin of the smuggler ship.

"The remora is down. Arming it now," Arlin said. Relachik noted that Arlin also matched the ship's spinner to the target ship's drive.

"Here we go," Arlin said.

The remora discharged into the smuggler ship, causing an electromagnetic disruption meant to cripple them. Arlin moved the *Vandivier* up to dock. Relachik abandoned his probes and headed for the exit.

He found Cilreth waiting at the lock, holding a stunner. Relachik noted a projectile rifle strapped to her back. A grenade hung from a utility belt at her waist. Relachik nodded his approval. She handed him a gas mask and a stunner. He checked his pistol, which he already had on him.

Relachik felt remarkably calm. He knew it was the result of all the training. He felt their ship come into contact with the other starship.

"Something's wrong," Arlin transmitted.

There goes the training.

"What?" snapped Relachik.

"The remora hasn't disabled the ship. Somehow it's still mostly functioning in there."

"Can we fire another one?"

"Not this close. Wait. Maybe I can manage something..."

Relachik took a deep breath. Waiting at this point was painful. "I'm going to try and force the door," he said.

"Okay, but I don't think it will work yet. I almost have the last remora ready to try again."

Relachik prepared to pry the airlock doors.

We're giving them time to prepare for us.

"You might want to step outside our lock," he said. "You know, just in case."

Cilreth saved her usual wry comments and stepped outside the lock. Relachik opened the Vandivier's outer lock and commanded their invasion apparatus to move into place. The device attacked the lock door, but it remained firmly shut.

"The other remora is in place," Arlin reported. "Stand out of the lock and I'll activate it."

Relachik stepped back to join Cilreth. They heard a dull crack.

"There, that's better," Arlin said. "No, there's still something odd. Maybe they have countermeasures against it? It's not working right."

"This is Leonard Relachik," he sent to all local receivers. "I'm here to speak with my daughter, Telisa."

"Telisa. Elsewhere."

"What? Where are you? Open up," Relachik said.

"Telisa travels to collect, gather, harvest. Telisa return soon."

Arlin walked into the lock, holding his rifle and a grenade.

Odd speech. Could it be...

"Where are you from?" Relachik demanded.

"Planet below."

Relachik and Arlin exchanged looks.

"Are you thinking what I'm thinking?" Arlin asked.

"Telisa is working with an alien," Relachik said aloud. "Either that, or they want us to think she is."

And that doesn't surprise me much. I should have told them about it.

"Open the door. Let us in."

"Stop. Halt. Desist."

"We're coming in now, whether you like it or not," Relachik said. "Open it if you want your outer lock door to remain operational. If I have to cut it, it'll be destroyed."

The lock door opened. The second door beyond opened as well, leading into a perpendicular corridor.

"Ambush?" Arlin asked Relachik and Cilreth on a private channel.

"Masks. Grenades," Relachik answered. They slipped their masks on. Arlin and Relachik rolled their grenades into the airlock. Once activated, the grenades accelerated themselves, rolling along the deck to the corridor. Arlin's grenade broke left, Relachik's right.

"What have you done with my daughter?" Relachik broadcast.

"Mutually beneficial contract, deal, relationship. Recommendation: await her return."

The grenades reported their activation. The gas was invisible but Relachik's mask told him the grenades had worked a second later when it detected the gas in the air.

"Cargo should be on our right," Cilreth said. "I looked up this design. UED scout ship. We probably want the left corridor."

Relachik nodded. He and Arlin took the left route.

A golden thing stood in their way, ten meters ahead. It had more legs than Relachik could easily count. Its head was at the height of his chest, a featureless knob with tiny tentacles on the underside. Its presence struck him hard. Of course, he had not really doubted the existence of alien intelligences after the battle at the space station where he had helped Telisa escape, but seeing one in person was different. He knew he was not looking at a virtual feed.

Five Entities. The aliens are here.

The Terrans raised their rifles and pointed them at the thing.

Without warning, Arlin exploded across the deck. Relachik staggered, covered in gore.

Relachik raised his weapon and fired. His round said it acquired the target, but a second later it was clear the shot had no effect.

Cilreth cowered behind a carbon strut for a second, then she turned and ran down the right corridor.

She's going to find Telisa? Even braver woman than I thought.

A flash of pain erupted in his legs and rose into his gut. He fell to the deck.

What—

Michael McCloskey

Chapter 22

Magnus sat outside the vault, regarding the battle-torn cavern around them.

I'm a long way from home. Or am I? Where is home for me, anyway?

He shrugged to himself. Somewhere along the way, home had become an outmoded concept for Magnus. Telisa came out with some food bars. They started to eat.

"It's time to flip our thinking," Telisa said.

"We cost them a lot. It'll never work as well again. The destroyer machines do learn, though a bit slowly."

"Exactly. So we turn it on edge. Use the fact it won't work again to our advantage."

"How?" he asked.

"Suppose we put out a huge number of signatures again, ones that they are sure to ignore, and have one overlap the seed."

"Ah, that might work. They've learned to ignore our false signatures, so now they ignore the seed," Magnus said. "It reminds me of what Shiny said. He figured out how the Trilisk facility worked, then he used it against the destroyers. And they couldn't keep up with his tricks."

"If they manage to discern our false signals, it'll still be dangerous. Also, they're not totally ignoring the signals. Just moving much more slowly than before."

"I don't want to give them too much time to figure it out," he said. "I could toss in a few signals over destroyers again, too."

"But we don't want them to pursue it before we start the ruse either. All the fakes and our real one should become visible at the same time."

"Agreed. Okay. Let's get it up to the vault entrance and then we'll let loose," he said.

Magnus looked at the floating cache of artifacts and frowned.

"What?" she asked.

"That weapon you used. It saved us once. It might again. I know you can't take out the whole destroyer fleet with it, but it might make the difference."

Telisa nodded. She set the key down and let the shelves deploy the collection. The amazing container unfolded and spread the items out over the shelves. Telisa grabbed the weapon and put it over her shoulder with a makeshift sling she had added. Then she withdrew the key and it all collapsed again.

"We need to bring that thing along next time, if there is a next time," Magnus said. "It's so useful for carrying stuff."

"I hope it can float all the way to the surface. Otherwise, we're going to have to stop and grab everything again in the middle of all the action."

Magnus nodded. He strode back inside, seized the industrial seed, and carried it to the entrance.

"If you're almost out of ammunition, you don't have to carry the rifle, too," she said.

"I found more ammunition. I'm suspicious though, because of the Meer stuff. I doubt it's the ammo I packed."

"Okay. I guess it's worth the weight, then," Telisa said, making it clear it was his decision.

Magnus thought about the weapon. It was a bit out of date, but that was exactly what made it valuable to him.

"It's hard to replace. The newer weapons have a lot more control restrictions."

"I bet our friends on the frontier have ways around that," Telisa said. "Or we can make our own."

"I'll drop the rifle quickly enough if the need arises," he said. She seemed satisfied.

"Ready for take two?" he asked.

"Yes."

"Okay here we go," Magnus said. "Let's hope we picked our targets well."

The signals activated, lighting up on the drone detection network.

"It'd better work. Scout is running out of power again," he said.

"We might be able to find some power source like before."

"Let's get out of here!"

"Yeah," she agreed.

They double-timed it out of the vault chamber toward the first upward leg. For Magnus, it caused a strong déjà vu.

This time we'll be successful.

Scout led the way on the ascent. The spider-like robot flooded the area with its lights, then launched a smart rope and headed up.

Magnus and Telisa watched their game of cat and mouse with the destroyers through Shiny's drone network. At first, the destroyers did nothing. Then they moved out sluggishly.

"They're going to investigate."

"Slowly. We may have time!"

"I assume the artifact trove thing will float up with us as long as I carry this small leader device."

"You may have to drag it. Or we can use another rope. I can get a spare rope ready, just in case."

Magnus staggered a bit under the load as he grabbed the line ascender. Telisa steadied him and watched him rise into the darkness. Scout waited for him at the top. He saw her glance over her shoulder and sweep her light about behind her.

"Being in back is as scary as being in the lead."

"Then get your ass up here!" Magnus said.

Telisa ascended after them. At her side, the container levitated with her, following the key. Magnus nodded. It made sense for a Vovokan transport device. It had to be able to move anywhere in the tunnels to be useful.

"We could give Scout the seed and send him on alone," Magnus said.

"The idea is logical, yet I don't want to let the seed out of my sight, or my protection," Telisa said.

"I know. Scout could probably make it up a bit faster, though, unless there are new cave-ins or problems ahead."

"If Shiny is there to pick it up, he might grab it and leave us here. Let's keep going and be flexible."

I don't blame her for wanting to stay close and protect the seed, but what if we get killed because we're so close to the destroyer's target?

They emerged from the top of the first shaft. Things looked pretty much as they had on the way down. The refuse and bodies lay scattered about. Scout had spotted a few of the scavenger creatures, but so far, there had been no signs of large numbers of them.

The destroyers slowly intercepted many of the false signature sources. The machines still moved cautiously.

"If we have any real Vovokan machines left to distract them, now's the time," Telisa said.

"Okay, I'll use everything I have," Magnus agreed.

They moved out again at a slow run. The adrenaline and their physical conditioning made the pace easy to keep up. If it came to it, their packs held performance enhancers that could drive their bodies closer to the limit at the expense of some excessive wear and tear. Of course, doing that always held slight dangers. Pushing oneself with drugs could result in tendon ruptures, burst blood vessels, or even broken bones.

We're beyond slight danger at this point, Magnus told himself as he contemplated it.

They stopped to re-anchor the ropes. Magnus split his time watching the destroyer display, Scout's input, and his sweeps of the area with his light. He saw two small creatures, but they did not seem inclined to attack.

We can do this.

The ascent resumed. Scout had already reached the top of the next tunnel. Magnus decided to send it a bit farther ahead than usual and check the coliseum for activity. Telisa continued the ascent at a furious pace.

"Take a stimulant," he suggested.

"Already did, at the bottom of this shaft," she said.

He smiled. "Great minds think alike."

Magnus took a dose of the stimulant himself.

"Yes. This is a situation critical enough to warrant a chemical boost. I think we can make it to the top with only one more ascent through that hole over there," she said, indicating a break in the debris above them.

As Magnus sent another smart rope up to anchor itself for the next leg, he checked the information from Shiny's probes. They showed him what he did not want to see: a destroyer coming toward them.

Magnus responded by setting up two more false signatures between them and the destroyer. The fakes moved slightly away in other directions. The destroyer dispatched smaller machines to investigate.

"The coliseum-place is wide open," Telisa said. "There are many connections to it. A destroyer can get there easily."

"This distraction may work," Magnus said.

They pulled themselves out of the lowest shaft and found the door below the wide open space where they had fought the eerie, suborned Vovokans. Scout did not see any threats, though the area was still filled with so much sand and debris an ambush was possible.

Magnus's body worked smoothly. He felt strong and his head was clear. He knew this was somewhat the effect of the stimulant, but it also reflected on successful execution thus far. Other than a few minor bumps and scrapes, he remained in peak physical condition.

"So odd that with all our technology, so much is still riding on our physical capabilities," Magnus said over his link.

"That's the frontier for you, I guess," she said.

"As you said, we need more robots for the next expedition."

"The *next* expedition? Ha. But yes. We could even stay up in orbit next time."

"That would be no fun."

Magnus carried the seed into the sandy interior of the spherical coliseum. Telisa had already shot a smart rope up to one of the exits of the huge chamber. Shiny's probe hovered nearby, disturbing the sand as it moved. Scout had an anchor rope ready to ascend, but Telisa had asked it to wait a moment.

In case her zombies attack again, Magnus guessed.

He stared at Telisa's weapon. It had saved them once.

"I wish Scout could use that, but I think that weird double-handle is beyond his manipulation capabilities," Magnus said.

"Let's get out of here," Telisa said. "I'll keep it as our last line of defense."

They emerged from the coliseum, out one of the dozens of entrance tunnels with the strange handholds. Magnus noted a grim picture on the probe network display. The nearest destroyer had picked their trail back up. Other destroyers had cleaned up a lot of the real targets. Some of them were returning to the surface, while others still slowly hunted ghost signatures.

The seed carrier must be a stronger signal than most. I think another one is veering this way from the far side.

"It's getting uncomfortably close," Magnus said.

"Then suicide a Shiny drone at it."

"No, I think we need Scout to do it. I can paint it with a Vovokan signature. We're almost out."

Magnus didn't feel any frustration at the prospect of losing Scout. It was a machine, and expendable. That was half the point of its existence. Besides, superior Vovokan-based Scout parts awaited him on the *Iridar*.

Scout scampered down a side tunnel toward the destroyer that had been dogging them.

"Let's hope that does it," he said.

Telisa and Magnus attacked the last major ascent in their return leg. They shot their ropes up and started to climb.

Suddenly a tremor passed through the entire shaft. A distant rumbling came from below. Debris rained down. Magnus felt his rope slip. Something struck his shoulder, but he gripped his ascender and made his silhouette as compact as possible. A burst of adrenaline raged through him, spiking his heart rate, but the rope did not slip farther.

"Are you okay?" he asked Telisa, coughing in the aftermath of the sandy rain. He heard Telisa cough in reply. A few seconds later she could speak.

"Doesn't the complex usually explode at the last moment just as the heroes pop out?" Telisa asked.

"It seems to be a bit ahead of schedule," Magnus said.

Activity flowered across his internal display of the house. Many destroyer machines reversed their courses. New signatures appeared and a few disappeared on the display. A couple of destroyers' red dots winked blue and disappeared.

"What the hell?" Telisa asked.

"I think Shiny is putting his last resources into the effort," Magnus said. "Maybe even some real Vovokan weapons out there."

"He knows we've almost got it!"

Telisa's ascender ground to a halt.

"It says it's out of juice," she reported. "We need another power pack."

"There are no other packs for that," Magnus said. "We'll have to do this ourselves," Magnus said.

"I found one right here," Telisa said, holding up a new power pack. It told his link it was fully charged.

"There were no other packs," Magnus said.

"You must have—"

"No, Telisa. I'm telling you. There were no other packs. This is another random event like my ammunition or the appearance of our friend Meer there on your back."

"What do you want me to do, toss it down the shaft?" she asked, but she quickly installed it. Of course Magnus did not stop her. He knew how badly they needed to get out.

A few meters farther up, Magnus had almost ascended to the top of his current rope position when his ascender died. Following Telisa's lead, he checked his backpack.

"No such luck for me," he said.

Telisa said nothing. She stopped next to him and pulled her backpack around again so she could look through it. After a few moments, she brought out another one.

"Okay, you're right. That definitely wasn't in there."

"Weird, but good," he said. His voice sounded disturbed.

She handed it over. Magnus had no choice but to drop the old pack and slap the new one into his ascender. They resumed at the fastest pace possible.

At the top of the first pit, they checked their entourage. Shiny's probe and the artifact cabinet were still with them, showing no signs of damage, though a bit of dust and sand had settled atop the cabinet.

"Remember the screw tunnel? Just ahead," Telisa told him.

They did not hesitate this time. Telisa jumped right into the tunnel and crawled forward. The tunnel sensed them and moved them along a bit faster, revolving in the opposite direction this time, to convey them toward the other exit.

Will this tunnel attract a destroyer? Or is it so mundane even they don't bother to destroy it?

Telisa's thoughts must have mirrored his own. "I hope we haven't provoked the destroyers to the point of making this tunnel a target. After all, it has some power storage or it wouldn't be working."

Magnus watched as Scout encountered a destroyer machine down below. The destroyer apparently did not quite know what to make of the non-Vovokan machine that looked like it was talking on Vovokan frequencies. It hesitated, shining lights down upon the robot it had discovered. Magnus decided to get its attention. He selected the most lethal grenade Scout carried: an incendiary warhead. Scout launched it at the destroyer machine.

The rest happened faster than Magnus could follow. There was a flash, which Magnus thought was the grenade, until it disappeared a second later. Then the feed from Scout went dead.

"So much for my first expeditionary helper," Magnus said.

"It was a great machine. I'll remember it fondly if I get out of this place alive," Telisa said.

Michael McCloskey

Chapter 23

The surface of Vovok had not changed in the time they had spent below the rocky surface. Telisa and Magnus emerged and found cover beside a pair of boulders. She did not see the *Iridar* on her tactical map. She scanned the blue sky, looking for signs of an approaching ship.

"It feels good to be above ground again," Telisa said.

"Shiny isn't responding."

"Oh, no. Is he going independent again? We're going to be stranded. With the seed!"

"No. The seed is exactly what he wants," Magnus said. "Let's just hope that once he gets it, our leverage is enough to protect us."

"Then what could be wrong? Destroyer interference? How long can we expect to be here before—"

"Hold on. The *Iridar* is coming in to pick us up."

"Maybe he's afraid to talk to us now that we have the destroyers all stirred up," Telisa said.

Magnus nodded. "I don't know. He could reach us with Terran comm systems now. Let's sit tight."

Telisa hugged the stone, trying to make her profile narrower. It was probably a futile action, given the incredible detection technology the destroyers possessed, but it was her only recourse. The drones showed some enemy activity. Magnus moved many of the underground decoys deeper, drawing the enemy forces away. He added a handful of false signatures on the surface, many kilometers away, trying to lure any above ground destroyers in the wrong direction.

"Good. Exactly what we need," Telisa said.

"The *Iridar* is coming down right over there," Magnus pointed. "Still no response on our channel to Shiny."

The ex-scout craft plummeted through the atmosphere. The destroyer capital ships ignored the ship. Telisa did not see any destroyer machines moving in on them.

"He's not screwing around!" Magnus said. "I'm impressed."

"The destroyers are ignoring us now—and the other surface signatures you gave them. They know the Vovokans aren't surface dwellers."

"I wonder if they would have had a chance if they'd surfaced en masse when the invasion came?"

"I doubt it. The machines would have learned in time. Besides, if you were a destroyer-maker, wouldn't you have come along to oversee the initial attack? They probably left once the Vovokans were crushed."

The *Iridar* became visible.

I can't believe it. It looks like we're going to make it!

They stood clear of the thrusters as its gravity spinner ran down. Telisa noted a few rocks flying around low to the ground. She felt her weight shift in throbbing waves.

I can feel the Iridar's spinner. It should be almost completely off by now.

"Damn! He's serious about getting in and out in record time," Magnus said, pointing out the debris. Close to the *Iridar*'s landing position, a boulder shifted and bounced away from the thruster's airstream like a rubber ball.

Magnus signaled to her and they ran for it. The artifact cache fell a bit behind, but Telisa knew it would take a moment for them to get up the ramp anyway. As they approached, her weight and the objects nearby returned to normal. Her footsteps became sure as the ramp descended ten meters in front of them.

They entered the *Iridar*'s cargo bay. Most of the parts left behind by Magnus and Shiny had been packed up; things looked relatively stable inside. Telisa stood at the top of the ramp to make sure it did not retract before her cache floated into the vessel.

I'll be damned if anyone is closing that ramp before my stuff gets in here!

Magnus let down the industrial seed with a grunt. The sound of takeoff already filtered in from outside. Telisa steadied herself.

"Mission successful."

"I think so," Magnus said aloud.

"Stay alert. This is a possible Shiny swing point," Magnus sent her on a private channel.

They walked out of the cargo bay. Magnus stopped short and unslung his rifle. Telisa was about to say he was going too far when she took a peek past him and saw a human body on the deck ahead.

"Five—"

Magnus clamped a hand over her mouth.

"They have to know we're on board," Telisa responded with her link. She stared at the form on the deck. Whoever it had been, he was obviously dead now.

"Maybe. Maybe whoever it is doesn't have control of the ship," Magnus said.

"Telisa?"

Telisa turned. A woman emerged from a crash tube. Telisa leveled her weapon and examined her. The stranger was thin in hands and face, with silver and black hair. She stood slightly taller than Telisa.

She's older than me. How old, I have no idea.

"What's happened? Why did you attack?"

"Telisa. Your father is here. I work for him."

"Liar! My father is dead!" Telisa snarled.

Magnus remained vigilant, covering the corridor in the other direction. Telisa brought her stunner out and pointed it at the woman. She noted in horror that blood spattered the deck.

"He lost his captaincy," the woman said. Then her voice hardened. "Don't take my word for it, kid. He's around here somewhere. That is if your damn pet alien didn't splatter him over the decks like it did to my crewmate Arlin."

Telisa wanted to rejoin the statement but she needed to find her father, or his body. The thought was unbearable.

"Where *is* he then?" demanded Telisa. "There's blood everywhere!"

"Calm down. We'll find him. We'll find him," Magnus urged. "Try the cargo hold again. Maybe we missed something. I'll check the storage cabinets down by the spinner, and my quarters, even though it should be locked."

Telisa ignored Magnus's attempt to divert her to safety and ran into the mess instead. There was even blood in there. She opened the food storage area and ordered the interior light on. The large circular rack held a lot of food, and the shelves were too tightly packed for anyone to hide inside.

Her link received a message from Leonard Relachik. *Five Entities!*

She crouched on the mess floor and read the message hurriedly.

If you can forgive me, I think we could work together. We're no longer at odds. You want to learn about the aliens. Especially the Trilisks. It's no longer my duty to uphold the law, but I'm still a Terran and I have a duty to help protect Terrans. The* Seeker *was destroyed by aliens. We have to give the Space Force all the help we can. But that doesn't stand in the way of what you want. You can learn about the aliens. I can pass along what we learn to the Space Force anonymously.

"Yes, yes, I agree," Telisa said.

But her link didn't see her father's link so she couldn't respond directly.

"Yes, I agree!" she yelled. "I agree, where are you?"

It might be a trap. It's too good to be true. There's blood everywhere.

Telisa started to cry.

"I agree, where are you?" she called again. She rose and walked toward the cargo hold.

"I found him," came a voice. It was the woman.

Telisa rushed back out to find her, wary. But the woman was still alone in the corridor, on her knees.

"Where's Shiny?" Telisa sent to Magnus.

"He's right here. Wait a moment," the woman said.

Telisa looked again. The woman held her arms in an odd way before her.

"Shiny is here. He's not trying to kill me, either," came Magnus's reply.

"I don't know how to get it to turn off. But he's here," the woman said.

"What?" Telisa snapped urgently. She jumped over to where the woman worked. The light was not right. Telisa reached out with her hands.

She felt something invisible. "This is my father?"

"Yes. He has a stealth suit on. Obviously, the monster got him anyway."

"The alien was defending himself against you. You came in here armed and tried to kill him, I'm sure," Telisa said.

"Magnus, we have him," she transmitted. "Get in here and help us take the stealth suit off!"

Magnus stepped into the corridor seconds later. Telisa searched for a front release on the stealth suit. Her hands were slippery with blood.

Michael McCloskey

Chapter 24

Leonard Relachik slept in a white bed in a small compartment of the *Iridar*. Telisa sat beside him. She stared blankly at the perfect white sheets. The air smelled sterile.

His legs were gone to the knees. Telisa was afraid of what he would say when he woke up. But she sat and waited.

Relachik stirred. He looked around. Then he saw Telisa watching him.

"Hi," she said in a small voice.

"Telisa!" He started to get up. She watched the realization cross his face. His legs were gone to each knee.

"Oh no. I'm a bit shorter."

She tried to laugh at his brave joke, but tears came out instead.

"I promise, dad, we'll get you someplace they can fix you up—"

"I know you will!" he said dismissively. "I lost an arm a couple years ago. Very inconvenient. Can you imagine what it must have been like when Terrans had to just accept being maimed? There was a time when almost anything could go wrong and you'd drop dead, you know."

Telisa smiled. "I know. You told me about it when I was a kid."

A cloud crossed his face. He took a deep breath. "I came to apologize to you. For being a lousy father. I know I was gone most of the time, and when I wasn't, I ran the apartment like a ship. I treated you like a recruit."

"You came all this way to apologize?"

"I came this way to make amends. To help you. To start to make it up to you."

Telisa smiled and squeezed his hand. She felt tears run down her cheeks, though she still smiled. "I'm so happy.

When we heard about the *Seeker*, I thought you were dead. I realized I wanted to be your daughter again."

"Now is our chance," he said.

"I got your message. Though honestly, I can barely remember what you said, I was so freaked out. I guess you said we could work together. I appreciate your offer. I'll take you up on it."

Relachik smiled, though Telisa saw fatigue—or perhaps the fog of medication—in his expression.

"Earth needs what you have. It needs all the alien tech it can get. The Space Force has to protect humanity against these hostile aliens, and we're behind in the technology race."

"Then I can find some more," Telisa said.

"What?"

"I can find more technological secrets. We can pass them on to the Space Force and help humanity. But I'm not going back. I'm going to keep looking. Keep learning. Our positions aren't in conflict. We can be allies instead of competitors, like you said."

"What about the alien?" he asked. "Is he on another side than the ones who attacked *Seeker*? Is he from a different race? How many alien civilizations does he know?"

"We'll find out. He knows of at least one other active civilization. I can fill you in bit by bit. It will take days, though. Right now, rest. Know we're safe," she said.

"Are we? Does the alien still want to kill me?"

"He should be fine. He shoots first and asks questions later. To survive. His society can be cooperative, or very competitive."

"Okay. Good. That, I can understand," he said. He sighed and coughed weakly.

"Enough. Rest now. I'll be back. I'm going to find out what's happening now, and I'll report back to you what I learn once you've started to recover."

"Are you in danger, Telisa?"

"Rest for now. I'm going to go find out what's happened and where we stand with Shiny. The alien."

"Shiny? I get the name, but not why you'd risk working with it."

"It's a 'mutually beneficial cooperative relationship,'" she said, parroting Shiny.

"What?"

"Never mind. Just rest."

Her father closed his eyes and fell asleep. Telisa watched him for a while, trying to absorb the fact that he was back in her life.

After a while, she decided to join the others. Although she had not come to terms with her father's awful injuries, so much was going on. Her father's friend was still alive on board somewhere, and Shiny had the amazing artifact.

Predictably, Shiny was in the cargo bay. Magnus was there, already tinkering with robot parts again.

Telisa didn't waste any time. "Shiny. Where are we going?"

"Asteroid."

"Why? To hide?"

"Shiny requires raw materials, supplies, resources to fully utilize artifact. Provides easy access far from destroyer devices."

"Shiny. That damn thing you sent us after is a Trilisk artifact, isn't it? How could you neglect to mention such an important piece of information?"

"Shiny, Telisa, compete to control same item."

"I'm in cooperative mode, Shiny. I won't take it from you. Tell me about it so we can accomplish more. If I trust you, then I provide more benefit to you, understand? What does it do?"

"Trilisk mind. Artificial, Trilisk-designed, scientist-constructed."

Telisa's mouth dropped open. Magnus stood in shock as well.

"Five Holy... let me get this straight: Your giant city-size house—ravaged by alien machines, filled with suborned members of your race, crawling with hungry scavenger bugs the size of my arm—had a Trilisk AI in it?"

I can't believe how much we don't know about Shiny.

"Very valuable. Very useful. Saved Shiny many times, provided, secured, aided."

"I want to talk to it! I don't see it in my link! What does it know? What has it taught you?" The questions spilled from Telisa and she only stopped them with an effort of will.

"Trilisk AI does not speak, communicate, inform. Only listens, examines, deduces."

"It has to be able to tell us what happened to the Trilisks."

"It is designed, prepared, constructed for other purposes. It provides, secures, nurtures."

"Then it can *provide* me with some answers!"

"Be careful, Telisa," Magnus transmitted. "Don't become a liability to Shiny."

"Not designed for information. Designed to provide useful food, tools, fulfill material needs. It is industrial seed."

"You've enslaved it to work for you? Is that what that Vovokan box is around it? A prison?"

"Trilisk device designed to provide. No enticement, payment, coercion required."

"Is it dangerous? If it's smart, can't it compete with you?" asked Magnus.

"Trilisk AI stays in cooperative mode. Shiny suspects, thinks, hypothesizes this is Trilisk intention."

"What is the Vovokan part here? You've merged something with it."

"Shiny limited competitive interference by filtering, screening, choosing input. Interface with Trilisk AI possible only from within Shiny house. Others blocked."

"You can do that? Tell us how," Telisa demanded. "How do we interface with it?"

"We already interfaced with the artifact, didn't we, Shiny?" Magnus interrupted.

Telisa looked at Magnus questioningly.

"Affirmative, correct, accurate statement of fact."

"What do you mean?" asked Telisa.

"We got weapons and supplies from the artifact. We didn't even know they came from it. And for all we know, it helped us a dozen other ways."

"Shiny, we get what we want simply by *needing* it?" Telisa asked.

"Wish, desire, pray," Shiny said.

It took a moment for that to sink in, then her mind raced. She could pray? She could get anything she wanted?

"Your modifications kept anyone outside your house from praying to it?"

"Shiny additions prevent AI from receiving, listening, fulfilling prayers from competitors."

"Please help me get my father's legs back," Telisa said. "Do I have to pray, or can I just want it?"

"Specific want. Requires high familiarity, understanding, knowledge and detailed prayer. Request likely too complex for Telisa ability to use, access, employ this device."

"That explains why the power packs we got were barely workable. It was a close thing," Magnus said. "Their insides were very primitive. Just enough to work one time."

"So the Trilisk technology supports prayer," Telisa summarized aloud, still absorbing what she had learned.

"Affirmative, correct, accurate statement."

"They must have reached a level of technology that could fulfill their every wish. Like the prayers of their ancestors."

"Shiny believes Telisa has reversed cause and effect. Unlikely Trilisk ancestors used, applied, employed prayer. Prayer developed as easy, convenient, effective request format for advanced technology."

"Really? In my race it was very common in many cultures and persists even to this day."

"Telisa ancestors used, applied, employed prayer to obtain items from Trilisk device operating on Earth. However, apparently unable to stop, cease, give up after device stopped functioning."

"On Earth? On Earth, how could it be? We prayed for—but my ancestors didn't have whatever they wanted, did they?"

"Likely limitations: primitive understanding unable to provide specifics for advanced constructs, power requirements of Trilisk device, possibly limited range. Also, possible Trilisk interference, regulation, oversight."

"I'm still trying to wrap my head around this. Primitive understanding. You mean, a witch doctor wouldn't know to ask for a flying car?"

"Must understand object intimately to obtain useful, usable, operational item."

"Oh. That's why I can't get a new pair of legs for my father."

"Affirmative, correct, accurate statement."

"Why did the Trilisks do that? Were they trying to turn us into an advanced race at an accelerated pace?"

"Motivations unknown. Competing theory: Trilisks visited, invaded, occupied Earth, required basic infrastructure."

"I see. We don't know if they were helping us or helping themselves."

"Other possibilities exist. Shiny terminate conversation. Seed requires attention."

"It requires your attention? Doesn't it pay attention to you?"

"Shiny in process of very complex wishes, desires, prayers. Requires full attention."

Telisa started to ask Shiny more questions, but she also felt a need to contemplate what she had learned. "Where is my father's friend? Is she dangerous?"

"I don't think so," Magnus said. "*Iridar* says she's in the mess."

Telisa walked off. As Magnus suggested, Telisa found her father's surviving shipmate in the mess. The woman was not eating but just sitting there, as if seeking company.

"I guess you know who I am," Telisa started.

"I'm Cilreth," the woman said, standing. She extended her hand and Telisa shook it. "How is your father?"

"He needs a real medical facility," she said. "But he's in a good mood."

"Of course. We came a long way to find you. Were you a prisoner or a willing participant in the smuggling?"

"Willing, though I have, at times, been at the mercy of our alien friend, Shiny."

Cilreth made a face.

She doesn't like Shiny and how can I blame her?

"Shiny is mostly a cooperative creature. Remember, you busted into his home. The only home he has left, really."

Cilreth nodded.

"Magnus and I just got back from an expedition. It was quite a surprise to come back to all this. But I want to thank you for finding my father and helping us get him patched up."

Cilreth's lips compressed a bit. "About Magnus. I've spent some time looking into the men of Parker Interstellar Travels. They're not all squeaky clean, you know."

"What about Magnus? You can tell me anything about him. I know him, he's a good man."

"Well, what do you know about him? Did you know he's a murderer?"

"Ridiculous."

"He killed a man in the war against the UED. A man on his side."

"Then he had a good reason for it. Why isn't he incarcerated if this is public knowledge? I know he hasn't been FBMed."

Telisa referred to forced behavior modification, usually applied as a form of severe rehabilitation. Cilreth remained calm, but she did not back down. She looked Telisa in the eyes.

"The Space Force didn't try him because his actions were supposedly affected by a toxic agent he'd received in an attack. In fact, the action wasn't ever admitted by the Space Force. But two veterans who made it out of there reported he'd done it before they got shut down by the Space Force."

"If anything, he's more ethical than I am," Telisa said. "And we're close."

"Then why hasn't he told you?"

"Undoubtedly because it's an unpleasant memory from his past. And I've hardly been receptive to tales about the war. Believe me. Magnus and I accept each other as-is."

"Then I envy your relationship. As long as he's not playing you. Were you a prisoner, at first?"

"No, I signed on to go find alien artifacts, like the ones we've been selling."

Cilreth held up her hands. "Okay. I wanted to know if you're all right. Your father was very worried of course, and we went through a lot of scenarios about what might have happened."

244

Telisa nodded. "Excuse me then, I need to figure out what happens next."

Cilreth smiled weakly. "Good luck with that."

Michael McCloskey

Chapter 25

Magnus walked into the room set up to care for Leonard Relachik. Relachik was awake. Magnus felt a bit awkward, but he faced the ex-captain squarely.

"Magnus Garrison," Relachik said.

Magnus tried to hide his surprise.

Of course he would know my name.

"Captain," he said.

"No more. Call me Relachik. Has my daughter been working with you of her own free will?" demanded Relachik.

"Yes sir. She joined us as a specialist."

"What have you been doing? I assume you collected artifacts to sell."

"We went to a new Trilisk site on Thespera Narres. We fell into some kind of closed environment made for aliens; it became a kind of trap for us. We worked with the golden alien to escape. We did manage to sell some alien artifacts to generate a lot of money."

"And this last trip?"

"We retrieved an amazing artifact for Shiny. The alien. It's a Trilisk artificial intelligence which apparently provides almost anything the owner can envision in enough detail. Or anyone whose thoughts it can perceive. The deal enabled us to collect a lot of other artifacts from the planet. Vovok, Telisa calls it."

"That's pretty amazing stuff. About this alien. It blew my man away. And took my legs. I take it we pressed it a bit too hard. My fault. But apparently you've befriended it?"

"Not exactly," Magnus said. "That's something I wanted to talk to you about. I think Telisa is in danger. All of us, in fact."

"You care about Telisa?"

"Yes. I care about her a lot. We became close. Went through some hard times on Thespera."

"What's the threat?"

"The alien. It has a history—a racial or cultural tendency, actually—of alternating between cooperative modes and a competitive mode. If it flips to competitive mode, then I believe it may at best enslave us, at worst, dispose of us. Telisa treats it with too much trust, handles it like a Terran, even though she of all people is actually the best equipped to understand it is very much not like us."

Relachik listened carefully. "She doesn't think she's in danger?"

"Telisa is smart. But young and naïve. Trustful of everyone except the government, whom she opposes fiercely, as I'm sure you know. What I mean is, though she hates the government as a nebulous entity, she trusts in individuals. She trusted us, her new employers, very quickly. Her loyalty is laudable, and I hope to return that loyalty to her, but I think in this case it's actually a dangerous flaw."

"So this creature may flip, you say? Has it flipped before?"

"Not on us. Not totally. He did take over our ship once. But by his own admission, he does whatever is optimal for himself at the time. There appears to be little capacity for lingering loyalty for old time's sake, or whatever you might call it. He said in so many words he was happy about most of his race being wiped out because of 'reduced competition'. Telisa and I hedged our bets by telling him if we died, a report would be sent to the Space Force. I don't know if it bought us much safety."

"Magnus, I want you to save her. If this alien is really like you say, we need to kill it before it kills us. We know it has the power to kill us easily if it decides it wants to.

Obviously it has no compunction against killing other sentient beings."

"Killing Shiny is easier said than done."

"What choice do we have? Sounds to me like it's a time bomb. We need to catch it by surprise. At least we need to somehow disarm it, cripple it."

"Yes, that, or figure out how to run away."

"I'm going to be slow getting back into action. Don't wait for me. Kill it or run away if you don't think you can. Take Telisa away from it. Do you need money?"

Magnus shook his head. "We have a rich haul from Shiny's homeworld."

"Your finances may have been complicated by a thing or two I did to get here," Relachik said. "I'll send Telisa details of my finances. Kill the thing, or get out of here."

"She won't abandon you."

"Her life is in your hands. If you really care about her, you'll take action. I'm counting on you."

He's right. Yet if I do as he says, Telisa may never forgive me.

"I'll see what preparations I can make. I'll try and estimate the odds of success."

Magnus left Relachik with even more on his mind. Magnus had been willing to let things slide because of the way Telisa seemed unwilling to fear Shiny. Now, he was not so sure.

Am I letting her put herself in too much danger through my inaction?

Magnus wandered back to the *Iridar* and stared at his robot parts, but he made no move to work on anything. All he could think about was convincing Telisa to run away.

If Relachik tries to make her leave whose side am I going to be on? I think we should leave, but I can hardly force her to leave can I? I think I would have to side with her. Even though I don't agree with staying.

Magnus went to Telisa in her quarters. He felt a bit weary, though he doubted he could find sleep with so much on his mind. Telisa lay in her web, her eyes staring at the ceiling.

Obviously in the same boat: heavy thoughts.

"Hey," he said. "Are you thinking about the AI?"

"Of course. Well, that and my father."

"I want you to reconsider about sticking around. We should take the cache of items and leave."

"I need to learn more about the Trilisks. I'm not going to try and steal the seed from Shiny, if that's what you're worried about."

"Shiny is still dangerous, even if you leave him the seed. Your father doesn't want you in danger, either."

"Too late. My life has been in serious risk quite often lately."

Magnus slipped into the web and held her. Something felt different. Telisa was tense.

Something more is bothering her. Just wait. She'll mention it.

"How many people have you killed?" she blurted out.

Didn't see that one coming.

"Three."

"In the war? Were they UED?" she asked.

"Two of them were. Saboteurs, sent in by the UED to destroy critical installations."

"And the other?"

Magnus gathered his thoughts.

"I told you a bit about the fear. In the war," he said. "The other one I killed was a soldier in my unit. He got messed up on drugs to escape the pressure. During an attack by UED cruisers, we were in a bunker. He was high, totally out of it. He said he wanted to call home and get them to come pick us up. It was a radio silence situation, so the UED couldn't pinpoint us. They didn't know if we were there, in what bunkers; they wouldn't know where to strike unless he made that call. I stopped him. I should have done it some other way, but there wasn't time. He almost gave us away. The Space Force acknowledged my actions as those of a hero, rather than a murderer, because I had saved more lives than I took. I was backed up by the officer there."

Telisa relaxed a bit in his arms.

I think she believes me.

"I should have told you," he offered.

"No, I understand. It's all right. I love you."

Magnus started to reply but his link gave him an alert. The *Iridar* had gone into an intercept trajectory with a large object. As Magnus investigated, he discovered that the other ship, the *Vandivier*, as well as Shiny's starship, were all closing on the same target.

"Where are we going?" Telisa asked.

"A large asteroid," Magnus said. "Though there are hints of an installation there. I assume it's Vovokan."

Magnus felt dead tired. He'd only slept in short bits under the Vovokan surface.

"Maybe catch a bit of sleep before the rendezvous..." he murmured, already drifting away.

"Yes. Yes, sleep," Telisa said.

Michael McCloskey

Chapter 26

Telisa woke up alone. Her link told her the time. She had overslept by hours.

"By the Five! I need to go see what's happening," she mumbled. Telisa felt her way around the quarters to the shower tube and revived herself.

As she returned to alertness, she opened a channel to Magnus. "Magnus? What's up?"

"We're at the asteroid. I've only seen the main entrance and I'm already impressed. Can you come out?"

"Yes. What's out there?"

"You have to see it. I guess it's the result of Shiny's prayers."

"Okay, I'm out there in two minutes."

Telisa finished her shower, straightened up, and donned her Veer suit.

I've turned into the female version of Magnus, she thought, feeling how at home she was in the military skinsuit.

Telisa hurried to the cargo bay and walked down the ramp. Her eyes had to adjust to bright white light.

A huge atrium spread before her. Its walls were irregular, like a giant cavern, though white support struts ran along the perimeter. The *Iridar* was parked inside like a car on a street. Telisa could not see how the ship got into the space. Fine white sand covered the floor.

Cilreth stood a few meters away.

"A large asteroid huh? Very large, I'd say."

"Many kilometers long anyway," Cilreth said. "It's beautiful. Sandy, though," she grimaced.

Telisa laughed. "That's Vovokan for you. The sand is like their carpet, and their toilet, apparently. Or at least their wastebasket."

"Oh. That explains why my footprints sift away within a minute."

"How's my father doing?"

"Not well enough to come look. His body took a lot of damage, and we have only basic medical support. He should stay put for a week or maybe more," Magnus said.

They walked toward a set of tunnels leading out of the atrium. A bank of windows looked out into space.

"I assume the gravity is artificial, or else there's a singularity involved."

Telisa found link services and looked the maps over. She quickly grasped the general layout the asteroid's interior. It was an advanced factory... for what?

I wonder how much was already here, and how much Shiny got from the AI?

"Couldn't rule out the possibility of a singularity in a place this advanced," Magnus said. "I assumed it was a gravity spinner. It's amazing."

"More than amazing. It's ours now. Our sanctuary," Telisa said.

Magnus blinked. "You mean we should live here?"

"Why not? From what I can see of the overall design, it's camouflaged, provides plenty of power, and even has defenses. It's a perfect base of operations. Shiny can make ships that are way more advanced than the *Iridar*. With them, we could go where we want, when we want. No need to fear getting caught by the UNSF."

"Yes. I see what you mean," he said. "I don't think we should stay, though. We have so many artifacts, and this time they aren't knick-knacks. We could own a planetoid on the frontier."

Telisa kept poring over the map. "It interfaces with my link, you know. And there's a map service, and it shows Terran-style rooms!"

"Yes. This way. Let's check them out," Cilreth said.

They walked down a straight but rough-surfaced cave tunnel toward the Terran section of the base. They came to a square corridor and stepped up a few inches onto a pristine white tile floor.

"If the walls shift around I'm going to scream and run," Telisa said.

Magnus laughed and Cilreth shot her a curious look.

"Inside joke," Magnus said.

"I wouldn't be surprised if the walls did shift according to your prayers," Cilreth said. "I'm kind of opposed to praying on principle, but if I really get what I want, then I imagine I'll get over the discomfort pretty damn fast."

They came to a wide circular platform, overlooking a series of spacious white rooms with glass ceilings.

"A kitchen, dining room, VR training room, and... a dance hall," Telisa summarized at a glance.

"I see a workshop," Magnus said. "And I see Scout parts in it! This is too crazy!"

"Are they the parts from the *Iridar*, or new ones?"

"I don't know. It probably doesn't matter."

"It's wonderful. White and clean. Not a grain of sand, hah," Cilreth said.

"Yes. Beats sleeping in sandy tunnels. This is stylish. Like a five star resort."

They walked down into the series of rooms and wondered at the luxury of it all. Each of them found a spacious bedroom filled with soft furniture. Telisa came into a room and one wall became a hologram of an alien forest filled with grazing alien creatures.

At some point, Telisa noticed Magnus was no longer in their party. She called for him.

"Hi. Stay there, I'm coming to you," he sent.

Something in his voice caught her attention.

"What's up? And where's my father's room?"

"Stay there. I'm coming right to you."

Magnus returned within the minute.

"Sit down," he said.

"What happened?" she said, sitting on a white chair. She became alarmed as she saw the look on his face. He dropped to his knees beside her.

"Telisa, your father died a few minutes ago."

"No! He was fine! I—"

A part of Telisa flashed in anger at Magnus.

What a sick joke—

Just as quickly she knew it was true. Tears flooded her eyes. The way Magnus looked at her, she could see he knew what he was talking about.

"He was fine," she repeated.

"His injuries were serious. The kit had to keep him from bleeding out any further. It may have caused a clot, or he may have simply taken too much damage."

She cried on Magnus's shoulder for several minutes. She had not cried so much in a decade.

"There is something else you have to know," Magnus said over his link. "Your father and I were prepared to betray Shiny. I told your father what we know about his race. Your father wanted to kill him, to protect you. I knew that wouldn't fly with you, so I pressed for running away."

"It makes no difference now," Telisa replied. "He's dead. How can it hurt so much? I just met him again. I lived without him for years."

Magnus took a deep breath. "What I'm trying to say is, it may not be a coincidence he died after threatening Shiny. The *Iridar* has been dismantled. Just like that. I think Shiny did it with the seed. We can't leave, either. It's as if Shiny overheard our conversation and made both actions impossible."

"You think Shiny did it."

"I don't know. I know he dismantled the *Iridar*. He said the seed needed raw materials. He said we would be able to use Vovokan ships soon enough, and they'd be much better."

"But he should have asked us. By Terran rules, anyway."

"Obviously. But it's done. The ship is gone. The *Vandivier* is gone too. He says our personal effects are in the grand atrium."

I should be so happy right now. I was a few minutes ago.

Telisa felt fate had arranged to negate her victory as if overeager to enforce karmic justice. "We don't know anything. My father is dead and we don't know if Shiny did it. I don't know what to believe. I'm confused."

"He would have died if he'd been on the *Seeker*. This way, you two got to square things between you."

Telisa knew Magnus was trying to help, but his observation failed to console her. She told herself her father had already been out of her life, as if he were already dead, but no matter how she considered it, she felt only loss.

He held her on the soft white furniture while she cried. Telisa let herself cry it out.

After a while, Magnus stood. "I'm sorry to leave now, but I have to check on things. I'll be back very soon."

Telisa nodded and let him leave. She moved over to the white bed. Her thoughts ran over the memories she had of her father. She tried to convince herself her emotions were overblown. It had counted for more than she realized, knowing he was alive out there somewhere, even though they never spoke.

As she lay in the fairytale bed, something else started to bother her.

Magnus thinks Shiny did it. I don't think so.

She lay there, looking at the ceiling, but the odd feeling stuck with her.

Why didn't Magnus stay here with me? What's he going to do? He knows my father wanted to kill Shiny. Do I have to worry about that?

As soon as she had the thought, it hooked in her mind and would not let go.

What if I wake up and Shiny or Magnus is dead? I already lost my father.

She used her link to find Magnus. The services of the asteroid functioned and gave her his location.

I wonder if Shiny made that work because I don't know enough about link services to pray them into existence.

Telisa followed service directions to get back to the atrium. She caught sight of Magnus, Cilreth, and Shiny out on the sand. She walked toward them. They had not spotted her yet, or at least Magnus and Cilreth had not. She noticed Magnus trade looks with Cilreth.

Something passed between them. Magnus held out his hand.

Cilreth detached something from her belt and gave it to him. A long tube.

A sword tube!

"Magnus, what are you—"

Magnus stepped forward. Telisa stepped in front of him.

"No. Stop it, whatever you're doing, stop it," Telisa said over her link.

"He will betray us," Magnus replied over a private channel. "It's only a matter of time. He doesn't care about the death of his own race. Those bodies down there? They must have been his slaves. Running his house for him. The destroyers? Is it so hard to imagine what happened? Shiny's race must have betrayed them, too. Now he's destroyed the *Iridar,* the *Vandivier*, and for all we know, killed your father."

"I don't think he did it. You have no proof."

"Your father was strongly advocating Shiny's... removal by force."

"We don't know any of this. Besides, you can't murder a sentient being. He's done nothing but help us. He hasn't betrayed us."

"He *will*," Magnus transmitted. "He may already have."

"We'll make sure it's not to his advantage to betray us. We'll get more leverage and make sure he knows about it. He didn't kill my father. My father wasn't a threat to him anymore. He only shot them when they forced their way onto *Iridar*."

"A ship which no longer exists. Once he re-establishes himself here, he'll be so powerful he won't care about anything we could threaten him with. He might kill us."

"We can't expect to get along smoothly with aliens, but if we can learn to be tolerant of each other, there's huge benefit in it. Shiny will see that. You will see that."

Shiny moved back a bit and stared at them.

"He knows something's wrong."

"He probably thinks you and I have ended our alliance with each other," Magnus said.

"If you kill him in cold blood, then we have. I'll leave you."

"Your father—"

"Don't mention my father. I'm not letting you kill Shiny. Or get killed trying."

Cilreth watched the stare-down without moving. Telisa saw her breathing had sped up, though, obviously in fear of imminent violence.

"What do you think?" Magnus asked Cilreth.

"I think he was only defending himself when he killed Arlin. As for his future plans, I can't say. But I know he's dangerous. I'm not so sure you should try. See if he gives you a ship, like he says. Why would he have put our personal effects in the atrium if he was going to flush us?"

Magnus handed the sword case back to Cilreth. She visibly relaxed. Magnus walked away, back toward the Terran quarters the seed had created.

"My timing is lousy, but I'd like to join your team, if you'd have me," Cilreth said.

"My father said you're the one who found us," Telisa said.

"Ah, yes, that's true. I hope there are no hard feelings. It was just a job."

"No hard feelings," Telisa said. "If you found us, then you have skills we could use. We have a lot of work to do, without government oversight. And it's dangerous."

"I'm not exactly a hardened criminal."

"Neither are we, unless you ask the Earth government. Nevertheless, I intend to carry out my father's plan to help the Space Force. It is what he would have wanted, but it's also my duty to my race."

Telisa sharply felt his loss again. Once again she berated herself.

You hardly knew the man. He was your father, but you hardly knew him, so get over it.

"What would you have me do now?" Cilreth asked.

"Figure out how we can interface with Shiny's ship. It's ten times better than the *Iridar,* and he's going to make us more."

"Let me at it."

"My first order of business is clear," Telisa said. "It turns out that we have a resident Trilisk expert. Or at least someone who knows more than I do."

Telisa widened the channel to include the alien. She set her lips in determination.

"Shiny, tell me everything you know about the Trilisks."

THE END of The Trilisk AI (continued in The Trilisk Supersedure)

From the Author

Thanks for reading! As an indie author, I rely on your ratings and reviews to legitimize my work to those who have not read me. Please review this book online. Thank you.

Made in United States
Orlando, FL
06 August 2024

50030340R00147